Lyrics Between Us

Christa Tillman

Heart Ink Press

Lyrics Between Us
ISBN: 978-1-959441-00-7
ISBN: 978-1-959441-01-4 (ebook)

For information about special discounts for bulk purchases, please send an inquiry to special sales at iamchristat to book a live event, visit the iamchristat website.

Dedication

My doctor's faith and self-assurance boosted my faith; therefore, I dedicate this book to them.

Dr. Naveena Allada, MD –Hematology/Oncologist Specialist – **Dr. Joyce Shotwell, MD–** Pulmonologist, **Dr. Barry N. Wilcox, MD–** Oncologist, **Baylor Irving Hospital** – extraordinary **Critical Care RNs**. (Their morning prayer started my day off properly), **Naheed Vidhani–** RN, OCN, and Texas Oncology Staff **(Rosalyn, Susan, and the Receptionist)**. I look forward to laughing and seeing you ladies every week. **Kristin Smith** – Vista's CFO, for demanding I leave work and go to the doctor. Your concern saved my life.

Without God, my amazing doctors, physical therapists, family, and friends, this masterpiece would have never made it to the press. This book is an emotional love story.

I hope you feel my love, faith, fear, and happiness in each chapter.

Please be aware that this story contains sensitive topics. As a survivor of domestic violence I tried to handle this subject matter with the care it deserves.

Lyrics Between Us

"Not Tonight" (Remix)

Lil Kim

Miya

HE MELODIC LYRICS OF "THE MISEDUCATION of Lauryn Hill" stimulated dopamine sparks in my brain's nucleus, activating joy in my soul and energizing my body as I decorated the tiny apartment.

A knock on the front door interrupted, "Doo Wop (That Thing)." A glance at my watch confirmed it was Imani; she's always an hour early for any BAE event. I spun on my heels and shuffled over to the front door.

Since I launched the Black and Educated social group in high school, my girls have granted me the honor of hosting our tenth anniversary. Tonight's theme is Pajama Jammy Jam, and I expect us to party until the cops come knocking.

I hugged Imani before going into the kitchen to finish cooking. I danced all around the postage-sized kitchen while Imani twerked in her seat. Our voices coordinated as we started singing on cue to Gwen Stefani's "Hollaback Girl."

"Did you create a scorching playlist for us tonight?" Imani questioned, flinging her arms above her head while tapping her feet in celebration before dancing towards me.

Imani waved her hand in my face, cutting me off before I could answer, singing, "The BAEs are bananas. B-A-N-A-N-A-S!" I joined in on the excitement, dancing around the living room with my BAE until the song ended.

"Bring Em Out" by T.I. started blasting from the subwoofers as I headed towards the kitchen. Imani paused, pumping her fist at the song choice before she spoke.

"Okay, heffa, you're trying to kill us tonight."

I pumped my fist in the air, giving Imani her response as Imani fanned me, hyping me up more.

"Tonight is going to be hot because you are on fire!"

I plopped onto the barstool next to a panting Imani. She gazed at her watch. "I thought this event started at 6:30 pm?"

I frowned before sliding a bowl of chips in her direction, watching as she poured herself a glass of sweet Argentinian wine. "Can a BAE event ever start on time? Where is Naja?" she asked as she took her first sip. I frowned.

"How can you live where the party is hosted and still be late?"

Pausing the song, I rapidly chewed the Doritos in my mouth before I swallowed, then answered. "Imani, Naja is still getting dressed, and I know she can hear us because this apartment is a mere 725 square feet. Shit, I can hear the bugs at night creeping across the floors. Tamia is fifteen minutes out, and Lexi has to make her grand entrance."

"You will require a wider apartment if you keep eating all those chips."

We both snickered at her joke.

Imani headed towards the back bedroom. "Naja moved to the front. We switched rooms since her late-night booty calls with Dakari disturbed me." Imani paused and turned around. I whispered sneakily. "And girl, he always waits until he's at the front door to hold a full conversation; these pre-med students are long-winded."

Clapping her palms together, Imani probed excitedly, "Dakari or Naja?"

"Both of them!" I said, laughing at her reaction.

"Hey, BAEs!" Naja hummed. Her ebony presence dominated the space. "Did I hear someone call my name?" Turning at the sound of her voice in the narrow passageway, I took in the cheeky, black, long sleeve romper hugging Naja's curves as she danced into the living room.

Smiling joyfully, I leered at my two ebony queens, forever classy with a hint of seduction. I stroked my gear's comfortable fluffy fabric and wondered if my outfit was acceptable for tonight before swiftly waving the doubt away.

"Y'all in here jamming and talking shit!" Naja smirked, hugging Imani before making her spin around so she could comment on her attire. "I see you killing this sexy pink and black spaghetti strap cami. Sexy and elegant as usual. Are those lace pajama shorts made of chiffon or satin?"

Before Imani could answer, I did. "Those sexy shorts are silk."

Naja gave a crisp nod as her feet tapped the floor incessantly while gazing at the clock's green glow on the kitchen microwave. "How long before Tamia and Lexi arrive, Miya?"

I rolled my eyes. It always astounds me when someone who comes late becomes impatient after arriving. They tend to forget people felt the same annoyance waiting on them.

"Tamia is ten minutes away, and Lexi has not called," Imani informed Naja. "She's probably fighting Paxton off so she can walk out the door. Every time she tries to leave, Paxton goes through separation anxiety."

Imani was forever defending Lexi in some way or another. Since I was eight and she was ten, I had been rolling my eyes at Imani's comments. We were best friends first, but like always, Lexi stole her away.

Glancing back as I headed to the front door, I caught Naja smiling ear to ear as I walked by, and I felt a bit disappointed hearing Imani compliment her on her sexy ensemble and mention nothing about mine.

My cousin Lexi stood there as I opened the door, dropping the white dress shirt she wore to the middle of her torso. She placed her hands on her hips and greeted me, revealing a lace bralette set featuring a multi-strap neckline with spaghetti straps and gold O-ring accents. The backside was hardly conservative as she twirled, flaunting the far from modest attire, displaying more flesh than material.

"Oh, shit, Diva," Tamia shouted, walking up to us. "Sexy Lexi!"

Running her hands over the high-waisted garter belt with the same accents as her bralette, Lexi caressed the material around her thigh as she modeled the matching panties with cutout panels.

"I know I live in the Trojan apartments, but did you have to walk in here looking like you're ready to get fucked?"

I rolled my eyes as Lexi twirled once more, smirking at me.

"Girl, I need to take pictures of you against this red door. You look like a sexy dominatrix!" Tamia continued.

"You want some red-light action?" Lexi joked, posing before the door. "Girl, I need to take some pictures of you too!"

These heifers were acting like my apartment door was the champagne room, and those satin pink and gray capris Tamia wore with that gray lace bra and matching robe could not contend with Lexi's sexy attire. I had no more words for Lexi and Tamia.

Stepping aside and allowing them to sashay into the apartment, I watched Imani and Naja's reactions to Lexi's outfit, their jaws dropping briefly before praising her attire.

Silently, I stood there, watching them pass around compliments. When Lexi cast her eyes upon me, tingling warmth filled my limbs. I stared down at my empty hands when she addressed me. I smoothed out my leopard onesie, my lower lip sticking out in a giant pout. The circle had already declared me the crybaby, and I battled with pride, struggling to suck my lip back in.

"Lexi, I cannot believe Paxton let you out of the house!" Imani shouted, forcing me to lower the volume.

Lexi snickered. "Girl, Paxton was not at home."

"Explains the outfit," I replied rapidly.

"No, it does not, smartass," Lexi snarled before fixating on Imani. "Do you remember the outfit I bought last week for tonight?"

Imani snapped her fingers in agreement.

"Girl, Paxton found the satin gown and demanded I model the outfit. I tried to protest. I even told him it was for my BAE event tonight, but no matter what I said, he insisted he wanted me in that gown," Lexi stated, running her hands over her body, carrying on with her tale. "I showed him this outfit; he tossed it on the floor. Sick of arguing with him, I conceded and slid my phat ass into the damn baby doll gown. I was going to buy another outfit today, but work swamped me." Lexi's arms waved in mock exasperation as she said, "Paxton had three tests today, which meant I was his last-minute study buddy."

"Girl, Paxton is your hubby, and you would do anything for that man just like I would do the same for Winten," Imani stated.

I wanted to tell them that calling Paxton and Winten their husbands did not make them wives. But as always, Imani and Lexi dominated the entire conversation and turned it into the Sexy Lexi Show.

Blushing, Lexi cooed as she spoke. "On top of that, I had a report due by 3:00 pm. By the time I arrived at work, I was exhausted. I contemplated what to wear and spotted this outfit on our bedroom floor. Being rebellious, I jumped into the outfit, Paxton tossed out like trash."

"They say one man's trash is another man's treasure," Tamia interjected.

We all stared at her, shaking our heads and erupting into laughter.

Lashing out, I snidely quipped, "I don't think that statement is related to nipples covered with dental floss." Lexi fanned away my witty remark. Annoyed, I poured myself a glass of wine before giving the bottle to Naja. Once everyone had a full glass, we toasted to the BAEs.

"We have snacks, wine, and a massage therapist coming in an hour. I have food in the oven."

Tamia placed one hand on her hip with an attitude. "You mean five massage therapists."

I matched her condescension and reiterated, "One!"

"Good thing I brought two blunts. Bitch, we will be here until tomorrow if we all want a massage," Tamia asserted as the other girls nodded in agreement.

Sometimes I wonder why I was even friends with these ungrateful heifers. I walked to the counter and turned my playlist on, making Lexi jump up. Dropping her derriere low, she popped it as Snoop Dogg and Pharrell's "Drop It Like It's Hot" thumped from the speakers. Tamia lit a joint, passing it around while we danced to Destiny's Child's "Soldier" with Lexi. We were tipsy when 50 Cent's "Candy Shop" blazed from the speakers.

I whined my hips to the beat, making Tamia point and chuckle at me, and soon they were all laughing. Grumbling, I rolled and popped my hips harder.

"You don't have to be stiff," Tamia gibed.

"Heffa, leave my cousin alone! She will get a swerve in her hips once she starts having sex," Lexi countered.

"I know why she's still a virgin," Tamia proclaimed loudly.

Rolling my eyes, I remained silent because she would enlighten us with her distorted opinion, regardless of my reply. I stopped the music, plastering on the fakest smile I could muster.

Tamia pulled on my outfit. "A man cannot find the pussy under all this shit. Look at what the rest of us are wearing. Now glance at what you have on. What man will get hard? Miya, why are you running around dressed like a teenage little girl?" Naja and Imani agreed with Tamia while Lexi kept a straight face.

I examined my outfit again. It was toasty and comfortable, and I honestly didn't see the problem.

"I bet I'll be the first to get married," I fired back, wondering why those words popped into my head. "Men love a woman that hasn't been stepped in. Men marry women that keep their goodies on lock and only reveal them in the bedroom."

Tamia gawked at her fingertips, rubbing them together as she spoke. "The men I deal with don't expect a woman to be a virgin. Then again, I wouldn't expect you to know what a real man is."

Being a virgin used to be a badge of honor. Now it means you are a nerd or unfuckable, and I was neither. I surmise men have lowered their expectations, or promiscuous women have become the social norm.

Hell, men had hinted they wanted to taste me and sleep with me. However, I promised my mother and father I wouldn't have sex until I graduated from college to ease their hood statistic concerns. Most girls in the neighborhood were pregnant by the age of sixteen.

Lexi and I made a similar declaration at eleven years old, vowing not to have sex until marriage. The summer before high school, I went off to music camp, but Lexi stayed at home. When I returned, Lexi had transformed into Sexy Lexi, the girl engaging in sex. Imani followed shortly after.

"I will be the first to get married," Lexi remarked, leveling a confident gaze. "I've been with Paxton since middle school."

Lifting myself off the floor and onto my knees, I waved my hands in Lexi's face. "Newsflash. Invested time means nothing. How many stories have you read where athletes leave their childhood, high school, or college sweetheart to marry a white girl after signing their contract?"

We all high-fived in agreement except Lexi.

"That will not be Paxton and me," Lexi barked. "And heffa, I am half white; he can marry that side. Shit, we've invested time, unlike the rest of you!"

Surprisingly, Naja rolled her neck, snapping her fingers. "Dakari and I have more time invested than any of you youngsters. We have been bathing together since we were two years old in Jamaica. Our parents have been planning our wedding since puberty."

"Time means nothing," I stressed again before bringing my point home. "If it did, Imani could claim the third spot since she and Winten met in high school."

The memory of the day Winten Johnson walked into my classroom at Locke High School captivated me. I was mesmerized by his flawless, bright skin and pearly white teeth. I created a playlist for him full of love ballads and songs declaring I wanted to be his girl. I didn't recall adding Biz Markie, "Just A Friend," yet he referred to me as his little homie.

I invited him over to my house to ask him if he had a girlfriend, but when I walked into my room, I caught him and Imani kissing on my damn bed! It turns out they met while I was at music camp.

My crushes viewed me as their homegirl but never a girlfriend. The girlfriend title only applied to Lexi and Imani. Yet, the title wife will be mine. A sly grin graced my face.

My mind drifted to my wedding and courting playlist. My cheeks turned rosy as I blushed when I added Ginuwine's "Pony." The sides of my mouth curled upward, and I struggled to cover my excitement as I mentally jotted down Mariah Carey's "Emotions" and K-Ci & JoJo's "All My Life." This time, I won't demonstrate the same shyness towards my future husband as I did with Winten. I will pen daily love notes for my husband while rocking Aaliyah's "4 Page Letter." The idea of marriage and beating Lexi ignited my soul with passion.

Breaking out of my thoughts, I shook my head, holding firm to my original statement. "I will be married first!"

"Miya, I agree," Tamia proclaimed, catching the other BAEs off guard.

I smiled, stretching out my arm for Tamia to slap my palm. She pretended to hit it, then pulled back. "But! Your husband will cheat. You will not be able to satisfy him in bed."

"Tamia, show me the stats. What number of men cheat on their virgin wives?" Lexi demanded, sounding like statistical Naja.

And on cue, Naja interjected. "Forty percent of married couples are impacted by infidelity. Studies show that a partner who is sexually experienced knows what they enjoy and chooses someone with whom they mesh sexually. However, other statistics have revealed that sexually experienced partners prefer to teach inexperienced partners their erotic desires."

"Damn, Lexi. I am only playing with your cousin. And Naja, not everyone lives by facts and statistics like your analytical ass," Tamia countered, trying to drive her point home. "Seriously, the order of marriage will be Naja, Lexi, Imani, me, and then you, Miya."

Unanimously, we all rolled our eyes at her comment.

Damn. What a joke. Even Tamia believed she would marry before me. She should find a man who loves her first. Tamia always chooses men out of her league. Even worse than that, she mistreats the men who adore her.

Tamia advertises my virginity whenever we are out and jokes about me having a chastity lock to embarrass me. Naja once said that Tamia does it to protect me from the dogs out in these streets. A couple of times, Tamia had explicitly told men what she would do to them, and if the guy still showed interest, she would degrade him. Her goal was to make men crave her, not protect me. She is the only BAE that represents five personality types in our group. She's the "I know somebody" friend and the "flirty, funny, mother hen, and turn-up" friend. I used to be surprised each time a new personality trait appeared. Before realizing every group of friends has a Tamia.

I stepped back into the conversation when my girls agreed Lexi or Naja would be the first to marry or have a double ceremony. It was a tossup between Imani and Tamia, but I always... somehow always placed dead last.

I sulked, sitting cross-legged on the floor as the girls circled me, expressing why they believed I would be last... the first reason being my fear of having sex, then my fear of talking to men. The third was the fact that I expressed myself through music too much. They emphasized that most men did not have the time to listen to a playlist to see how I felt. I couldn't recall the fourth through tenth reasons because I zoned out.

My competitive nature got the best of me. I was ready to place a bet. "Okay, why don't you put your money against your hypothesis. We all have good jobs. We will drop a hundred dollars each month into an account for the next five years. The first two people to get married will get the money in the bank," I propose.

Naja huffed. "I am too old to be betting on my future."

"Heffa, please!" I taunted, "I have seen you bet on your parents' marriage. It's okay to admit you fear losing."

"My problem is the prize doesn't seem fair," Imani muttered. "I think the first person who gets married gets half of whatever is in the bank. The second and third person gets half of whatever is left in the bank each time they get married. The fourth person will bleed the account dry, and the fifth person gets nothing but congratulations."

"Don't you think this is childish?" Lexi exclaimed. "Besides, I do not want to take all of your hard-earned cash."

Scowls of various styles graced our faces, contemplating Lexi's words before declaring we were all in.

Hopping off the floor, I retrieved paper to write out the terms. The first guideline stated that we could not get married until 2007 because Tamia and

I were a part of USC's Trojan class of 2006. *Go Trojans!* Naja will graduate from USC Keck School of Medicine, earning her third degree. Lexi and Imani graduated two years ago with dual degrees but were still validating their positions at work.

The second rule declared that engagements did not count. You must walk down the aisle to win the bet. And if you elope, you must present a marriage license and pictures. My mind implored me to add another clause. I omitted the clause since no BAE would dare marry without her sisters present.

"Are we done partying?" Tamia asked, signing the contract, making it official.

Resuming my playlist as the answer, we all danced, singing along with the music, marveling at how Naja sang the hook and performed Busta's part of "Touch It." The girl could flow. If she ever gave up on medicine, she could be the next Missy Elliot.

"*Run This Town*"

Jay-Z

Malik

IN JANUARY 2006, I WAIVED MY senior college season and declared myself eligible for the NFL Draft. My mother was livid. She is a firm believer in always having a backup plan; according to her, that's a college degree. Since childhood, football has been my sole plan. My sports manager—Kyle—incorporated an education clause into my contract to ease my mother's anxieties. He assured her we had the leverage to achieve this goal since various teams were scouting me.

Numerous commentators predicted San Francisco would draft me to achieve a formidable offensive team because I was the NCAA's top-ranked wingback for three years.

Two months later, at Radio City Music Hall, the Atlanta Falcons signed me as their new running back the evening before the draft.

After announcing my new team to the world, I stepped off the stage and dialed my mother. I was bouncing on the tip of my toes, listening as her words filled me with pride. Pops snatched the phone from my hand, saving me from my mother's charitable wish list. I made a mental note to bless her church and two charities because everyone knew I would run through the fiery pits of hell to make Mary Ann Walker proud.

A few commentators declared the 2006 NFL draft was the worst in NFL history. As a rookie, I was determined to prove I was worth every penny of my $52.5 million contract. Reebok reported receiving over ten thousand orders for my Atlanta jersey the following day. However, my number wasn't assigned yet. Thanks to my mother and Kyle, I secured over five million dollars in endorsements within a month, which allowed me to purchase my mother's dream estate in Temecula Wine Country.

During minicamp, I bonded with the Atlanta Dirty Birds. The team accepted me, but the city had doubts. During the first game, the fans showered me with love, cheering as I performed the Dirty Bird dance. I dedicated my first touchdown to the state, earning my team's respect and the city's love.

I thought life couldn't get any better until Sabrina Bollinger made me her target of affection. I tried to stay away from her and focus on my first season and senior college year. However, Sabrina was aggressive, and that intrigued me. Whenever I lost a game or struggled with school assignments, she would appear to alleviate my stress.

Some players have lucky socks, drawers, and undershirts. I had Sabrina. I stockpiled 140 yards against New York in the first game Sabrina attended, and the Falcons won. Every game she attended, I massed massive yards. Sabrina became my good luck charm.

Sitting on the jet, rehearsing my speech, I was headed to my parents' twelve-bedroom horse ranch in Temecula, California, to get my grandmother's wedding ring and my mother's blessings. After dating Sabrina for over a year, she's confident she is the woman for me.

I approached the back entrance of my parent's home, and the aromatic scent of sauteed vegetables smothered the atmosphere. Placing my bag on the ground, I leaned against the stone wall as the melodic sounds of horns and trumpets wailed by the pool. My eyes devoured the horse stables, two villas, two guest houses, and the rock cavern. Last month, my parent's massive estate was featured in Temecula Wine Country's Modern Ranch homes edition.

I closed my eyes and swayed from side to side as the piano's bold, rich tones dominated the song. Music has been my therapist, lover, and closest friend. Musical notes connect my DNA strands. Music was always a building block for my father and me. A man of few words, he allowed music to express his moods for as long as I can remember, and I could always tell if my father had a beautiful or a horrible day at work by the songs he played.

His favorite thing to say to me was, "Son, embrace the musical language. Music can help us express emotions that are hard to verbalize."

I adore the way my pops love my mom through music and actions. I had vowed to love Sabrina the same way. First, I must get her to enjoy songs that speak to her heart, not her twerking skills.

As usual, the sliding French doors were wide open. I knew I could genuinely surprise my queen. I slowly crept into the dining room. My mother stood at the stove cooking, and Pops sat on a barstool singing to her. My father noticed me sneaking into the house and smiled.

I placed my index finger on my lips. I eased behind my mother and planted a kiss on her wavy black tresses. Pops smiled brightly.

"Mark, we will never eat if you keep getting fresh."

I could see how my mother could get me and my father confused. We're twins. He's about two inches taller than me.

"Oooh, Ma. You and Pops are undercover freaks!"

She spun around, waving the serving spoon at my father and me before squealing while jumping around the kitchen island. "I missed you, Queen." I kissed her on her olive cheeks. My mother wrapped her petite arms around my waist, squeezing tightly.

"Mark, did you know Malik was coming?"

My father hunched his shoulders. I called him a week prior and told him I was coming this weekend. My father promised to have my mother floating on cloud nine upon my arrival – a small task since my mother stays ecstatic.

Growing up, I recall my parents having eight quarrels. I asked my parents what kept them from arguing. They both shared similar advice. "I seek God's guidance before jumping to conclusions," Pops admitted. He continued to say, "The same time it takes to think of something negative to say, I could kiss my wife on the cheek and calm the both of us."

He advised me always to take my problems to God concerning my marriage and life. Then, he joked how he reminded God that Jesus gave him this woman, so they both needed to keep her in line.

My mother proudly acknowledged maintaining a peaceful home by being a snitch. I recall thinking, "Who was she telling?" It must be Granny and Papa, but Papa was too old to spank my dad's butt. I will never forget the sincerity in my mother's eyes when I asked her the same question.

"I tell God about my problems. He is the only being who can change hearts and minds. God directed your father to me. So, God needs to provide him with the knowledge and wisdom to lead this family and provide for us."

Faith and music have preserved the peace and love that fills my parents' home. The thing I admired most about my parents was their hearts. God directed their paths towards each other, and I think God did the same with Sabrina and me.

"Are you here for the entire weekend, Malik?" my mother questioned.

I smiled brightly, revealing my pearly white teeth. "No, ma'am. I leave tomorrow. I came here on a mission with a purpose."

"Oh no, I recognize this smile," my mother teased. "It yells, 'Mom, I hit the pole at school in your brand-new car. Please forgive me!'"

My father chuckled at my mother's theatrics, then walked into the living room and sat in his oversized recliner.

"Mark, why are you moving away? Malik Walker, I hope you're not here to upset me."

I raised my eyebrows and frantically shook my head. "Mary, love, can we eat?" my father asked.

I winked at him.

After I helped my mother set the table, I ran to the cellar and retrieved a sweet red wine. My mother looked at my father while I opened the wine bottle and allowed it to breathe.

"Mark and Malik Walker, are you two up to something?" My mother glared at Pops and me. "All week, my king has been singing to me nonstop. Now don't get me wrong, singing is regular for him, but it raised my suspicions when he sang me a bathroom teetee song."

My father's eyes ogled. He hunched his shoulders. My mother continued, "Now, you are overfilling my glass with wine while giving me those lost puppy dog eyes."

I smiled brightly at my mother and winked.

My father reached out his hand to my mother and me to say grace. After we prayed, my mother was even more skeptical of Pops and me. I gawked at my father's choice of words. Did he have to ask God to allow cooler heads to prevail and intercede between my mother and me?

"Malik, have you changed your mind concerning your college degree?" I attempted to answer, but my mother plowed on. "College tuition reimbursement is a part of your contract outside your twenty-million-dollar guarantee."

"Mom, I am still attending school. I came tonight.... Because. Well. God has sent my wife, and she will replace you as my queen, and I wanted Grandma's wedding ring so I can propose to her."

My mother placed her fork and knife on the plate. She finished chewing the grilled chicken in her mouth, taking a nip of water, then two sips of wine before tilting her head towards the ceiling. "What queen do you have in your life? The only person you have been dating is that little gold-digging white girl."

I ran my clammy hands over my jeans, then rested them on my lap under the table. "Mom, white women can be queens, too."

My mom's eyes rapidly fluttered. My father shook his head, leaving his seat to walk over and stand behind my mother. He kneaded her shoulders as she heaved with anger. My mother began caressing his hands as my father kissed her forehead before releasing her shoulders and strolling over to the bar.

He raised a cognac glass in the air. I held up two fingers, requesting a double.

My mother cleared her throat. "Her color has nothing to do with her not being a queen. Do you know the name of the most powerful chess piece on a chessboard that resides adjacent to the King? This piece can move in a straight line vertically, horizontally, or diagonally. She is not limited to one space. Furthermore, she can cover twenty-seven squares on the board, and she goes by the name of Queen!" My mother educated me.

My knees bounced up and down under the table. Getting this ring was not going to be easy.

My mother wagged her index finger in the air as she spoke. "Your grandmother's mother, my mother, and I are queens. Against all the odds, we continue to move vertically, horizontally, or diagonally no matter what life has thrown at us. We remain the most powerful players in our homes, school, and the boardroom. In a time where women had to fight for an education, the female rulers in your family tree independently fought so you could inherit wealth and a birthright."

"Mom, I understand—" My mother waved her index finger above her head and then balled her hand into a tight fist. Instantly, a knot formed in my throat, and I ceased talking.

My mother continued her speech despite my interruption. "Now, you have the nerve to attempt to destroy my mother's, mother's, mother's legacy by coming in here, asking for my mother's ring to give to a high school dropout."

I glanced over my mother's head and witnessed the sun dipping low.

The night's blue hue elevated itself towards the sky, and so did my mother's mood and tone.

"For Pete's sake, Malik, the girl follows NFL players around like a job!"

My mother shoved her plate forward, and it collided with her centerpiece. My father stepped toward my mother, but she fanned him away with her index finger. Pops froze.

"Mom, she has a GED, and she works. She's a receptionist," I exclaimed.

My mother closed her eyes tightly, speaking through clenched lips. "Did you consult God, son?"

I lowered my head.

"We are Walker's. That means we never look down. You can never move forward, traveling backward," my father said.

My father was right. Slowly, I lifted my head. I was afraid to question God concerning Sabrina being my wife. What if God did not send Sabrina? I was not ready to be without her. I refused to ask the question. My eyes trailed upwards until my eyes met my mother's golden-brown ones. I contemplated telling her the truth but knew it would not bring me closer to getting my grandmother's ring. So, my response could only be what I hoped.

"Mom, God sent her to me," I whined.

"Son, sometimes people think God sent them a gift when it's a distraction from the enemy to obscure their view from their blessings."

"I did not have to ask God if he sent her. I feel it in my heart," I honestly admitted. "I have been praying you would too, Mom."

"God's acceptance is all you two need, not ours," my mother retorted, aiming a finger at my father, then at herself. "Malik, besides Denise, this is the only woman you have fornicated with, correct? I still do not know what happened between you and her to this day. She was a good Christian girl."

Getting over my first love rocked my belief in true love. After we separated, I called her house once a week, never speaking. I only played Brian McKnight's "Anytime." I didn't stop calling her home until her mother called my mother complaining about me blasting her ears with "I Miss You" by Aaron Hall. My mother was livid, but my father understood my anguish.

I glanced at my dad, shocked he didn't tell my mother about my college days. Women threw themselves at me every day in college, and I was a fat kid sampling their cake until my father busted me with a girl getting head. He gave me a speech about being a better role model for my baby brother.

Before I could tell my mother what had happened to Denise, she continued speaking. "Do you think it's lust or love? I am sure Susan is doing unimaginable sexual things to you, considering she has more experience than you. Do not allow sex to distract you from your blessings." My mother pointed a finger in the air as she paused after each word in this last statement.

I eyeballed my father. "Sorry, Son, I don't keep secrets from my wife. I hope you will not either," my father informed me as he looked at my mother. "Usually, your mother doesn't share what I confide in her."

"Sorry, my King, but this is my baby."

"Mom, I am not a baby anymore. I am a grown man. Can I get the ring or not?"

"Not!" The pitch of her voice made me and my father shudder.

"You raised me to make solid decisions, and my life indicates that," I shrieked. "Can't you trust me and stand behind this decision?"

My mother reached her hands across the table. I turned my palms upright, and she laid her hands in mine. I engulfed her hands and instantly felt a surge of love exuding. She peered past my exterior into my soul. The innocent little boy dwelling in me crumbled.

"I raised you to be a king so God could direct you to your strong queen. In this world, a black king needs someone to have his back. Life will get tough, but a strong queen can make it better with a simple hug or smile. Her light can brighten his darkest path, and when her king's compass breaks, she becomes his navigation. She is his bridge to God when he's spiritually wounded or churched out. She pulls her king back under the umbrella of protection after he wanders too far away from God's grace and mercy."

"Amen," my father shrilled, cutting my mother off.

Pops continued where my mother stopped. "They say a man changes after he finds the right woman. A man changes once he finds his queen. A king recognizes his queen because her light shines like a beam guiding his path."

I caressed my mother's hand, and Proverbs 18:22 invaded my thoughts. My heart sung. *"He who finds a wife finds what is good and receives favor from the Lord."*

I slumped in my chair as the words danced across my heart.

"Son, God does not send a woman to find her king. He directs you towards her. A man is drawn to her essence because it is familiar to him. In her presence, he feels solidarity. His missing half will reunify his body, mind, and soul. He is confident she will pour into him. He understands his job is to pour into her mentally, physically, emotionally, financially, sexually, and spiritually.

He will safeguard her crown at all costs. Understand, a wife can only give the world what her king gives her. That means you will pour into each other daily, but you should always pour more into her. Is Sabrina strong enough to refill you after you have poured into her and the world?" My father paused, waiting on my response.

"I have only met her a few times; however, she comes off egotistical and destitute. A wife must restore and refill her family. One of her jobs is to be her husband's helpmate. Your mother and I have raised you to uplift, provide, protect, and pour into your queen. Can this girl refill you, Son?" Pops asked again, differently.

I bucked my eyes at my father. "Damn, Pops!" I mouthed.

My mother's superpowers kicked in. "Do you have something to add, Son?" I shook my head.

My mother can genuinely see and hear all, even when no words are swirling in the air.

When I attempted to ask my mother if Pops could return to being a man of minimal words, my tongue twisted in knots. He had tons to say tonight, and they were all directed to lash me. I did not have the bravery to voice my thoughts. Instead, I confessed. "I am not sure if she can refill my soul, but Sabrina is ready for us to be married."

My mother snatched her hands from my grip. "I will give you my mother's ring after Sabrina tells me what it means to be a Proverbs 31 Woman and a queen."

My mother stepped away from the farmhouse sustainable hardwood table before I could continue to plead my case.

"Malik, I love you," she voiced her back towards me. "However, boy, the next time you ask for my mother's ring, I pray you are ready to be a husband because God has presented you with your wife and not because a woman is demanding to become your mate."

"God in Me"

Mary Mary

Miya

BARELY MANAGING TO ROLL OVER, I snatched the phone off the hook. Tamia's voice rang clear even as I adjusted the receiver's cold plastic to rest on the base of my neck, nestling it against my ear.

"Wake up!"

My eyes danced until they landed on the digital clock on the mahogany dresser. My eyelids flutter shut as I struggle to focus on the illuminated red digits, revealing a dancing six and two blurry circles.

While most people lay snuggled in their beds, plunging into a profound realm of sleep, I am up at three in the morning on the weekdays producing the hottest morning show in Los Angeles, CA.

A typical Saturday morning consists of voiceovers and pre-recording syndicated advertisements. My evening ends with me snoring in a Salon chair or in my bed. On Sunday, I attend the early morning church service. On my way back to bed, I stop at my Aunts to eat breakfast leftovers and snag myself a lunch plate.

"Miya, did you hear me? Heffa, wake up!"

Voice still groggy with sleep, I questioned, "For what…? It's Sunday, and I plan to curl in my bed and indulge in a delightful book." I pulled the hunter green and gold jaguar comforter to my chin. I was not going to church or anywhere else today.

Tamia smacked her lips. "You don't want to see God or get a plate of food?" she responded to her questions. "Yes, you do. Then, you can thank him for blessing yo' black ass with your promotion."

"Girl, I thanked God before and after they informed me of my promotion and every day since."

"Mmmmkay if you say so," she sarcastically replied. "First, I want you to meet my boy from school, and second, because I said so."

"Girl, God is everywhere for one since we are counting. Secondly, I acknowledge God in all I do. Furthermore, I can thank Him at home for all the blessings He has bestowed upon me."

"Okay, then come meet my boy."

My brows furrowed as I grew frustrated.

"Why are you pushing him off on me?"

"I am trying to bless you with a husband. He was joking about marrying a virgin, and I would have told him that was impossible, then I thought of you."

Tamia always had a boy she wanted me to meet.

A pinched expression clenched my face.

"Interesting," I hummed.

"Last night, Lexi told me they may trade Paxton to LA. They will marry on the 4th of July if he returns to LA. Girl, the MLB draft is in June of this year. So, you have four months to beat Lexi to the altar," Tamia whispered.

"Why aren't you trying to beat Lexi to the altar? The MLB draft has nothing to do with Paxton. The season starts in March, and they will trade him before the draft," I educated her. "Didn't you say you would be married before me?"

"Competing is you and Lexi steelo, not mine."

I sat on the bed, replaying the night we all wagered on who would be the first BAE married. So far, my journey to marriage playlist included heartbreak songs from Mary J. Blige, Keisha Cole, and Faith Evans. Things were not going well.

"I have a couple of men I'm dating. I still haven't found my husband yet," Tamia confessed. "At least if you win, I know we are going on a vacation at your expense. We should have enough money to go to Rome in style. Who suggested the deposit go from one hundred to two hundred monthly?"

I hunched my shoulder, assuming Tamia could see me.

Thinking back, it was Imani. She probably told Winten the bet details, and he accrued the cash towards their wedding budget.

Damn! We have been out of school for nine months, and nobody is married or has secured an engagement ring. Everyone thought Lexi would grace the altar first. Paxton opted to leave college and play for Atlanta Regulators, obliterating that dream. Sadly Lexi did not relocate. Somehow they are managing a long-distance relationship because my cousin refused to leave her LA Public Relations job. Outside of Paxton, she has some big stars on her roster. Whenever an athlete or an entertainer gets into some shit, they call Lexi to spin the story. The girl is the problem-solver in our clique.

According to Imani, Winten made them a five-year plan. In 2007, they were to buy a home. Winten neglected to divulge that they would be in separate homes. In 2008, they were supposed to get engaged, marry in 2009, buy a bigger house, and rent out their homes. In 2011, they would conceive their first child. I imagine he decided to give my judgmental/ mother hen BAE a break in 2010.

After graduating, Dakari and Naja were supposed to start their residency, but Dakari chose to do his residency abroad, and Naja refused to go. Naja disappeared for two weeks after they broke up. Every BAEs was worried except Lexi, which led me to believe she knew Naja's whereabouts.

After her second disappearing act, Naja returned, praising their rekindled relationship. She and Dakari cope with a global relationship through Skype and overseas booty calls. After all, they could afford international travel; they both come from inherited wealth.

Naja's father is filthy rich, and he knows everyone in Hollywood. During my second year of college, he helped me get a job at LA's hottest radio station as a junior music producer. Now here I am, a radio talk show producer. I could have never accomplished my goal if I were worried about a man or getting married.

I don't see how Tamia manages to be in everybody's business. As an investment banker associate for a private equity company and a party animal, she is busy seven days a week. She absolves herself of the past six days of sin every Sunday morning, acting holier than thou.

Six months ago, the church buzzed about her scandal with Deacon James.

The BAEs called an emergency meeting and demanded Tamia end her affair with Deacon James or find another house of worship.

Since Lexi and I were three, our mothers were a part of the Holiness Church of God in Christ congregation. We were never a part of a church scandal for decades until we invited Tamia to join our church. Tamia promised never to make another congregation member a financial contributor. The girl has a fetish for married men of God.

Tamia would never marry first unless it were as a sister-wife. The conversation in my head was entertaining as I laughed loudly.

"What is so funny?"

I shot from the bed, surveying my surroundings, placing my hand over my mouth.

"Are you going to church to see a Deacon?" I asked, avoiding giving her an answer directly. "And did you sleep with this guy? I am not trying to be rude, but remember you slept with Rodney and then tried to hook him up with me."

"Fuck you, Miya. I cannot comprehend why you guys assume I fuck everybody. Girl, you know I only talk a good game."

I pursed my lips as she continued to appeal her case.

"Well, for your info, he is a brother to me. His family moved to Atlanta when he was thirteen. He moved to LA a couple of months ago, and we bumped into each other at a work event."

"Is he a banking analyst?"

"No!" She paused for a dramatic effect, but I remained silent like a church mouse. "My boy is a personal financial advisor. He has been dating, but these LA girls are too complex for him."

"Okay, I will go to lunch with him."

"Are you able to come to church today to meet him? He needs an unadulterated woman like you. Please come and meet him today at church," Tamia begged.

First, she teases me for being a virgin and too pure for any man. Now my virtue is perfect for her childhood friend. I can comprehend why I am friends with the other BAEs, but I ponder why I'm friends with Tamia. I am sure I was not the only BAE contemplating this.

"All right, Heffa, but I am not making any promises concerning us dating. Make sure you wake up Lexi and call Naja and Imani. If I am going to church today to deal with my family, we are all going," I retorted before ending the call.

I turned on my Bose stereo system, inviting the spirit of the Lord into my bedroom, singing along to "Never Would Have Made It" by Marvin Sapp.

Musical notes inundated my veins, reaching across generations. Whenever racial segregation and discrimination arose, the spiritual hymns and folk music that played a vital role in slavery and the Civil Rights Movement filled my heart as I fought for equality and justice.

When trouble or tragedy invaded my life, gospel music helped me release the pain and allow God to fill the emptiness in my heart.

Music rhythmically binds the world together. It crosses nations and aids in sharing our cultures regardless of race and gender. How often have you watched a YouTube video, witnessed a young Asian kid singing and dancing to Michael Jackson, or spotted a Russian man spitting Tupac lyrics?

Music is selfish. It is a vessel for expressing and sharing feelings. Music merely cares for itself and the emotions it conjures within you. The right song could evoke emotions and influence your interaction with people. Every human being can describe a situation in their lives where music altered their mood, provided them with an answer to a question plaguing their mind, or increased their knowledge.

Hell, Aretha Franklin taught most of us how to spell respect, and Anita Baker taught us how many days there are in a year.

"I Won't Complain" by Rev. Paul Jones came on. I stood there, frozen in place, allowing each word he sang to minister to my soul.

"God, you have truly been good to me!"

I cried with my eyes raised towards heaven, reflecting on how exceptional God was lately. "Lord, please send me a good man. I would love it if you sent me a husband. I want to be the first one married. Can you allow the last to finish first?"

"Lord, Tamia, and nobody else has to remind me how good and merciful you are. I acknowledge that you are my provider, protector, and best friend. I could not imagine my life without you, Amen!"

"*You Brought The Sunshine*"

The Clark Sisters

Miya

SWEAT DRENCHED MY IVORY TUNIC DRESS as I shouted and praised the Lord. Pastor Sutton's sermon ignited my soul.

Attempting to make a beeline for the bathroom and freshen up but was deterred with each step I took. People patted me on the back, thanking me for giving my testimony. One woman visiting our church said she appreciated me for letting go and letting God.

Filled with joy, I smiled inwardly.

The congregation reminded me why I loved coming to this tiny church. It is always on fire for God. I could feel the spirit of the Lord still enveloping me, and I couldn't care less about my appearance.

Halfway to the bathroom, Tamia approached me with a massive grin.

"Miya, the Lord certainly got a hold of you today. I am glad you listened to me and came to church. You would have missed your blessing if it were not for me."

I started to inform her that God would bless me at home or church because he is concerned with my heart's position, not my geographical location. Tamia and people like her perplexed me, assuming others would never receive a blessing or accomplish anything without their existence in our lives.

Every day I thank God for Naja's help and appreciate her father's connections. That one opportunity opened doors for me from global traveling to my current position. I'm grateful Naja never vocally stated that I would not be a radio producer if it were not for her or her father.

Since college, Tamia was famous for taking the recognition for anything good in anybody's life. It was always because of her prayers, because she invited you somewhere, or simply because you were her friend.

People need to comprehend that what God has for you is for you and only you. Thank the people who led you to your blessing, but God is the only person you owe everything to in the end. God would have used somebody else if they did not allow God to use them.

As an alternative, I smiled brightly, allowing my Shekinah glory to eclipse any darkness around me.

"Girl, what are you wearing?" I asked Tamia, inspecting her. The black floral lace cap sleeve dress was not a church dress. I was sure of it because I bought her this freakum dress for a BAE club event.

Tamia was a size seven like me, but her butt was a work of art. You could set a cup and a saucer on it. Tamia was drop-dead gorgeous with her flawless gingerbread skin. I've witnessed men standing in awe once they noticed her luscious lips, round chin, high cheekbones, and solid square jawline. Her light brown almond hooded eyes and naturally long lashes were cascaded by her long dark brown hair, which she wore in a soft flip to her shoulders.

Somebody said, "Child, you cut a rug today."

A glowing smile graced my sweaty face. "Yeah, the Lord was in this sanctuary today," I replied, frantically patting down my seventy-five-dollar press and curl.

My cousin Lexi started walking toward Tamia and me. The short red floral chiffon beaded neck dress hugs every curve on her body. The three-inch stilettos gave her legs for days.

Gawking at Tamia, then back at Lexi, I slowly spoke. "Did you guys wear these outfits to the club last night?"

Tamia snigger's.

Shoving Tamia aside, Lexi fluttered her hands in the air rearranging the space between us before greeting me. I attempted to return the salutation but halted when Lexi started wiping the mascara off my streaked cheeks.

I pulled away.

"I am a big girl. I know how to clean myself up," I barked. She was always treating me like a naive little girl.

"Miya, I am trying to help you look presentable. Girl, you a hot mess," Lexi jokes, yanking my hair. "Do not make me use foul language in the house of the Lord."

The words hot mess would never describe sexy Lexi. The young boys in our neighborhood nicknamed her. My cousin turns both sexes' heads with her vanilla wafer skin and heart-shaped face when her red bottoms walk through. God blessed my entire family with breasts and round derrieres, but he gave Lexi a double dose.

God could have stopped there. But oh, nooo! He made her five-foot-nine and a perfect 135 pounds, and most of it is breast, buttocks, and hips. She has never had acne breakouts or unruly hair days. The heffa even smells like a fresh floral bouquet after an intense workout. God desired sheer allure when constructing Lexi, hence the oval oceanic eyes, perfectly pouty lips, long eyelashes, and lengthy blonde hair with natural golden highlights. He even gave her the perfect father.

When men meet my cousin, they are speechless because they do not see the mischievous glare behind her smile as I do. Even my parents said, "her smile lights up any room and can entice any man's heart." My cousin's tantalizing aroma diverts men from her evil intentions of constantly outshining me.

"Cousin, I heard of the term getting ugly for God, but you took it to a whole different level today," Lexi acknowledged. I braced myself as my cousin belittled me to make herself feel superior. "How will you meet Tamia's friend looking like a hot mess?"

Tamia and I whipped our necks towards Lexi. While getting my praise on, it slipped my mind that Tamia had invited her friend.

"He might love the hot mess between her thighs," Tamia voiced with a snicker.

"Damn, you almost made me curse. Fooling around with you will get me a one-way ticket to hell," Lexi asserted, rolling her eyes at Tamia and me.

"Silly me, I imagined shaking your butt in every Hollywood, Santa Monica, and Long Beach club would send you to hell on a first-class ticket." Lexi stood there, itching to curse me while Tamia and I chuckled.

"Tamia, I do not understand why you are snickering and shit. I was out clubbing because you begged me to go. Unlike you two, I have a man. And for your information, Ms. Innocent, I use those club visits as an opportunity to network. I landed two clients last night," Lexi snapped. "You two don't have to network to build your empire. I do! Both of you are men less, so who cares if Tamia goes out and shakes her ass to snag a husband."

Unlike Tamia, I only engaged in relationships with men that are husband material. If her friend is not, I will cut it off before it begins.

Since I am always working, I found it better to date men ready to get married. They seemed more prepared for the commitment I wanted. They were financially sound. Christopher was the first guy I dated. He broke it off with me because I was a virgin and didn't want to be responsible for my virginity. Whatever the hell that meant.

Next, I dated Curtis from the Art Department. He was a gentle soul. He was always drawing me abstract pieces. According to Barber, the hairstylist who has the hottest tea, Curtis was a down-low brother.

One of the radio show's co-host advised me to stop dating the men I work with after Eric, the sound tech. He tried to sabotage the show after telling him I was not giving him my virginity until he placed a ring on my finger.

When I showed him my wedding binder, he flipped out, ranting and raving about wasting months of his life.

I wanted to tell him my notebook was minor compared to Imani's yellow book-sized binder. She started planning her wedding at ten years old. Her binder has grown immensely in the last year. The bet sparked innovative ideas. The only thing missing in her book is her wedding date.

"Where is Imani?" I inquired, changing the subject.

"I called her, but she never answered," Tamia exclaimed with an attitude. "Her lovestruck ass is probably somewhere under Winten."

"I pray she stops putting Winten before God and herself. Imani worships Winten. She believes he can walk on water. Her world will crumble when she finds out he is merely a man. Heaven have mercy on her soul," Tamia preached and then huffed. "Shit, even though I went clubbing last night, I brought my ass to church."

I wanted to disagree with Tamia, but you cannot tell Imani that Winten is not a saint. I have watched her and Winten debate, and even if she is right, she will degrade herself to feed his spoiled rich ego.

"Watch your mouth, girl," Lexi warned Tamia. "We need to go outside before God hits all of us with a lightning bolt."

"Do not worry. God sent Aunt Geraldine instead," I announced to Tamia and Lexi, pointing in Lexi's mother's direction.

My aunt waved at us, and Lexi rolled her eyes. My auntie is the only person that can put Lexi in her place and then demand money afterward.

"Hello, ladies," Aunt Geraldine greeted us, smiling from ear to ear. The grin slowly dissipated as Auntie's gaze fell on Lexi. "Lexi, only God can describe what you are wearing. Did you leave the club and come straight to church?"

I laughed, but Tamia refused to express any amusement at Lexi's expense.

"What do you think Paxton would say regarding his future wife dressing like a harlot? Paxton is the best thing that has happened to this family. Do not come running to me if he drops you."

My mother joined the circle, ranting. "Niece , do not bend over. I am afraid we will all catch a glance of your goody pie."

Lexi smacked her lips. The piercing glare in Aunt Geraldine's eyes forced our smirks to diminish.

"Mommy, do you need some money? Did you cook?" Lexi quipped.

Annoyed, Aunt Geraldine threw her hands in the air. Before she could respond, my mother grabbed her by the arm and dragged her away.

"Love you, Mommy," Lexi yelled smugly.

Auntie turned around and smiled cunningly. "I hope you all are coming by the house for lunch. I cooked tons of food. Lexi, bring me a thousand bucks. Thanks for offering." She took two more steps and then turned around again. "Tamia, bring your polite friend, and I didn't forget your repulsive outfit. Lord, you and Lexi are not clubbing with Jesus. Lexi, I love you more, baby." My Auntie and cousin always argued, but Lexi is her heart, and she loves her to death.

"Miya, I think he is single," my mother whispered loud enough for everyone to hear. My body instantly diminished. All I could do was shake my head.

Tamia squeezed my hand. "My mother embarrasses me all the time. Your mother is culturally unaware, so she gets a pass. Ghetto describes my mother." I have met all my BAEs' families except Tamia's. Sometimes I see a glint of sadness in her eyes when anyone inquires about her family.

My heart became overwhelmed with emotions as I yanked Tamia into my arms. Instantaneously, she reminded me why we are friends. I love her crazy ass.

"Speaking of Tre, he's headed this way," Tamia announced. I turned entirely towards Lexi, allowing her to clean my face.

"Typical heifer behavior. First, you want me to stop treating you like a child. Now you want my help. You better be glad you are my favorite cousin, and I love you."

I poked Lexi in the side.

"I am your only cousin."

I pleaded with my eyes for Lexi to hurry.

Tamia's friend's voice drew closer to my ear. "Tamia, thanks for leaving me by myself. I received an invitation for lunch," he announced.

"Tre, this is my girlfriend, Miya," Tamia said while tapping me on the side. Lexi's fingers moved faster. I slowly eased around to face Tamia's friend.

"Miya, stop playing. Tre can still see your beauty. He is a Christian man and understands getting ugly for God. You have a timeless beauty and could never look ugly, girl," Tamia complimented me.

I turned to Tre, and he placed a hand over his heart. "Tamia was right. You have a timeless beauty. I love the shape of your face. It's like a heart, the same as Sophia Loren. I adore how your skin, eyes, and hair are honey-brown hues. It reminds me of the singer Natalie Cole. Wait! You have a beauty mark above your succulent lips like Cindy Crawford." If he kept going, I would remind him of a beet. I could feel the heat in my cheeks rising.

I extended my hand. "Hello, my name is Miya. It is a pleasure to meet you."

Tamia's friend had a sexy baby face, but his juicy lips drew me in.

"I am Tre, and you, my dear, are an angel sent from God." Tamia smiled at Tre and me. I could tell she was pleased with her matchmaking skills. I could not believe I blushed at his corny compliment. I struggled to keep my mind on the Lord since I was still standing in his house.

"Can you do me the honor of going on a date?" Tre questioned.

My skin heated another degree, and I fanned my face.

"We have to go to my momma's house right now," Lexi interjected. "You realize she will kill us if we don't show our faces."

"Tre, do you mind going to my aunt's house for dinner?"

He swiped his hand over his jet-black fade, and his hazel brown eyes gazed off in the distance, contemplating the invitation.

He ran his hand over his smooth chocolate skin and perfectly trimmed goatee. He seductively licked his succulent lip and responded, "I will follow you anywhere."

I glanced at Lexi and Tamia, who appeared smitten by his hackneyed response. The brother was fine, and his black suit was hanging precisely right on his sylphlike physique.

Eyeing Tre, I recognize God was in the prayer answering business. He was attractive, and I could already foresee him as my husband.

"Feenin'"

Jodeci

Malik

RB POURED US A DRINK. "BRUH, promise you won't allow the ghost of Sabrina's past to stop you from having fun this weekend," Romello "RB" Brooks grunted.

The mere mention of her name made me grunt.

"Don't allow Sabrina to taint our Las Vegas trip," RB insisted.

The sound of Sabrina's name twice in the same sentence created bile in the back of my throat. I puffed on my Cohiba, deciding to let go of the past and enjoy the weekend.

"RB, this Behike stogie is smooth," I bragged.

RB turned me on to cigars, and the diversities of flavor based on the regions were astounding. Visiting cigar lounges had become our thing.

"I'm happy you like the taste," RB replied, passing me a glass of cognac. Dusting off his shoulders, he continues. "Malik, I'm glad you agreed to come. I'm calling this trip the players' weekend."

"I appreciate everything you've done for me," I voiced, sipping on my cognac while RB texted on his phone.

RB and I met in Oakland, California, years ago when he played baseball and football in San Francisco. Before being picked up by New York after two years, he became my teammate when they traded him to Atlanta.

The truck stopped, and I puffed on my stogie several times before bouncing out of the vehicle.

RB patted me on the back while we walked into the Venetian. "I'm glad your ass didn't resist. I was prepared to kick your ass if you didn't get on the jet."

Both of us chuckled.

Walking through the Venetian hotel, a couple of women noticed RB. Women also recognized me, rendering me speechless as they pleaded for us to sign their breasts and hands.

My mind screamed. *Whatever happened to autographing a piece of paper?*

RB high-fived me as the football groupies encircled us. It was astounding how women could slip a room key and a number into your pocket without you even feeling it. I have found business cards, pictures, and room keys in my pants after a night out with RB.

I smiled politely at the women, then quickly turned away. The last thing I needed was another football groupie girlfriend.

Shit, I wanted to date a woman who didn't recognize me and confused a touchdown with a layup.

RB and I approached the club entrance, and the bouncer waved us to come straight to the front. Smiling from ear to ear, the bouncer declared, "RB, you guys have been killing it on the field." He and RB saluted each other.

He glanced over at me with a remorseful look, then greeted me. "Sorry about your injury, Malik. You'll be back on the field gaining mad yards soon." RB smiled at him. I struggled to keep my torso in a vertical line.

No matter how much I attempt to forget about football, fans always remind me of what I frivolously lost. I appreciate the words of encouragement and them shouting, "You will be back soon." However, they don't understand the pain attached to inspirational words.

Six months ago, I tore my knee's ACL, MCL, LCL, and PCL ligaments during a game against New York. A couple of weeks after my injury, I flew to Los Angeles to see a specialist another player recommended.

Dr. Allen claimed I could return to the field in a couple of months, depending on my dedication and hard work, but he needed to perform another reconstruction knee surgery. It was the best news any man could hear. Once I healed from knee surgery, I decided to marry Sabrina. Eager to tell Sabrina, I grabbed the first flight back to Atlanta.

An eerie feeling engulfed me when I entered the mansion. Attempting to shake it off as I hopped through the massive North Buckhead estate searching for Sabrina. Both of her cars were home, and I recognized her hairstylist truck tucked away in the back of the house.

I hopped on the elevator to search her glam room; a sharp pain shot through my leg. The throbbing in my leg slithered up my body and landed in my chest. I froze in place.

I stood there for what seemed like a lifetime, watching Sabrina on her knees in my wine cellar, giving my teammate fellatio in my fucking house.

The old scab of Denise and Tre having sex on my bed reopened. Sabrina's slurping and my teammate's moans of ecstasy bounced off the walls as my blood pressure shot to the 10 ft ceiling. I blinked, and the world went black.

The broken neck of the cabernet bottle in my hand, paired with the blood oozing down Bryant's face, was my first memory of striking him. Sabrina jumped to her feet and started crying. They both tried to convince me this was the first time it had ever happened and would never happen again.

Bryant begged to leave to seek medical care for his head injury. He promised not to tell anyone I had hit him, then ran from my cellar. I didn't care if he told the entire world because he deserved that beat down. I gave Sabrina three days to get out of my house. She tried to say that none of this would have occurred if I had stuck to my schedule. What a fucking joke! Something stirred within and hatred brewed from the pit of my belly.

The slurping sounds of Sabrina's betrayal echoed in my head, driving me to my final decision. She was leaving with nothing except the clothes on her back.

I flashed her the ring I was going to give her. I didn't appreciate that my mother was right. Sabrina was not a queen. Had I not torn my ligaments, I would have proposed the weekend I got injured.

She cried and begged for forgiveness, but anger had dug a hole in my chest and its roots wrapped around my heart, implanting itself fully. A sinister smile crept across my face. Sharing my thoughts, I divulged her wardrobe, and my car stayed.

"I am going to kill myself, Malik!"

I shrug my shoulders before dialing RB. Moments later, he pulled into my driveway with his sister, Raven, and her friends in tow. RB instructed Raven and her friends to restrict Sabrina from taking anything out of the house. Before I could speak, he insisted Raven would oversee everything. I examined my footsteps as I followed my friend to the gaming room to shoot pool.

Raven and her friends had hauled all Sabrina's stuff away by the time the sun was setting. Raven handed me a bag. Glancing in the bag, I spotted the five-carat earrings that Sabrina was wearing today.

A massive sigh escaped my core. "Did you guys take the trinkets and garments off her back?"

RB folded his hands across his chest. "Raven did as I instructed by allowing Sabrina to leave with the outfit she was wearing."

Silence floated between me and RB.

"Raven, did you get the car keys and call her an Uber?" I queried.

Raven's gaze went from unfocused to confident. "We watched her leave in the Uber."

My body collapsed as I wondered how my mother would react to me standing by and allowing a woman to be thrown away like yesterday's garbage. A downward gaze plastered upon my face as I attempted to convince myself a cheater didn't deserve to flaunt my hard-earned money.

Raven's timid voice yanked me from the pits of remorse. "I replaced all the locks and changed the security codes. I even changed the code to the garage," she bragged pridefully.

I wondered how many times she had done this for her brother.

RB snapped his fingers in my face, pulling me back to the present. "What are you drinking?"

I bit down on my lip as I gawked at the waitress. Noticing my apprehension, she provided her favorite drink options. When I raised my left eyebrow, she suggested a glass of cognac, and I agreed.

RB placed his hand on my shoulder and gently squeezed it. "I try to imagine how hard it is not playing right now, but bruh, you have to get back to the land of the living," RB said genuinely. "I realize these last couple of months have been rough on you."

"It is uncanny, dawg. I have small endorsement deals for now, but I went from a chaotic daily life to nothing. My primary goal was to be a professional football player. I miss the intensity I felt every game. I even miss the camaraderie."

"Bruh, you're still a football player. You have been rehabbing your knee nonstop. You will be back on the field soon."

"Man, I went from being a part of the team to a quintessential taxi squad player."

Being a practice squad player was a step below the guy in the equipment room, washing the dirty laundry between practices. I am grateful for the opportunity. Who would refuse six figures in six months? I wasn't sure if this was something I could do for years. Seeing the other players take the field constantly reminded me of how I recklessly allowed my dream to slip through my fingers over a woman.

"It is not your fault. It was that bitch, Sabrina," RB assured me.

"I am a good and upstanding dude. I constantly self-check myself, but seeing Sabrina and Bryant together makes the vein in the middle of my forehead pulse. Hopefully, he gets traded or skips offseason workouts."

"Hopefully," RB rapidly replied. "Sabrina and Bryant will get what is coming to them for what they did to you."

Previously I blamed Sabrina for my NFL dream ending, but it was all my fault. I deserted life, not her. Sabrina was looking for money and status, not unconditional love. I yearned for me and her to have what my parents shared.

However, Sabrina is nothing like my mother. She was a shiny object that the enemy dangled in front of me to convince me I was unworthy of God's blessings.

I slowly drifted into the darkness of depression until it became my haven. I was sulking in the house for weeks waiting for God to save me; instead, he sent my parents.

My father hovered over me, pointing at a controller. My subwoofers and Bose house system roared "I Have Nothing" by Whitney Houston, Dru Hill's "In My Bed," and motherfucking "Games" by Chuckii Booker.

My mother yelled over my brokenhearted soundtracks that had been playing on an endless loop for five days. I thought my mother was about to curse me out. Instead, she demanded I get up and reclaim my life by allowing Dr. Allen to perform the surgery on my knee. I started to protest, but the concern etched across her face broke my heart.

It took a week for my mother to rebuild my confidence in myself, people, and love. However, my faith was rocked when Dr. Allen assessed my knee damage. My odds of playing again went from ninety-five percent to sixty percent because my PCL scar tissue was in the formation stage.

My parents reminded me of my faith and who had brought me thus far.

My mother temporarily relocated to Atlanta and cared for me until I was physically and spiritually healthy enough to stand independently.

My speed had diminished during my practice run, but I was determined not to give up. God blessed me with a talent, and in honor of this gift, I decided to work hard on my craft and leave the particulars to Him.

"Continue to stay focused on offseason workouts. Coach will get you back on the field," RB declared, reassuring my thoughts. "Trust the process." I nodded. "Now, enjoy the beautiful women here."

Two girls twirled their half-naked bodies in front of me as the club's blaring bass rattled the champagne flutes sitting on a table next to me.

What was the purpose of VIP if they just allowed anybody entry?

RB tilted his head towards the two girls, whose bodies were now entangled as one.

"Do you like these ladies?"

I raised my eyebrows. "Shit, they wear more clothes in the strip club!"

RB chuckled. "That's because they want you to take the bands off those stacks. Once the band comes off, so do the clothes." He shrieked at his statement. "Bruh, you are not here to find a wife. You're here to have a good time."

My shoulders rose to the ceiling, then dropped to the floor as I inhaled a gust of air into my lungs.

"Bruh, I'll pay all your fucking bills this month if you fuck one woman here tonight. No names, no strings, only sex."

My spine stiffened as I straightened my posture, contemplating his offer. I cupped my right ear with my hand. "So, let me get this right. If I disrespect a woman here, you will pay all my bills totaling eighteen thousand?"

"Damn, fool! Why are your bills so fucking high? I have a monthly budget of seven thousand." RB studied the wide smile that graced my face, continuing. "Yes, that's my damn proposal."

I shook my head. RB yanked me to my feet, leading me to the VIP section's front. Sighing, I rested my back on the gold rails as my boy scanned the room. He elbowed me in the side whenever he spotted a woman he thought I could bed.

I was getting ready to return to my seat when I spotted her bent over, waving for the bartender at the bar. My strength jerked, pressing firmly against my zipper.

I tapped RB, who had started a conversation with some girl standing close to the VIP entrance. "I found her, I found her. I found my queen, dawg."

"Bruh, you're supposed to find a woman to have sex with, not a wife," Romello snorted. "Now, point her out."

I scanned the bar, but she was gone. The neon beams in the ceiling did not give off enough light. Two strobe lights whirled across the dance floor. I followed the lights, hoping they would land on her.

After twenty minutes, I noticed her on the opposite end of the bar, surrounded by four other ladies. My gaze cruised her figure.

Barely telling RB I'd be back, I sprinted in her direction before he could respond. I bumped into a couple smothering each other on the dance floor. I apologized but never took my eyes off my future queen.

Her friends started gathering their bags, and I tried to push my way through the crowded dance floor faster.

Shit, if I had to chase her around the Las Vegas strip, I would because her essence was luring me like a moth to a flame.

"Red Light Special"
TLC
Miya

ARSPLITTING MUSIC, TATTOO-STAMPED HANDS, DRUNKEN NIGHTS, and two-hour naps signified my and Lexi's 22nd birthday invasion.

Hollywood may be full of glitz and glamor, but Las Vegas was overflowing with pizazz and sin. I was having a blast; however, I missed my boyfriend, Tre, whenever I spotted a couple canoodling through my boozy haze.

Since the day Tamia introduced us, we have been hanging out nonstop. He has a marvelous sense of humor, and I find his overprotective demeanor priceless.

Tre calls or texts me all day to remind me to eat lunch or make sure I make it to my destinations safely. Recently, he started sending flowers to my job every Tuesday and Thursday with lovely poems. I catch myself laughing as I replay one of his corny lines in my head.

Since I arrived in Vegas, I could only get him on the phone once. Our call lasted less than five seconds. I've left numerous messages, but he hasn't called me back. I wondered if he was still upset about not spending my birthday with him.

I explained how my and Lexi's twenty-first birthday consisted of pizza and frozen drinks at my cousin's house due to finals and Lexi's rocketing career. Therefore, we had to celebrate together this year. I couldn't bring him alone because nobody else was bringing their man.

I walked towards the ceiling-to-ceiling hotel window, wondering why Tre hadn't called me in two days. My shoulders slumped against the window. I persuaded myself he was thoughtful, allowing me uninterrupted time with my BAEs.

Imani leaned her body on my right side. She waved her hands in the air as she spoke. "Millions of lights are shining on the BAEs' four-day birthday weekend." I weakly smiled.

"Vegas has over a hundred and fifty casinos, and I will hit big before leaving. I also plan to shop until I drop at the outlets giving Vegas back every penny I win. Are you in?"

I stared at her blankly for a minute.

"Answer me. Say something, Miya. How are you holding up, youngin'?"

I smirked at her comment because she never calls Lexi a youngin.' Imani and Lexi graduated high school and college together because Lexi joined a high school program where she completed her sophomore year over the summer and skipped the sixth grade. None of this mattered because she was still the same age as me, and I entered the exact sophomore program.

Imani twerked against my rigid body. My demeanor softened as I hip-bumped her back.

I softly giggled because I was placing too much emphasis on age these days. When we are young, we say we are older than others and vice versa. Most women stop counting after thirty-five. When I'm fifty, I plan to scream it loud and proud because my uncle never made it to forty or fifty years old. His life was cut short at thirty-nine. My uncle Lexi and I were the three Musketeers and all Aries.

"Aries nation," Tamia yelled. "We're getting turnt up all day."

"I'm a bit exhausted," I admitted.

We had been running around all day, and by the time everybody had gotten dressed, we were all starving, so I suggested the BAE's favorite diner. Whenever the BAEs are in Vegas, you can usually catch us at Blueberry Hill restaurant around 4 am, eating pancakes or muffins to soak up the alcohol after an exhilarating night.

After I inhaled an omelet, a side of bacon, and two blueberry muffins, I was ready for a nap, but Naja and Imani wanted to go shopping.

After shopping, we returned to the hotel and danced between our conjoined suites while getting dressed. We headed downtown to Fremont Street as lavender and orange rays coated the skies.

Fremont Street's bright illumination drew us towards the zip line kiosk. After taking turns, we made a beeline for the first daiquiri stand we spotted.

I ordered a thirty-two-ounce strawberry daiquiri while the rest of the gang ordered a hundred-ounce drink. Naja ordered tube shots for the group right before Tamia got us jello shots.

When the girls tossed back their shots, I hid mine and held my hand out to collect everyone's empty containers, camouflaging my full ones as I disposed of them in the trash.

We arrived in Vegas on Wednesday, and I could only recall drinking two glasses of water. Everything else I drank was a sweet mixed drink or shots of tequila. I was giving my liver a break today.

I remember a girl in my music appreciation class telling me how she got fucked up in Vegas with her girlfriends, and they left her on a bench after she passed out. I liked to think the BAEs would never leave me behind, but if all of us were drunk, who could say what would happen?

As we walked towards the car show at the short strip's end, I babysat the drink in my hand. We stopped at a few small clubs and danced our butts off along the way. Tamia kept shouting it was Lexi and my birthday to anyone that would listen.

While taking pictures of a 1964 canary yellow VW Bug, Naja walked over to me and draped her arms across my shoulders as she spoke. "Pudd, do you think Tre is holding out until marriage due to his itty-bitty dick being the size of a thumbtack?"

She struggled to balance herself before sticking her thumb in the air and ramming it into my nose. I wanted to tell her that her thumb was more prominent than a thumbnail. However, I knew it was futile to debate with a drunk because their intoxicated haze makes them knowledgeable beyond measure.

I smiled and attempted to evade her intoxicating foresight.

"Tamia told me he is not a virgin, so why can't he break you off? Girlie, do you genuinely want to buy a car you have never taken for a test drive?" Naja made a vroom sound, then snickered at her drunken wit.

At that moment, I realized Naja had left the building, and her drunk Gemini twin, Eboni Dream, had joined the conversation. I loved Eboni. She has no filter.

"You should have a paradise lover as I did," Naja slurred. "I fell in love, but he was a liar and a cheater. Make sure Tre is not either."

"Okay, I will."

"Girl, these men will steal your heart and panties." Naja paused as she struggled to balance herself. "And your pussy will betray you and get soaking wet for his tall chocolate tattooed body. Your tongue will salivate because it desires to trace his collarbone and chiseled abs that always take center stage."

I nodded, wondering who Naja was talking about because Dakari had no tattoos on his body.

"So, are you going to call Tre and tell him to come to Vegas and blow your back out?"

I giggled, contemplating her question for a while. She had no clue that these questions had been floating around my head since Lexi's conversation with me the week prior.

Lexi came over to my house with a Bordeaux wine and dark chocolates. As kids, Lexi and I confided in each other about everything. Her father's death bonded us at the hip. Lexi would hand me a tissue before I knew I had to sneeze. We felt each other's fear, pain, and happiness.

It was either puberty or the change in our environment, but Lexi changed. I was the outgoing and popular cousin in elementary, and Lexi was quiet and observant. I caught the first whiff of jealousy when we entered junior high.

Paxton, Lexi's boyfriend, smiled at me during gym class, and I smiled back brightly. Mainly because he made my sister-cousin happy, and he was family. Lexi lashed out, slapped me, and accused me of being jealous of her.

I told her that day. "I am not jealous of you, and I will marry a man better than Paxton before you two get married." I must make it to the altar before my cousin because I claimed my destiny as a teenager.

Once she and Imani had sex, they excluded me from many conversations. They shared inside jokes. I slowly felt pushed aside until I was a complete outsider. The BAE's social group brought us back together, but not our bond.

Once we were both a little drunk and feeling good, she suggested Tre and I get tested before engaging in intercourse.

I informed her that Tre wanted to wait until we were married to have sex. She raised her eyebrows and didn't probe any farther.

My mouth hung open when Lexi revealed Paxton was not her first. It turns out they separated the summer she lost her virginity. I could see the regret on my cousin's face as she explained how she never confessed her indiscretion to Paxton.

Lexi tried to tell Paxton the truth. However, his swooning about being her first lover dried her throat, and she could not speak.

I was stunned. I never imagined Lexi would confess all these things to me.

Pressing Lexi for her lover's name was fun, even though she refused to divulge it. I could feel the tension dissipating as we laughed at her revelations. She did disclose his dick was the size of a baby's pacifier. She implied Paxton was much larger, and sex with him hurt.

I slowly sipped on my drink while in deep thought. I eyed my cousin curiously.

"Is sex always painful?"

She didn't laugh or crack jokes at my expense; instead, she revealed, "It will hurt a little…but once the pain passes, it will be pleasurable."

"Are you ready for marriage and sex every day, Lexi?"

"Marriage is a flaming fire, full of heart and passion. If you stoke it with love, it'll keep you toasty and your core warm. But if you neglect it, the flames will consume your entire life spreading like a California wildfire."

Her response confused me, but I fired off a million more questions like a greedy child, hoping to gain insight about sex and love.

At the end of the conversation, I understood that size does matter; the first couple of strokes will be painful, but my body will open if I relax, and the pain will diminish. The most important thing I learned was to get tested before engaging in sex and always wear a condom.

That day reminded me of our old cousin-sister union.

Tamia appeared out of nowhere, startling Naja and me with her screeching tone. "What are you guys discussing?"

"The thumb between Tre's legs," Naja gushed. "We are wondering if it is bigger than my thumbnail." She held her hand up to Tamia. Tamia laughed viciously, then hunched her shoulders.

"Girl, it could be the size of a thumb. But! It is the first and only thumbnail Miya will ever have. SO, it will be massive to her," Tamia informed Naja.

I glanced at Naja and then at Tamia. "How do you guys know?" I questioned. "You cannot decide if it is the size of a thumb, thumbtack, or thumbnail."

"Your virginity reveals a lot," Tamia reiterated. "Has he called you since we've been in Vegas?"

I remained silent.

"Hell naw. Nope. I see it in her eyes. Girlie, some bitch is sucking on his thumb-nail-tack as we speak," Naja, Eboni, or both of them yelled.

Tamia and Naja tried to high-five each other but ended up spilling their alcohol on my outfit. I froze, rage spreading as fast as the red and blue sugary syrup soaked into my white shorts and shirt.

Tamia reached into her crossbody bag and passed me a condom. "Okay, big girl. Get you some random Vegas dick. Then you will have someone to compare Tre, too," Tamia whispered, then glanced around. "And if he is getting his dick sucked, you can say you got your pussy licked. Then you can drop the mic on his triflin' ass!"

I shoved Tamia and Naja and stomped towards Lexi like a five-year-old child, placing my hands on my hips. "Cousin, these drunk heifers spilled alcohol all over me! I am going back to the hotel to change."

"Wait, Miya. We will all go," Lexi declared, wrapping her arms around my shoulder, kissing me on the cheek. "Are you enjoying your birthday?"

I nodded. I could sense my cousin was angling for compliments. I slowly slid from under Lexi's arm. "I was until they spilled their drinks on me. Overall, you did a wonderful job."

"Well, thank you! I just wanted you to have a wonderful birthday, Cousin!"

Once we arrived at the Venetian, we changed, then strolled down to the hotel club. Tamia ordered Patrón shots. She gawked intently, forcing me to coat my throat with brown liquid heat.

I walked to the other end of the bar, leaned over, and whispered in the bartender's ear. "Can I get an iced tea with lemon? Can you pretend it's a long island iced tea when you bring it over?"

I thought the bartender had forgotten my drink when Naja ordered the fifth round of shots. I didn't know how many times I could pass Naja and Tamia my shots to drink before they detected my trickery.

"Hey, sexy ladies," the bartender said. He laid a napkin on the bar. "Here is your long island iced tea, beautiful, and I made it extra strong."

"Thank you," I squealed, passing him my credit card. "This is for the drink; take a twenty-dollar tip and one more round of Patrón shots, please."

"We wondered if you would buy a round of drinks," Tamia slurred, struggling to maintain her balance. She waved two shaky fingers in the air. "You owe me for one round. I bought two."

I sighed in frustration.

"Okay, enough alcohol," Lexi declared. "I'm ready to go club hopping."

I rolled my eyes. "This is our last night, I'm exhausted, and only sleep has stopped us from partying. I think I have had five hours of sleep since we were here, so I will go to the room after I finish this drink and get some rest."

Tamia hovered over me and screamed, "Girl, you have gotten more sleep than us."

Lexi pushed Tamia away to kiss me on the top of my head.

"If you need me, I'm a call away, cousin," she announced, leading the BAEs out of the club.

"Too Close"
Next
Malik

ENTHUSIASM INUNDATED ME, PUSHING ME THROUGH the crowd in pure exhilaration. Her lips kissed the straw as she sipped on her long island iced tea. Holding on to the bar's edge, I observed her as I struggled to fill my lungs with air.

She closed her eyes, popping her body to the bass of Jay-Z's "Blue Magic," my eyes traced the curves of her body as she moved. I scanned the empty shot glasses clustered on the bar in front of her. She and her girls had guzzled thirty shots. I hoped she wasn't drunk because I wanted to know her.

With my breath hitched in my throat, I tapped her on the shoulder. My eyes bulged in astonishment once her eyes fluttered open and locked with mine.

Her beauty was soulful, sophisticated, and sultry, like an Anita Baker soundtrack.

I nervously yanked a shot glass off the bar and shoved it in her face. My chest swelled with air. I attempted to give her a smoldering stare and hit her with my Denzel's voice, but my first syllable cracked.

"What were you drinking?"

"Patrón," her silky voice echoed. She continued to rap Jay-Z lyrics. Her melodic tone sent tingles sailing across my spine. I wondered if Jay's verse 'Push money over broads' was a subliminal warning. My heart punched my mind instantly, reminding me this woman was not Sabrina.

Uncertainty danced in my mind as I patted my hands together. My heart wanted this woman. She enticed me, but my soul was frightened of her. I felt the urge to walk away but could not force my feet to move.

My voice was trembling as I mustered up the courage I needed. "Can I buy you another drink?"

"Sure," she coyly replied, giggling.

I struggled to catch my breath. My wobbly legs refused to support my weight as I plunked onto the barstool.

"I can tell you have had too much to drink already."

Waving her assumptions away, I assured her I was okay, running my hands across my body.

"All this is because of you."

She raised a curious brow.

As corny as it was, I invaded her space and whispered my truth in her ear. "You are taking my breath away."

She laughed childishly, and the warmth of her breath nestled against my neck, slipping to my heart. I eased back and focused on the innocence in her eyes.

"Your essence is forcing my heart to thump wildly."

A bashful smile gyrated across her face, and she fanned my comment away.

My heart was about to erupt into fiery flames of passion; I pulled my gaze from her enticing beauty and feverishly waved my hand in the air. Before she could speak, the bartender approached.

I yelled, "Dawg, can we get two shots of Patrón."

The bartender cast his eyes on the beauty, still dancing in her seat next to me. She gave the bartender a nod of approval.

"Do you know him?" I prompted, questioning the minor act of communication between the two.

A spark shot through my body when she leaned over and replied. "Nope."

Her round breast peeked over the rim of her shirt. Not knowing where to look, my gaze wandered.

"You smell heavenly," I announced as her floral scent engulfed me. I wondered how I missed that earlier.

The spotlights in the club swept around us. Each loop revealed another flawless feature. I wondered if she was this stunning under natural light. Escaping into her honey brown eyes ignited a spark in me, and I could feel my strength rising.

She leaned back and admired me. I thought she recognized who I was or noticed my swollen manhood for a moment.

"You have the physique of a football player. You must stay in the gym. I have to force myself to go." Her beautiful voice made everything sound sultry and sexy, like a Schumann romance opus.

Patting my six-pack, I clarified. "I live in the gym."

"I can tell," she said flirtatiously, running her hand over my stomach muscles.

My heart stopped beating. I was lightheaded and drunk with passion. Stumbling over my words, I requested her name, scanning her hand for a ring.

"How about tonight we go nameless," she insisted, winking at me before she continued. "I always wanted to meet a man in a bar and enjoy each other's company without the stress of asking for names, what you do, and what brings you here?"

I nervously scoffed.

She leaned in and slightly tilted her head. The gesture was slow but seductive. "Honestly, do you care what I do for a living?" Lust hitched in my throat as she licked her succulent lips. "I'm here to party like everyone else. Going nameless is for the mystery, and the allure of what happens in Vegas stays in Vegas." She ran her hands over my brawny shoulders.

I unfastened the top button of my shirt as a flat gaze rocked my face. I studied her body as she crossed and uncrossed her legs repeatedly. I massaged my chin as she nibbled on her bottom lip, waiting for my response. Her body language and words did not match. I could tell she had never played this game before.

Smiling to myself, I thought, *Fuck it! I will play along.*

"Don't look at me like that," she insisted. "After tonight, you will never lay your eyes on me again."

A scowl crept across my face. I wanted to scream, hell yes, I will! After this encounter, my heart was ready to bask in her essence and gaze upon her beauty. Instead, I remained calm. I didn't want to scare her away.

"Do you want to waste tonight pretending to care about the shit I talk about?" she questioned.

I lost myself deep in her eyes for a long time. Praying I would sink directly into her heart and soul.

She stood, leaning against my body, placing her ample breast in my face. The contact of her body against mine made me weak to her seduction. Her nipples hardened, pressing against the thin black fabric of her top. I pressed my body tightly against hers in response.

I brought her face closer to my lips, whispering in her ear. "I would spend the night making you claw at my back while you scream my name." Visions of me entering her invaded my mind, and a quiver formed in my gut.

"No names," she muttered into my ear.

"Then call me Mr. Good Dick," I cockily replied.

Her legs trembled, and her chest contracted at my response. My heart rate quickened as I grabbed her around the middle of her back.

"Would you like to come to my room?"

"Do you want me to come to your room?" she countered, gliding the tip of her tongue over her top lip.

Her tongue and lips had my brain feeling waterlogged. The blood loss in my brain made me agree with a simple kiss on the crest of her breast.

"Can I presume that's a yes?" she replied, placing her pillow-soft lips on mine.

Our lips locked, and time stood still. A brief sadness soared above me when she pulled away. Hungry eyes swept over her body, and the corners of my mouth touched my right and left ear. She winked at my joker's face.

"I need to freshen up, don't leave," she announced, easing out of my embrace. "Then we can go to your room."

As she faded into the crowd, I instantaneously felt incomplete.

I threw my head back, tapping my feet on the bar in sync with the bass, and contemplated what was transpiring. The blood rushed back to my head, reminding me I needed a room.

I texted RB.

Me // 9:15 pm: I need you to rent me a luxury king suite here. I will transfer the funds to your account later.

RB // 9:18 pm: Why? We have a villa at Caesars Palace.

Me // 9:18 pm: She thinks my room is here.

RB // 9:25 pm: She will be happier if you take her to the villa.

Me // 9:25 pm: Fuck my bills, dawg. Get the room & we are good. I'll pay you back.

RB // 9:34 pm: Stop sounding desperate, fool. Do you need Lou to come over?

Me // 9:34 pm: For what?

RB // 9:36 pm: A smash contract. You don't want her screaming rape tomorrow.

Me // 9:36 pm: NO! SHE NOT LIKE THAT!

RB // 9:37 pm: You don't know shit about her. But OK. Player. Smash her! Do not marry her, okay?

Me // 9:37 pm: OK! Okay!

RB // 9:39 pm: Meet me in 15 mins by the entrance for the key.

Me // 9:39 pm: BET!

I sat at the bar, twisting and turning on the barstool, observing the restroom hallway. She had me burning with passion, and I prayed that she had not changed her mind. The last thing I needed was another tragedy in my life.

A woman attempted to take my mystery lady's seat, and I told her someone was sitting there. Struggling to lean her body against mine, she pretended not to hear me. She blew in my ear, requesting I repeat myself. Bumping her back, I repeated myself.

She shrugged her shoulders, mumbling something about it being my loss, then walked away.

"Dawg, can I get a glass of cognac?" I asked the bartender.

She tapped me on the shoulder again as he sat my glass down. I turned around, ready to repeat myself. I smiled. My sexy mystery lady had returned smelling sweeter than when she departed.

"Was there a lengthy line, beautiful?"

Instead of answering me, she shifted her glare toward the girl who had walked away. I don't understand what made me explain myself, but I did—recounting every moment since she walked away.

I held her hand as she adjusted herself on the stool. Taking a sip of my drink, I examined her body language.

"I explained to the girl. Are you going to speak to me?"

She folded her hands across her chest. "You're a handsome man. Women will lean their breasts all on you," she said as a matter of fact.

"But I'm not a player," I pause, watching her brows knit into the faintest frown. "I don't want you to think I do shit like this all the time."

"The bathroom was nasty, so I went to my room. Once I was there, I freshened up," she said, addressing my first question and ignoring my comment.

Forming my lips to speak, yet saying nothing as I stopped short, checking the message my phone's vibrations just alerted me to.

"Are you ready to go upstairs?"

My eyes turned big as saucers. I laid my hand on hers and gently kneaded it. "Yeah, but I need to let my boy know I'm leaving first," I told her.

She blew me a raspberry kiss. I leaned in closer, prompting her to wrap her warm, slender arms around my waist. Blasted with desire, I cruised my hands up and down her spine. Her mysterious stare drew my lips to hers.

The constant buzzing of my phone caught my attention. I pulled away. I needed to meet up with RB.

"I will be right back." I kissed the top of her head before departing.

I approached RB by the entrance. Rocking my head and hunching my shoulders as he reminded me this was a one-night stand, not a love connection. He attempted to give me another speech about Lou drawing up a smash contract. Recognizing my annoyance, he shoved the keycard into my chest.

Thanking him for the room, I rushed back to my mystery lady, ecstatic about my first one-night stand, all because she agreed to a shot of Patrón.

"Nice & Slow"

Usher

Malik

LEANING AGAINST THE ELEVATOR WALL, **HELD** hostage by her presence—lust, passion, and desire developed in my gut and fired off like missiles. I engraved every inch of her body to memory, right down to the beauty mark that lived on the left side of her upper lip.

She was drop-dead gorgeous, and I was ready to ravish her.

In a tangle of limbs, we stumbled into the room. Pushing her body against the wall, I parted her lips with the tip of my tongue, joining hers in dance as we explored each other.

I growled, pleasure fueling me as I savored the sweet juices pooled on the sides of her cheeks, tongue, and gums. She struggled to maintain the speed of my torpedo tongue as my hands skated up her silky honey-brown legs. The more I willed my body to calm down, the deeper I kissed her.

Our passion-filled kisses slowed, turning into locked, warm lips.

My hands instantly floated across her arms, causing her body to plank against the wall.

I eased away, my heart pounding like a tribal drum in my chest as I rested my back against the adjacent wall. I watched as she wrung her hands together before running them along the side of her skirt repeatedly.

"Are you ok, beautiful?"

Instead of answering me, tears flowed down her cheeks.

Fuck, I thought, *the last thing I need is a woman crying rape.*

I was pissed I didn't allow Lou to write up a smash contract.

Pleading for her to tell me what I had done wrong, I could tell she was struggling to breathe as she squeezed her eyes shut, covering her mouth and nose with her hand. Her chest jerked, causing her chin and bottom lip to shiver.

I adjusted my jeans and then tugged at the tip of my shirt. I urged her to remove her hands from across her mouth and nose in a serene tone. I slowly approached her with my hands held above my head.

She peered at me skeptically.

"Smell the roses and blow out the candles."

I inhaled deeply through my nose, shaped my lips in a perfect oval, and expelled the air. Her gaze penetrated my soul, and even with skeptical eyes, she mirrored what I was doing until she calmed.

I swept the hair dangling in her face aside, tucking it behind her ear before kissing her forehead.

"Do you want to go?" I assured her she was free to leave and no harm would come to her before she could even say a word.

With eyes cast to the floor, she shared her feelings. "Your kisses felt aggressive like you were punishing me for coming to your room."

I stepped back, fumbling with the buttons on my shirt. My gut sank at the sight of her watery eyes. I was embarrassed by my behavior. Her soaked face was slightly calmer as she continued sharing how she felt.

"Some of the stuff I said at the bar were things I heard my girlfriend say to men. She's joking most of the time, but I meant everything I said."

I approached her again, reciting a quick prayer, placing my index finger under her chin, lifting her head slowly until our eyes met.

"I'm a virgin," she muttered. "I expected my first time to be magical, not brutal."

I knew I had to choose my words carefully. As I rolled my shoulders and cracked my neck, I asked God for help.

A vision of my mother reaching her hands out to me and gently immersing them in the palm of my hands invaded my thoughts. I could feel the serenity it always brought me.

I stepped closer and reached my hands out to her. She slowly lifted her hands. I turned my palms to the ceiling, tucking her petite hands inside mine before gently caressing them.

"If I had known, we would have spent the entire night talking."

Her gaze lowered to the floor, both of her shoulders leaning forward until her chest formed a hollow shape. I stroked her hand, but she refused eye contact.

I squatted down until our eyes met once again. I gradually rose from the floor so did her stare. She rested her forehead on my chest and swung her twitchy gaze upward.

I kissed her forehead. "We always hold our heads high."

Smiling at me, she spoke. "It is not your fault. I'm a big girl. I wanted to experience a magical night with you. At the bar, heat surges ripped through my body, and I thought —"

"And I robbed you of an amazing experience because my body was burning with lust and desire," I confessed, cutting her off. "Are you sure you don't want to tell me your name? Maybe that will make this feel a little more personal."

Her lashes swept up, and she blinked. "Can you slow down? Ever since we left the bar, I've felt more like an object than a woman. Just acknowledge my presence for a moment. Women are more than slabs of meat, you know?"

My glare traveled with unnerving diligence. "I'm sorry," I faintly spluttered, then kissed her hands. "My mother raised me to respect women and treat them like the queens they are. I never meant to offend you."

It was time for me to use what my Pops had taught me. I scanned my brain, thinking of a song to get me out of this mess and express my fascination for her.

"Can we go to the sitting area?"

She nodded her head. I let go of one of her hands, leading her through the bedroom.

I stumbled on the steps leading to the sitting room.

"Watch your step, baby," I warned her. I saw her descend down the two steps leading to the sitting room. I instructed her to sit on the sofa while searching the room for a docking station.

I tried not to fumble around the room for too long, not wanting her to realize this room was unfamiliar to me. I could have kicked myself when I realized the clock radio was the docking station.

"Don't Be Afraid" by Aaron Hall bounced off the walls in the suite, then shot around my body.

Kneeling in front of her, I basked in her beauty while allowing the song to intercede on my behalf. I reached for her hands, and she wrapped her silky ones around mine before kissing them.

"If you want, we can listen to love songs and cuddle in each other's arms."

She yanked me off my knees without responding, and I plopped down on her side. She gazed at each, then erupted in laughter.

The glitzy gleam of the Vegas night sent flairs of light shooting around the room, bathing her in the dim light as one persistent ray seemed determined to show me her radiance.

She was angelic with flawless makeup-free honey brown skin that complimented her radiant golden eyes, paired perfectly with her honey-brown hair. God took his time crafting this lascivious angel.

"You are sexy."

"Do you tell that to all the women you sleep with? How many women have you bedded? We both know I am a virgin."

I hesitated because I had never had a woman ask for my number. "I've had two serious relationships and slept with a handful of girls in college."

"So, seven?"

"Seven to ten. In college, I didn't keep count. I stopped sleeping around because my father warned I needed to serve a better example for my brother and that every woman I bed, I invite their spirits into me and mine into them."

"Do you want my spirit?"

"Yes, when you are ready. Tonight, I want to hold you close."

She extended her neck and kissed me before she snuggled into my chest, coaxing an involuntary whimper from my throat.

The soul-shifting vibration of the O'Jays quaked my core like five strikes to a timpani drum, and my heart leaped from my chest into my hand. I was ready to offer her my heart. The assurance of our destiny and my soul's completion could only be felt in After 7's "Ready Or Not" lyrics. I hankered to be and give her everything.

My eyes greedily drank in the beauty nestled in my chest. I kissed the tip of her nose as we listened to my playlist.

"Freak Me"
Silk
Miya

HIS VOICE WAS DEEP AND MELODIC, like a guitar bass. Each time he kissed my forehead, he fed me small doses of himself via energy surges that shot from his lips to the bottom of my feet and then back up, landing between my thighs.

I laid my head on his smooth muscular chest while listening to Luther Vandross, Anita Baker, The Whispers, Janet Jackson, and Tevin Campbell. He massaged my scalp. I purred like a seductive kitten.

As The O'Jays' "Forever Mine" played, my body was smoldering with lust.

Easing away from him, I rose. I stood before him as I angled my body's curves to catch the dancing rays of light flitting through the glass windows.

My Aunt's behavior during her card parties finally made sense to me. Because I wanted to waive a glass of Hennessy in the air with my eyes closed, gently swaying to the melodic vibe of "Tonight Is the Night" by Betty Wright as I indulged in this man's warm sensual strokes.

As I posed, I felt like the R&B singer Tweet, baring myself before him. I pulled off my shirt, exposing my ample breast, striking a pose, allowing his gaze to bounce around my curves.

He licked his fleshy lips at the sight of my plump breasts. "Mmhmm, you look good enough to eat."

I blushed at his comment. Sashaying towards him, I yanked him to his feet, wrapping my arms around his neck, then placed my lips on his.

He resisted pulling away. "No! We—we shouldn't do this."

I slowly advanced towards him again. He stepped backward, bumping into the loveseat. I pulled him back into my embrace, and his touch became my life's anchor at that moment. I was terrified yet excited. My soul suffered an incompleteness when he pulled away, stealing a piece of me.

His playlist could have been a Miya creation. The songs he played triggered deep emotions. Music was connecting our souls.

I closed my eyes and listened to "Don't Say Goodnight" by The Isley Brothers. The lyrics engulfed every inch of the suite. A surge of sexual desire briefly washed my body.

My hips swayed to the beat. Overtaken with passion, my hands explored my neck before touring my physique. I rolled my body slightly, opening my eyes, noticing the lustful daggers shooting from his eyes. I allowed the song's lyrics to convey my emotions.

His smokey gray eyes fixated on me; I beckoned him with a slow curl of my index finger. Obeying, he crept towards me, his pace zombielike. Twirling my body against him, his hands wrapped around my waist and then retracted. I slowed down my twirl and locked both of my hands around the back of his quivering thighs.

I involuntarily bit down on my bottom lip. I swung my head back, and he saturated my neck with warm kisses.

Seductively, he whispered, "I will be gentle." He softly tugged on the soft flesh of my earlobe with his teeth. "Let me know when you want me to stop."

He pulled his hand tighter around my waist. I inhaled the sweet aroma of his woodsy cologne, and we danced up the two steps into the bedroom. I massaged his burly neck and shoulder blade when The Isley Brothers' "Spend the Night" played, igniting my body temperature another degree.

The fire looming between my thighs echoed as I was ready to spend a night with this chocolate king. The heartbeat in my panties was faster than the one in my chest.

"Yes, I will," I replied, answering the song's hook.

When his lips graced mine, the world halted. The tip of his tongue parted my lips. His tongue was like smooth R&B seducing my soul.

He unfastened my skirt, gradually sliding it down my thighs, and never took my eyes off his sexy form once.

"Oops, there goes my skirt," I purr while kicking the skirt off my ankle.

He slid down my lace panties before bringing them to his aquiline nose. He inhaled.

"I am taking advantage of you," he muddled, taking another whiff of my panties. "Sweet vanilla candy." He licked his luscious lips. "I am a decent man. I usually don't do things like this."

"Me either," I exclaimed, half out of breath.

"Can I touch your breasts?" he asked tenderly.

Turned on by his polite demeanor, all I could do was place his hands on my hot mounds. He nuzzled them before placing sweet kisses on the flesh that formed the curves of my bosom. An earth-shattering jolt shot through my body, coaxing a soft moan from between my lips.

He sucked on my tongue and bottom lip. "Can I suck on your nipples the same way?"

I nodded repeatedly.

His mouth was warm as he gently nibbled on my nipples before devouring them completely. My body sailed into a frenzy of involuntary trembles as warm breath blew on my puckered buds.

"Oh, God…umm—Oh, God."

He sucked, licked, and nibbled. His featherlight lips propelled me into a spiral of pure ecstasy.

I unbuckled his pants and slid his shirt down his bulging biceps, placing soft kisses on his chiseled physique. He pulled away from my embrace, leaned against the wall, and admired my naked frame.

Shivering with unease, I sat on the ottoman.

"Do you want to stop?" I queried a smidge above the melody.

His response was action. He kneeled in front of me and swung my legs onto his creamy, smooth shoulders in one quick motion. My thighs and backside rested on his chest and stomach while he placed kisses on my inner thighs and abdomen.

My heart leaped out of my chest as he swept me off my feet. I locked my legs together, and his enormous hands cradled my back. Overwhelmed by the kisses assaulting my outer lips, my fingers laced tightly behind his head, fearful my twitching may cause him to drop me.

I blushed as Quincy Jones "The Secret Garden (Sweet Seduction Suite)" played, wondering if he could see all the freaky things I wanted him to do to me. A cool breeze sailed over my rosebud, plunging my head unwillingly backward, pulling me from my thoughts.

My thighs tightened as the urge to urinate attacked my bladder. A warm sensation started in my toes, landing between my womanly folds.

"Tell me how it feels. Tell me what you want. Do you like what I am doing to your body?" he asked in his Barry White tone.

Struggling to breathe, I shoved his head away from my honeypot, unable to recall the command that allowed my body to breathe so easily mere moments prior.

He lowered me onto the bed, kissing me. "Do you love the way you taste?"

The woozy haze clouding my mind rendered me speechless. I reached into my purse and pulled out the golden wrapper Tamia gave me.

"Can I put my mouth on you before we have sex?"

He laid back and cupped his hands under his head. I whirled my tongue around the sweet nectar dandling on the tip of his penis. A throaty moan escaped his body.

I closed my eyes and replayed a scene from a porno Eric had shown me one night. He had hoped the video would rouse me into having sex with him or at least prompt me to give him oral sex. Who knew those tapes were getting me ready for this night?

I gripped his love shaft with my hands and massaged his penis up and down. I slid his ego into my warm mouth.

Maybe it was euphoric, but he tasted like Godiva's milk chocolate. Trying to fit his entire length into my mouth caused me to gag. Each time I choked on his magic stick, my mouth produced new salvia, allowing him to sail deeper down my throat.

His eyes were closed, and the soft grunts leaving his lips did nothing to tell me if I was doing this oral thing right or not. His reaction was nothing like mine, and as I explored his penis, tracing the large vein with my tongue until I reached the crown, his moans inspired me to expand my limitations. Flicking the tip, I utilized my tongue to run laps around his mushroom top. Lapping at his glands, the more he groaned.

"Aw shit," he grunted.

Urging me to go faster as I sucked, flicked, and spun my tongue around the tip of his chocolaty lollipop.

He placed his hands around his pole and lightly shoved my head back.

"Do not make me cum. I want to experience your sugary walls gripping my strength!" He exclaimed.

I drew in a massive gulp of air.

"You are thick and long. I want to ride you. I've seen women on TV do it all the time. If they can ride, so can I."

He arched his eyebrows at me, then gave me an eloquent smile.

"If it's ok with you, beautiful, I'll take it from here. I promise to go nice and slow. I will never hurt you."

I passed him the condom. He kissed my earlobe and then glided down to my sweet spot.

"Your yoni is the most beautiful thing I have ever feasted on," he stammered.

He slid his lips tenderly around my swollen bud without pressing down on my love button, and then he placed wet kisses on my yoni. He licked the inner crest of my thighs and tenderly bit on them, placing wet kisses on my body as I quivered.

Whenever I became inundated by his touch, he retreated and observed my body shuddering in pleasure.

He slowly approached my yoni again, blowing gently on my most intimate area, softly pulling my lips apart before probing the inner regions, circling them with his fiery tongue's warm, wet tip.

"Aw shit!" I hollered.

His tongue ran laps around my yoni's exterior a couple more times. He went dangerously close to my nucleus' center only to blow on it twice; the warm moist breeze engulfed my entire body in passion. Each time he purposely skipped, my pearl rendering me speechless with anticipation. I tugged at the sheets and yanked my hair.

His teasing lit my body with desire. I bucked, wiggled, and squirmed, trying to guide his tongue towards my sweet spot. He graciously pulled away and waited for my body to stop gyrating, only continuing once I calmed down.

He pulled away again, and I clawed at his shoulders, trying to pull him back to the gates of my ecstasy. He smiled mischievously.

Pleasure rippled through me as his tongue sank deep inside my sugary canal. His lips French kissed my yoni. Dawdling lovingly, my body instantly responded by sending billions of neurons transmitting sparks in my brain as they glided down my spinal cord in a spidery tingle. My back arched off the bed, and I voiced my desire.

"Make love to me," I demanded.

His hooded smokey gray eyes squinted at me.

"You are not ready yet," he declared. "I want to please you until you erupt in utter ecstasy. I'll know you're ready when I hear the secret code."

"I am ready! Yes, I am," I fired back.

He ignored me and went back to work, polishing my pearl with his tongue and fingers. I lifted onto my elbows to tell him I couldn't take anymore, yet no words would escape my lips.

He peered at me before stretching my yoni open with his fingers. My rosebud popped out, waving hello.

"There goes my sweet pearl," he slurred. His face beamed with drunken passion before nuzzling it between my thighs, flicking his tongue against my sensitive flower. He licked, slurped, and smacked on my clit until my legs quivered with pleasure. My toes curled before my back slammed against the mattress.

"Peaches & Cream"

112

Miya

MARVIN GAYE'S BALLOT "IF I SHOULD Die Tonight" hopscotched up my spine as his fluids entwined with mine. An isolated tear rolled down my golden-brown cheek.

He sent my body into a convulsive temperament. "Oh...my...god!" I yelled into the ceiling.

Kicking, I retreated towards the headboard. His firm grip yanked me down until his mouth hovered over my lovely folds again.

Overstimulated, I yanked at his hands, trying to pull him up and away from my sensitive rosebud. No matter how I bucked, he kept his lips snugly wrapped around my delicate flower, constantly blowing on it. My heart pounded so hard I thought it would explode.

I always thought breathing was a natural reaction, but I kept forgetting the simple inhaling and exhaling technique. My body was an inferno, and I was ready to explore this thing called intercourse. If his mouth pleasured me to this degree, I knew sex had to be mind-blowing.

I raised my torso off the bed, entwining my hands in his dreadlocks. I gently tugged on them, hoping my actions would make him release me.

"Make love to me, Mr. Good Dick!" I yelled. "I want to feel my warmth around your strength."

He yanked me down by my hips and kissed my stomach, trailing up to my neck. "Now, you are ready for me," he whispered. His deep baritone voice sent earth-shattering sparks down my spinal column and exploded between my thighs.

He slowly eased the tip of his love shaft into my dripping wet canal.

"Oh God," I whined, tugging at the sheets, struggling to escape his grip after his joystick knocked on the door of my sweet spot.

My body granted him entry regardless of my fearful dissent.

"Am I hurting you?" he inquired. "Do you want me to stop?" I shook my head in protest. "Relax your muscles and allow me in."

I took a deep breath, relaxed my muscles, and eased my legs further apart.

"Fuck," he yelled while turning his head away from me.

His sharp cheekbones and square-cut jawline revealed the perfect silhouette, which could chisel granite.

"Fuck!"

His outburst tensed my body into one knot, making him turn his head towards me. "Baby, what's wrong?"

I struggled to keep the tears from falling. "I'm sorry," I whined.

He ceased movement and straddled my body in a pushup position.

"You have nothing to be sorry about," he assured me.

"Then why do you keep yelling fuck and laughing at me? I am sorry. I'm a virgin." Instead of getting upset or reacting to my tone, he placed kisses around my heart-shaped face.

"I keep saying fuck because you feel amazing, and I'm struggling to control this beast." He licked his provocative lips. "But fuck. This shit—right here. I need to savor every half of a second with you."

Before I could say anything else, his tongue locked with mine. My heartbeat rose to the rhythmic beat of our kiss.

He sat on his knees between my legs and slowly eased inches of himself inside me while playing with my rosebud. After a couple of slow pumps and my umpteenth orgasm, his love shaft punched my yoni's back door.

"Oh, SHIT!" I screamed.

Whimpers of pain and pleasure escaped my lips. The pain vanished slowly, and pure joy conquered my mind, body, and soul.

I snuggly wrapped around his rod and gently sucked his magic stick deeper into my interior.

Struggling to contain my passion, I tugged on his golden-brown dreadlocks. The bleached blond tips sparkled like gold. With each thrust of his magic wand, my yoni captured and cradled it like a newborn baby safely tucked in his mother's arms. Out of condoms and exhausted, we laid together, panting uncontrollably.

He adorned my head with more kisses. "Nothing in my life has ever felt this good. Your sweet vagina felt as if a vacuum resided in your tunnel. Each time I tried to pull away, your yoni thrust life back into my strength. Shit!" He shouted, then moaned. "No woman has ever pleased me in this manner," he confessed. He wrapped me in his arms and planted kisses all around my face.

Resting on his burly chest, he kissed my forehead, and energy ran down my spine. "You have the sweetest yoni I have ever tasted. You must be the wettest woman I've ever been with," he continued. "I need to know your name. We have to do this for the rest of our lives."

"I will answer all your questions in the morning. I'm exhausted, lover. Can we go to bed?"

He kissed the top of my head as we drifted off to sleep.

Around five in the morning, I stumbled off to the bathroom with a throbbing pain echoing from between my legs. This feeling was the embodiment of pure satisfaction in my book.

Fuck! How am I going to walk back into my hotel room? The BAEs are going to ask twenty-one questions.

Standing over his naked body, I struggled with myself. I wanted to wake him up and answer all his curiosities, but I was dating Tre.

What if I woke him up, and one of his questions was, "Do you have a man?" Would he ever trust me in a relationship after I sexed him on the first date? Hell, we haven't even gone out on a date! We were the bar's last call hookup.

I watched him sleep. The man's thighs, back, and stomach had to have been sculpted by Michelangelo. Every angle on this man was razor-sharp precision.

After all my crying, I was too embarrassed to leave my name and number.

"I don't know your name, but Mr. Good Dick will do for now," I mumbled, then kissed his chiseled jaw.

"Thank you for a fantastic first time. You were indeed the perfect one-night stand. If we are destined, we will meet again," I whispered before leaving.

I cautiously opened my hotel room door, trying not to wake up my girls, but the room was empty, to my surprise. I opened the door to the other suite, and nobody was there. Those hoes never came back. I wonder if they had a fun time like me. I pondered if I should tell the girls or anybody else about my Vegas fling.

"What happens in Vegas stays in Vegas," I yelled as I danced around the room.

"Right and a Wrong Way"
Keith Sweat
Miya

ROLLING MY EYES AT THE SOUND of Tre's shriek, I stomped down the stairs in search of him to serve him a piece of my mind. He beckoned for me as if I was a damn servant.

"Mimi, what is all of this?" he questioned, pointing at the burning candles surrounding the house.

Since my encounter in Vegas, I have longed to experience those emotions again. I found my hand slipping past my waist, exploring my body before withdrawing from bed in the morning, in the shower, and before bed. Nothing resembled the euphoric feeling I experienced in Vegas. Why didn't anyone tell me sex was addicting like drugs?

I was sexually frustrated whenever I spent the weekend or a few days with Tre because I couldn't explore my body.

I twirled the edges of my hair. "I wanted to set the mood before you came home."

He kissed me on the tip of my nose.

"Aww, how sweet," he chimed. "But baby, you need to set the candles in a votive. The wax is destroying my furniture."

Resisting the urge to remind him, I bought the sofa and tables.

"Sorry, baby," I uttered, then blew out the candles on the table. He walked around the family room, blowing out the candles in the votives.

I huffed and silently stood there in dismay as Tre dashed around the house, blowing out candles, then ran upstairs. I didn't move a muscle until he returned.

"Damn baby, did you buy every candle in the store?" he joked, pulling me by my wrist towards the kitchen.

Pushing his hand away, I took a seat in the family room adjacent to the kitchen as he grabbed a beer from the refrigerator and then joined me.

Slightly annoyed, he had ruined my romantic setting; I barked, "You could have brought me a glass of wine." Stunned, he turned around and got me a glass of white wine.

He sat in the recliner, and I gawked at him. He caught the hint and joined me on the sofa.

"Baby, you've been different since you came back from your Vegas trip. One minute you're trying to rip my clothes off. Then you're treating me like a helpless baby the next minute."

For a moment, I wanted to confess that I had slept with a guy in Vegas, but I didn't want to lose him. I had deep feelings for Tre; my mystery man was a fantasy. I will never see my Vegas lover again.

"I'm sick of you constantly turning down my advances. Being rejected hurts my feelings," I rasped. "You are going to give me low self-esteem issues. I do not understand why we can't have sex before marriage. Are you truly all right with buying a car you have never driven?"

He tightened his lips so tight they disappeared. "Self-esteem starts with self. So, you need to check yourself. Most importantly, those words sound like one of the BAEs, not you."

I rolled my eyes at his response. Although he was right, the question still had merit.

He placed his hand on top of mine and squeezed. "I love you, Mimi."

I cut him off. "Why do you call me Mimi? Nicknames are supposed to be short because a person's proper name is hard to pronounce. Miya is four letters, just like Mimi, and easy to pronounce!" I expelled a lung full of air. "Now, say it with me, Miya!"

Everything he said and did was pissing me off.

He bucked his eyes at me and continued his speech. "Miya. I fell in love with you the first day we met." I smiled and batted my eyes at him.

Tell him you love him, Miya, my mind urged. My heart refused to surrender and lie. Since my heart and soul were not on one accord, I remained silent.

"What happened today with your girls?"

I grumbled, then tapped my feet on the floor, contemplating if I should lie or tell him the truth. Would he agree to marry me faster if he knew me and the girls were betting on who would walk down the aisle first, or would he overanalyze the situation?

Staring at me pensively, I could tell he was waiting for me to speak. Dropping my head, I rubbed my forehead. "They teased me all day."

He groaned.

"They all agreed you will never marry me, and you don't want to have sex with me because you have a tiny penis." I peered at him, petitioning my eyes to produce a tear, yet nothing rolled down my cheeks.

With bulging eyes, his nostrils flared out. "Are you sure they weren't joking around? I don't see them viciously trying to hurt your feelings. Maybe you misunderstood them."

Realizing I needed to turn up the heat some more, I continued. "Besides Tamia, I don't believe the others think you will ever marry me or make love to me. Tamia was hopeful because you're her friend. They think I'm wasting my time with you," I lied. "Lexi agreed to give us ten thousand dollars if you marry me before June."

His eyes greedily widened.

I didn't feel too bad about lying since some of what I said were facts. The girls and I did go shopping today. They also teased me about returning to the room and watching TV in Vegas. I couldn't tell Tre I had an urge to slap those smug heifers in the face with specifics about my Vegas lover. I couldn't articulate how our night together danced on the tip of my tongue. I resisted because those heifers would not believe me. They would think I was creating my Vegas lover to win the debate.

By the time we arrived at La Barca Mexican restaurant, Lexi had confessed she had heard Paxton on the phone telling his jeweler to come over this week so they could design her engagement ring. Naja and Tamia were excited for her.

I was surprised Imani did not ooh and ahh over Lexi's news. Instead, she confessed to catching Winten looking at rings on his computer and thought he would propose this year instead of next year.

Imani was confident she would win the bet and beat all the BAEs to the altar. Lexi and Tamia joked that he was probably figuring out the wedding cost so they could start budgeting. You would think his parents weren't worth millions, or he wasn't a trust fund kid the way he forces Imani to split every bill with him. His family should pay for everything since Imani's only family was the BAEs.

Imani squealed. "I'll give the first BAE to get married an extra two grand."

I pursed my lips, and Lexi batted her eyes rapidly at Imani's statement.

We all ate in silence until Tamia insisted Lexi and Imani discuss what had transpired earlier. They both looked around the table, confused.

Blurting out, Lexi doubled down. "Whoever marries before me gets ten thousand dollars."

Naja drummed her nails on the table while sipping her margarita on the rocks. I assumed Naja felt the conversation was beneath her or her unwavering confidence made her victorious. Maybe superior. Either way, she was convinced she was the winner already.

Tre shouted while snapping his fingers in my face. "Hellooooooo! Miya, did you hear me?"

I pushed his hand out of my face and snapped back into the present.

My eyes turned black, then tightened. "I know you hate when I do that, but I need you to pay attention and stop daydreaming."

I smacked my lips.

"I will ask you again. Do you believe you are wasting your time with me? Can any of the BAEs testify to spending quality time with their mates? I'll wait. Nope, they cannot because you are the only one who spends quality time with your boyfriend. We are never at home. The only thing they have is sex. We have a genuine connection."

Right on cue, tears sprinted down my cheeks. I got off the sofa and walked over to the sliding door to the backyard. Thunder rolled over the house, and lightning lit the crackling sky as I pretended to cry.

He approached me and wrapped his hands around my waist. "We're not buddies having sex. We are two friends who will get married because we love each other. We can have sex after we are married."

My fake tears turned into actual tears because I was ashamed of my behavior. He loves me, and I was behaving like a brat.

He brushed his pelvis against my backside. "Does my dick feel itty bitty to you?" I hunched my shoulders slowly. He stood still. I reached back and slid my hands into his slacks. I stroked his penis. It stiffened. He pulled away.

"Miya, we have to wait." This time my pride and self-esteem took a hit. I didn't know how much more rejection I could take.

"Are you attracted to me?" I wailed.

He fumed. "Woman, did you not feel how my body reacted to your touch? Fuck! I know God will favor us and bless our union if I do right by you. I need God to bless me at work. Some investments at work are not panning out the way I envisioned. I need to pay the back taxes on this house. The last thing I want to do is piss God off by deflowering you before we get married. You have the rest of your life to make love to me."

I swung around to face him. His eyes widened at my tear-streaked face.

"If your end game is not marriage, we need to separate now. I could help you with your taxes. We would have more money if we lived together."

He stumbled back as if I had struck him with my words. "You know marriage is my end game. I'm only asking you to wait until we get married." He walked over to the sofa and plopped down. "Do you know how hard it is holding you with you constantly grinding your ass against my dick all night? You're here every weekend. Shit, you might as well move in," he barked.

"This is hard on me, too," I admitted. "And if you don't want me staying here, then tell me."

He slammed his empty bottle on the coffee table. He sighed deeply, then patted the seat next to him.

"You can't miss something you never had. I have had pussy before, so I'm going through hell here, Miya."

"I know how it feels to masturbate," I professed. "Why can't we have oral sex?"

He rubbed his hands on the front of his slacks. "Your statement echoes virginity. You don't understand how impossible it is to stop after engaging in oral sex."

He flicked the tip of my nose with his index finger.

"Ouch."

"And oral sex is sex, so no to that also."

I threw my hands in the air. "Then marry me and end both of our torments! I'm attracted to you and want to make love to you." Before he could reply, I stormed up the stairs.

I turned on the radio, and Marvin Gaye's "Let's Get It On" played. I lay across the bed. He joined me in the bed and kissed my cheek. My physique softened until he yelled.

"Turn his ass off. You're always listening to music. It reminds me of my damn daddy and my fucking brothers' bond! Use your own words, not someone else's lyrics!"

I sprung from the bed and went to shower. He cracked open the door. "Don't molest my shower head."

"Ha...Ha...Ha," I retorted.

I found an empty bed when I emerged from the shower feeling revived and ready to cuddle with my snuggle bunny.

He stumbled into the house an hour before I had to get dressed and go to work. He stirred and then sprung up in the bed as I emptied my drawers.

"Miya, what are you doing?"

"I'll get the rest of my shit later," I snapped, aiming a shoe at his head. "How dare you whine about not wanting to make love to me? Begging God to bless our union and your job, and then you walk in here drunk, smelling like a cheap bitch."

Before he could respond, I was out of the front door in my car.

"Fuck you!" I yelled, then drove away.

"Doo Wa Ditty (Blow That Thing)"

Zapp & Roger

Miya

Y HEAD POPPED UPWARD. "MIYA! I have been calling your name for a minute," Imani yelled from the bottom of the stairs. "Are you ok?"

Lost in my thoughts, I barely heard Imani calling out to me. I planned to skate my blues away tonight, wondering if I should forgive Tre as I leaned on the balcony leading to the skating rink. He had been smothering me with flowers and gifts, begging for my forgiveness, and a sliver of my heart wondered if my Vegas lover would treat me the way Tre does or better. Flicks of our Vegas night played on constant repeat in my head.

"I'm good."

I wanted to tell her I was daydreaming about the guy I met in Vegas, but I didn't need her judgment. She has a heart of gold, but sometimes she comes off a bit judgmental and bougie. I picked my skates off the ground and descended the stairs. Embracing briefly, we greeted each other before entering the rink, already bumping to "Doo Wa Ditty (Blow That Thing)" by Zapp & Roger.

"Girl, this will count as my cardio workout," I told her.

"Mine too." She danced on the bench while lacing up her pink and white skates. I snickered, thinking about all the pink and white outfits in her closet, which she only wore to the skating rink.

We rushed to the floor when "More Bounce to the Ounce" started playing.

"Girl, this is a Zapp night," she noted, stating her observation as we glided in unison on the floor.

Imani turned around, her feet and body moving in tandem as she moonwalked, gliding across the floor with incredible smoothness.

"Show off," I yelled, swinging my hips in time with the beat, and followed where she led.

As the song ended, Imani locked her arm around mine to perform the routine we had created. A couple of guys skated circles around us, muttering about who gets to approach Imani. She glanced at me and rolled her eyes.

As the two shadowed us, I followed suit, led only by instinct as we continued to bounce to Parliament, attempting to ignore their presence. One guy even dared to run the sights of his handheld flashlight over us, scanning our now illuminated bodies with greedy eyes. After the second rotation following us, Imani elegantly exited the skating area, and I followed promptly behind her.

"Damn girl, you're wearing the shit out of those jean shorts," some guy voiced as I tiptoed to her.

Imani started ranting before I could reach her. "Who carries around flashlights? What if they didn't play this song tonight? Girl, I could no longer deal with those guys on the floor."

"Yea, they were extra," I echoed in unison, leaning on the rail.

"I noticed you had a new swirl in your hips. Did you and Tre, you know?" She asks, raising her eyebrow suggestively.

"Girl, No! He's sticking to the no-sex-before-marriage rule," I answered, debating if I should tell her my Vegas lover was responsible for the hula hoop twirl in my hips.

"I think that's sweet. Most men only want to hit it and quit it. At least you know he wants to be around for a lifetime." I hunched my shoulders. "How are you and Tre?"

Before I could answer or ask about Winten, she continued talking. "Winten has revised our five-year plan. I suppose we are going to be married soon. We're both making a profuse amount of money. It's way more than we projected at this point."

Was this her subtle way of telling me she would beat me to the altar?

Tre was not the man consuming my thoughts. My Vegas lover was. I wanted to get her opinion on love at first touch, but I couldn't reveal my mystery man's existence. It was clear to me. She was on team Tre, so I approached what I was feeling in a different matter.

"Imani, how could you tell you were in love with Winten?" I probed, firing off another question, interrupting her initial response. "Do you believe in love at first sight or touch?"

"Do you believe you are in love with Tre after a couple of weeks?" she queried.

I wanted to correct her comment about my relationship's duration but restrained myself. I always hated how people answer a question with another question, only changing the subject most of the time to spark a conversation concerning something else, and your original issue never gets addressed. Today was going to be different. I was getting an answer to my question.

"Answer my questions first," I insisted, "and then I can tell you how my heart feels regarding Tre."

"Love is a complex emotion. Falling in love is unchallenging for some people and the most complicated thing others will ever face in their entire lives. Most of us are emotionally disconnected from ourselves."

I leaned closer to her because I didn't want to miss a word.

"We lock away any emotion which feels hard to unravel. Giving away your body without exploring emotions is uncomplicated, which lures people into participating in one-night stands. Tons of people never consider the defragmentation that one night can have on their entire life."

My recent indiscretion forced me to look away.

"Then you have the fakers who claim they are in love, so they don't feel bad while engaging in lustful sex. These people hide their selfishness, abuse, and emotional issues behind the banner of love.

"Many people confuse the words love and lust. They both start with an L, but they mean different things. Lust is geared towards desires, while love is draped all around sentiments. Finding a genuine connection with someone outside the bed is the first step to discovering real love."

"If love and lust are a new emotion for you, how would you know if you're in love or lust?" I asked.

"Love is a feeling of affection, endorsement, protection, acceptance, friendship, compassion, honesty, intimacy, and utter respect for each other's feelings and views. Love is a feeling of addiction and passion at the same time. Love is a series of choices that will affect you and your partner. Love can sometimes make us reckless, and it will often have you questioning your levels of acceptance and intelligence. Love will evaluate your endurance, communication, and problem-solving skills. Love is blind to the physical; it sees the heart, not the outer shell," she explained.

I clenched my chin firmly with my hand. "And lust?"

"Lust is based on demands made around sexual desire, sexual appetite, sexual urges, and the yearning to please one's own sexual needs. It feeds itself at any cost. Lust's only goal is a personal compulsion, not marriage, not a relationship, and nobody's feelings matter apart from its own," she enunciated.

"So, you saying that love is blind and makes you stupid? In addition, love and lust are both selfish but for different reasons."

"Yes! Your experience with love depends on you and your partner. Too many people are in relationships, and their mates don't love them. So, they generate enough love to love themselves on behalf of their mates. They pray silently, hoping their mates will love them the way they've been schooling them. Their mate never knew the class was in session, so they weren't taking notes or paying attention. These people are in love with the possibilities of 'one day.'" she interjected.

I nibbled on my top lip, overwhelmed by this love and lust conversation. Imani patted me on the thigh, sensing my attempt to sort all these facts out in my head.

"Don't overthink it. Take me, for example. I understand Winten loves me, but I also acknowledge I love him way more than he loves me."

I smiled, wondering if I was in love or lust with my mystery guy.

"Loving Winten has aided in my growth. I learned how to control my emotions and not allow them to control me. Too many people miss precious moments overthinking or assessing the magnitude of love instead of bathing in its beams of light.

"Love can blind you to the point that you only see your surroundings' attractiveness. God won us over with love by sacrificing His son. Jesus set us free through love, so love will always be freeing."

She pulled her phone out and tapped on the screen. Passing the phone to me, she said. "Read 1 Corinthians 13:4-5 aloud."

"*Love is patient, love is kind. It does not envy, it does not boast, it is not proud. It does not dishonor others, it is not self-seeking, it is not easily angered, it keeps no record of wrongs."*

"That scripture is why I mentioned that love would test you. According to the word, remember that there is nothing new under the sun, Sis. The way music makes you feel. That's how love makes the average person feel."

After all the knowledge Imai had offered me, I was ready to tell her about my Vegas lover. "Imani when we were in Vegas…."

She cut me off. "Girl, Vegas was amazing. I wanted to tell you what we did while you were sleeping. However, last week when we were out, things became uneasy. Well, you know Lexi was Lexi."

She gazed off. "Anyway! I never saw you sleep in the airport, much less on a one-hour flight. You are always creating a playlist or working," Imani affirmed. "I should have been sleeping beside you. Girl, it took me three days to feel energetic again."

I was gearing up to interrupt her when Tamia approached us.

"Shit!"

My investigation of love and any plans of me divulging my Vegas tryst had to end. I quickly switched gears.

"What did you guys end up doing?" I campaigned, not genuinely interested in the answer.

"Lexi ended up running into one of her clients. He took the afterparty back to his mansion. Girl, I did not realize Vegas had luxurious mansions. He had two different parties going on in his house. The second floor was a VIP pool party, and he had a closet filled with brand new bathing suits in all sizes and styles. All the BAEs slipped on suits and indulged in his pool. He had an infinity waterfall pool that flowed from a stone wall on the second floor, dripping into two smaller pools on different levels. I was trying to figure out the levels, but I was too wasted."

"Girl, I ran up and down the stairs from the sophisticated party to the ghetto throwdown," Tamia ecstatically reminisced. "You would have enjoyed yourself. I know it was better than laying up in the room all night watching television dreaming about Tre."

I gazed at Imani and rolled my eyes. "I left my skates at home," Tamia announced. "Let me go rent a pair. I'll be right back."

"Imani, I wanted to talk to you tonight by ourselves. If I wanted Tamia to come, I would have invited her."

Imani placed her hand on top of mine. "BAEs don't keep secrets, Miya."

I didn't respond, so she followed it with, "Right?"

I smacked my lips and then agreed. "But you know Tamia cannot hold water. I can't talk about Tre with her here. I love the BAEs, but sometimes I want one opinion, not four."

"Every time Tre and I disagree, Tamia calls explaining his point of view. If I ask him where he's been, he says with Tamia. She calls me to cover for Tre. I never have time to call her about him. These days I call her phone if he doesn't answer. Most of the time, he's been with her.

"The last time she called, she explained why he missed my call. I politely told her to tell him to explain himself to me, not her. They both should have answered their damn phones, and she needs to stop answering my man's phone. I would have dialed her digits if I wanted to talk to her. Her excuse was that the club's music was too loud, so they didn't hear the phone, or she wanted to say hi to me, which is why she answered his phone.

"Later, Tre confessed they were in a strip club, and Tamia loves answering his phone, pretending to be his girlfriend. Do you understand the childish behavior I have been dealing with lately?"

I looked around for Tamia before I asked Imani my next question. Tamia was at the counter flirting with some guys.

"Do you think Tamia and Tre are more than friends? Would she betray me like that?"

Imani threw her fingers over her mouth, then checked if Tamia was still at the counter. "If Tamia had sex with him, she'll tell you if you ask. Tamia is shady yet truthful. The keyword is 'asking' since she'll never volunteer information. You do understand why we love her."

I nodded in agreement.

"I am sorry, Miya. I didn't consider her relationship with Tre when I invited her. I will never place you in this type of situation again. I should have known better since you only invited me skating."

Sooner than we could get another word out, Tamia joined us, and we awkwardly stared at each other.

"What?" Tamia inquired. "You heifers talking about me?"

"Girl, stop being paranoid. We are talking about G.O.D. — You down with G.O.D.? (Yeah, you know me)."

Tamia rocked to my lyrics, then started singing Naughty By Nature's "O.P.P."

"Fantasy"
Mariah Carey
Malik

I'VE BEEN MOPING AROUND SINCE RB and I returned from Vegas. I woke after the most fantastic night of my life with my mystery woman to a vacant spot in the bed. Either she was Casper — the friendly ghost, or she ghosted me. I searched the entire room for a note or evidence that it had not been a dream.

RB called and insisted I meet him in front of the Venetian as I scouted the hotel for my mystery woman.

RB joked about me being a good guy who said goodbye and didn't disappear on women like most men. I wanted to confess she had ghosted me, and I was in love with her. Embarrassment forcibly held my tongue.

The memory of my Vegas lover lingered in my head like Monica's lyrics "For You I Will."

My heart questioned my mind concerning love at first sight. I was a believer because I could recall every freckle on her face, even the solitary mole on her right hip. I smiled, remembering her fingertips raking across my butterfly back.

"Practice went well. I see a ton of improvement in your knee, bruh."

I took my eyes off the table and scanned the room for RB, missing the visions of Vegas in my thought. RB was at the wet bar mixing a drink.

"Are you going to daydream all day or rack the balls?"

I shrugged my shoulders before racking the balls on the billiard table when my phone buzzed. It was my brother, Tre.

Tre // 5:00 pm: Why are you playing? Open the front door!

Me // 5:02 pm: Give me a sec.

Nobody except Tre would climb all those damn stairs and knock on my front door. Did he think I would hear him in a 15,256 square foot home?

"Who Dat?" RB inquired. "I hope it's the girl you've been daydreaming over. I told you to smash her, but I think yo' ass in love again." RB chuckled.

"Have you ever met a woman that forces you to question if you ever loved anyone before them?"

Instead of answering, RB threw two ice cubes at me.

My phone buzzed again, and I forgot Tre was at the door.

Tre // 5:15 pm: Open the damn door! FUCK!

"What's wrong?" RB asked, reacting to my expression. "Bruh, why do you keep breathing like that? Who the fuck was that?"

I tried not to sound pissed, forcing a smile on my face.

"It's Tre! He is at the front door."

Romello sipped on his concoction. "You realize his uninvited visit will cost you a pretty penny. I'm telling you now I'm not investing in anything else his ass suggests. Every time Tre sees me, he asks to be my money manager. You would think by now he would understand there's no fucking way. If he weren't, your brother, I would have broken his legs over my fifty thousand."

We chuckled in unison.

"Dis fool trying to manage people's money and bad at managing his shit. Theoretically, both of us were to blame. He's always hitting you up for money, and I should have considered those facts before handing him my money."

I wanted to toss the eight ball at RB's head, hating that he was telling nothing but the truth.

"Well, umm…he's not that bad." I attempted to defend my brother.

RB struck multiple poses, pretending to take snapshots of himself. Each time his facial expression changed to show profound skepticism. After the third fake picture, he stopped and erupted in laughter.

"Well, both of us lost money," he said, walking close to the pool table and lowering his voice. "Real talk, you're still losing money. I would cut his ass off. Technically, he's not your biological brother."

I wanted to say mos' def! However, I knew my parents would kill me for that. They brought Tre into our family and demanded I love him. Overnight I became a big brother.

"He's not a horrible brother, dawg."

RB laughed, collecting his stuff before announcing he would see me tomorrow for practice.

"Why are you running off?"

RB chuckled before emptying his glass. "I need a shower, love from a fine woman, and rest. We must get you ready for the rookie minicamp in May. Fuck with me, kid, and you'll be ready in August for preseason games. But I'm not ready to fuck with Tre. My momma didn't demand that I take care of his freeloading ass."

"I'll be there. I refuse to be on the taxi squad forever. My knee is feeling better every day," I admitted honestly. "Dawg, walk to the front of the house and let Tre in."

RB threw the deuce sign in the air before making a right out of the game room, heading away from the front door.

"I parked in the back. Besides, your knee needs a workout. Shit, you can even jump in the sauna after your stroll to the door. You need to move out of this big ass house and move into a penthouse like the king!"

RB popped his shirt collar. I flipped RB off before strolling to the front of the house.

Tre only made his way to Georgia or San Diego to beg for money. After he visited our parents, they were always in need of cash. Our mother grants Tre whatever he requests, and I have to replace her funds. She has a soft spot for her baby boy.

The day Tre walked into my life is a day I'd never forget.

"Back in the Day" (Remix)

Ahmad Malik

IN THE EARLY '90S, I HEARD my first Opera geared towards impossible love concerning a man torn between two lovers and a woman's devotion to God and family.

In 1995, with a slight tilt of my head, the wails of a boy condemned to personal sacrifice rang in my ears as I composed the Walkers Opera's dramatic ending.

The first act started in my living room when Tre's mother, Tasha, knocked on my parent's door announcing Tre was my father's love child.

I was ready to ball my tiny fist and punch her in the mouth for lying on my dad. I held on tight to the staircase railing, waiting for my mother to slap the lie out of this woman's mouth. Instead, my mother invited her and her son into our home.

My mom fed them, inquiring about the wellness of her daughters.

Dang, how many kids did daddy have with this woman? I wanted to remind my mother that she was not her friend. She was the person you don't invite to your birthday party because they stink like pee-pee.

I walked over to my mother and asked if she was okay a thousand times.

We all watched TV waiting for my father to arrive home from work. My Pops walked into the house. It was standard for me to run to him and give him a big hug before my mom would hug him and take his coat and briefcase.

On this night, I didn't hug him. Instead, I placed a distance between my father and me with my arm, informing him he was in big trouble. Shaking my index finger, I stomped my foot and pointed towards the den. My father only chuckled.

I followed closely behind my father. I slammed into him as he halted, watching as he blinked and wiped at his eyes when he spotted Tasha and her son sitting on our sofa in the den. Walking over to my mother, he kissed her cheek and took a seat.

My father went to speak, but my mother caressed his kneecap, stopping him short.

"Tasha, I don't know what kind of trouble you may be in, but I can tell you, Maurice, and I will help you the best we can."

Tasha sat up straight on the sofa, gearing to speak. My mother cut her short and reminded her children were present. Tasha rolled her eyes at my mother.

"As I told you earlier, Maurice and I need to have a conversation concerning Tre," Tasha insisted. She pointed at my dad, herself, and her son. "This circle right here has nothing to do with you."

My father ran his hand across his forehead.

"Tasha, did you ever wonder how I knew who you were when you knocked on our door? You never introduced yourself," my mother reminded her.

Tasha frowned and flung her hands in the air, making my mother laugh at her antics.

Pointing to my dad, my mother asked Tasha, "Do you see this good man right here?"

"Of course, I see him. I'm not blind," Tasha retorted, batting her eyes.

My mother grinned. "Okay! Well, God gave me this man, and last night, my heavenly father warned me something was coming today to challenge my faith. He also warned me when I met Maurice. You see, a warning comes before destruction."

My mother beamed at my dad and then Tasha. "I know you and Maurice dated years before he married me. My good man laid out the details of your first encounter. According to him, he offered you a ride on a cold rainy day. He was heartbroken seeing you walking in the rain pregnant, struggling with two babies."

"Okay, we get it. Maurice is a good man," Tasha blurted, cutting my mother off.

"My king was present for your daughter's birth, and your other daughters became attached to him. I understand this, and a lot can occur within four years. Maurice also informed me of how he became attracted to you, and I see why."

Ms. Tasha was beautiful, but my mother was gorgeous.

"And your point," Tasha replied, cutting off my mom.

"I am a queen. I am secure enough to compliment another woman. Did you know your daughters used to call Maurice during our courtship? Most of the time, they needed food. One night they called to inform my good man you had left them unattended for the entire weekend, and they were hungry." My mother inhaled deeply; I could swear her eyes went pitch black.

Tasha hunched her shoulders. "Well, it is hard out there sometimes. I do what I must do to make money. I'll whip their asses later for calling you guys. What happens in my house stays at my house."

My mother nodded her head. "Did you know your daughters still call us?"

Tasha rolled her neck. "Did you know Maurice still buys them birthday and Christmas gifts?"

Tasha smirked at my mother as she anticipated her answer. I rested my elbows on my knees, awaiting my mother's reply. My living room drama was better than *The Young and The Restless* soap opera my mother watched daily.

"Don't forget the Valentine's Day jewelry or the Easter baskets," my mother corrected her.

I couldn't believe my father was buying other kids presents. On top of that, my mother was all right with Pops buying Tasha's kid's gifts.

"And you okay with that?" Tasha questioned. "I knew you were stupid, but damn, you dumb as fuck!"

My mother gently chuckled and wiggled her entire body, shaking Tasha's words off.

"That's right, Mom! Sticks and stones may break your bones, but whatever she says to you bounces off you and sticks to her like glue," little me whispered.

"I'm the one who buys all the gifts, so I am aware. I reminded my husband of the day he stepped into those girls' lives; he took on the role of shepherd to their souls. I've heard them screaming, 'Hey Dad!' through the phone. They've called us whenever they need something, and it has been a blessing to help them. We have entertained them and their grandmother."

I scanned the den for the picture of Shanice, Eboni, Aaliyah, and me. I wondered if they were my dad and Ms. Tasha's kids. That would explain why they spent last summer with us. I spotted one picture and took it to Ms. Tasha.

My mother snapped her fingers at me, and I retreated to my spot on the floor by the den entrance.

"So, my babies have been to your house. What does any of this have to do with Tre and Maurice?" Tasha questioned my mother again.

"I'm not saying my husband would never cheat on me and possibly make a baby, but I am saying this is not his son."

My father's eyes shot wide open, and he frantically shook his head.

"Queen, this is not my son. After all we have done for you, why would you lie, Tasha?"

Tasha rolled her eyes and smacked her lips.

"I told my wife we should cut all ties with you. She insisted it was unfair to your daughters because I was in their lives for years, and they call me Dad. I can admit I love those girls. It would have broken my heart to turn my back on them, but my marriage is my world.

"Yet, my wife would not allow me to hurt your girls or myself to please herself. That's why I agreed with my wife's wishes after discovering the girls lived with their father's mother. I should have never come to your house to help with your car. Again, it was my wife. The girls thought you were not visiting because your car broke down."

I wanted to jump up and rejoice when my dad announced I was still an only child.

My father balled his fists and shook them in the air. My father gaped at my mother. "Queen, some people cannot be helped." My father slapped his thighs, and my mother patted my father on the leg to calm him down.

"Walkout on the girls and your son, Maurice!" Tasha screamed. "You're supposed to be a Christian man. Tell her how you destroyed your marriage."

"Our marriage and home have a solid foundation built on God's word. The Man I serve would never allow the man He blessed me with to make a fool out of me because I put God before this man and everything else in my life," my mother proclaimed.

My mother raised her back off the sofa and slid to the edge of the couch. "My husband is a good man, and I wish every little boy and girl could have him for a father, but he is not your son's father."

"How the fuck do you know where Maurice's penis has been?" Tasha asked, causing me to blush at the word penis, and I wanted to ask my mother if she heard the nasty word I heard.

"No, I am not," was all my father declared.

My young mind could not understand why my mother was not beating this woman. She was using foul language. If that were me, I would have received three whoopings by now.

Tasha jumped off the sofa and started yelling at my mother. My mom remained calm as she scanned the room. My mother politely waited for Tasha to finish ranting.

She assured Tasha she would not yell or fight her unless she posed a danger to her family in the sweetest tone. My father stood behind my mother, massaging her shoulders.

I laughed.

My father was warming my mother's muscles the way they do wrestlers before a fight.

I screamed, "High-fly her, Mom, like Randy Savage does when he is wrestling." My mom scanned the room until she located me, demanding I go to my room and take the little boy with me.

My dad finally called me downstairs. Ms. Tasha was crying on my mother's shoulder. She stepped out of the house, reminding my mother and father that she was leaving her son in their care.

I waved for her to stop, dragging the little boy down the stairs, and ushering him towards the front door.

I will never forget the way my mother wrapped my little hands inside hers. A surge of love flowed from her heart directly into my soul through her hands.

"Ms. Tasha needs some help taking care of her son. Your dad and I have agreed to help. He is not your brother by blood but your brother in Christ. He will sleep in your room."

I wanted to ask my parents why I was responsible for this three-year-old boy at six and a half?

"If It Isn't Love"
New Edition
Malik

TRE POUNDING ON MY DOOR AND texting yanked me back into reality. His presence has been hammering on our lives since he was a boy. I can count how many arguments our parents had while growing up because they were always due to Tre.

Tasha would come to get him for the summer. Each time Tre returned, he would cry and pee on himself, which was the routine from the time he was five to eight years old. My mother placed him in summer camp or classes as an excuse for not sending him to Tasha in the summer.

My mother indulged him because she felt terrible about Tre living between two homes. My mother still babies him, and his sisters are still in our lives today.

Poor Dad has five kids he's accountable for, yet only one shares his DNA.

"Hey, big bro," Tre greeted me as I opened the front door. We bumped shoulders in a one-armed hug. He spun around the foyer, gazing at the ceiling and chandelier.

My posture stiffened. "Baby bro, why do you always come to the front door?"

He spun around on my marble floor, scuffing them with his shoes.

"I love the look of these soaring ceilings and this massive chandelier," he admitted. "I need a favor."

"What else is new?" I sarcastically replied. "You couldn't just call for this favor? You had to get on a plane?"

"Your brother is in love, and I'm ready to get married," he hummed.

Tre was a decent brother, but he always made the wrong decisions. I was gearing up to tell him all the reasons he shouldn't propose to a woman, and I remembered how I felt the day momma crushed me over my desire to marry Sabrina. I heard him out before casting judgment.

"I was going to ask Mom for grandma's ring, but then I remembered she wouldn't give it to you, and you had to buy Sabrina a ring." The nerve of him thinking he could get my grandmother's ring and I couldn't. A small part of me wondered if my momma would give it to him.

"You want me to ask Mom for you?"

He scoffed. My question was ludicrous to him. "Nope! I want you to give me the huge rock you bought, Sabrina."

This guy! I thought to myself.

Pushing up my sleeves, I inquired. "Tell me about this woman."

"Are we going to sit in the white room?"

I sat down on the white loveseat, ready to curse at him, but resisted. He knew my house rules, yet he failed to remove his dirty shoes before stepping onto my white carpet. My face contorted, squinting at his filthy sneakers on my white carpet. He stepped back, nodded, and then kicked off his muddy shoes.

I pointed to the white chair, waiting as he took a seat.

He opened his mouth, then closed it a couple of times. My knees bounced up and down while waiting for my brother to speak.

"Tre, today!" He sat there, scrutinizing the entire room. "Dammit, Tre! Say something."

"Oh...oh... ok. So, my Mimi is a Radio Talk Show Producer. She is a twenty-two-year-old virgin and Blackanese."

"And?" I pressed.

"And we have not had sex," he replied.

I had been waiting for him to tell me how much he loved this woman and how he could not live without her. Something regarding her characteristics and seal it with 'God revealing she is my wife.' Instead, I got. "Oh, and she is breathtaking with a banging body. I cannot wait to fuck the shit out of her!"

I nodded my head at my brother's vulgarity.

"Have you been working on your problem? How does she feel regarding it?"

Leaning forward, Tre's shoulders slumped as he placed his elbows on his knees, burying his face in his palms.

"Is that a, no?"

He cleared his throat.

"I have been going to the therapist you hired, and I am getting better," he stuttered. It was a nasty habit my brother displayed whenever he regretted his actions.

"Mimi has been asking me to have sex with her, and I told her to wait until our wedding night. I am trying to do right by her."

"I am proud of your progress. You're not alone, baby bro. We're all here for you," I assured him. "I need a stogie."

I told my brother about the sweet woman I met in Vegas and how I could not get her off my mind. He demanded her name.

Lying, I blurted the first name that came to mind. "Rudy." The cute little girl from the Cosby Show. I didn't want to appear irresponsible. That role depicted him, not me.

Our parents expected him to be unreliable but would kill me if they thought I was contemplating a reckless thought. When I was sulking over Sabrina, my mother slammed every verse in the bible at me.

The more he interrogated me regarding my Vegas mystery woman, the more I lied.

To end the lies, I gave him Sabrina's ring. Once he had the ring, he didn't ask any more questions about my mystery woman. Instead, he requested fifty thousand dollars to help pay for the wedding.

Was this fool, fo'real? Did he forget I agreed to give him a 3.5-carat ring for free?

"Bruh, no! I gave you an eighty-thousand-dollar ring. Sell the damn ring and buy a cheaper one," I demanded, hitting the sofa in disbelief.

His eyes bucked.

"I'm not marrying her. I haven't met this girl, and you want me to spend over a hundred racks on her?"

"Can you come to Los Angeles on April 26th?" Tre queried. "I am going to propose to her after her cousin's party."

"If you are proposing on April 26th, why do you need the ring now?"

"She's mad at me. I contemplated proposing now to buy me some more time. On the plane, I realized that if I waited until the end of April, all her family would be in town for her cousin's event. So, I'll save my money. I won't have to fly them out or put them in hotels. Her cousin will do that. I can propose during her cousin's event. She'll set the stage for me free of charge."

Tre was consistently exploiting someone else to get ahead. He tried to high-five me, and I shook my head, running my hand over my face.

Was it too late for me to snatch the ring out of his hand? Shit, he claims to love this lady but was too cheap to buy her a ring. Whoever she was, it seemed like she deserved better than my freeloading brother. He doesn't call it mooching or using people. He only saw them as free hookups.

"I tell you what. I'll bring the ring to Los Angeles after I pay for the resizing," I informed him, snatching the ring out of his hands before he could protest.

I was not going to give this fool eighty grand to rekindle his relationship with some chick he may never see again.

"Fine!" he uttered, twiddling his thumbs. "Well, this guarantees your attendance now."

He patted me on the back.

"Did you tell Mom and Dad? Have you taken her to meet them?"

He gestured with his hands as he talked.

"No, and no. Mimi and I have only been together for a short while."

"Why haven't you introduced her to our parents?" The more he talked, the more shit sounded suspect.

Tre lived in the Inland Empire, and our parents stayed in Temecula, a forty-five-minute drive, yet he had not taken this girl to meet our parents.

"Can you invite Mom and Dad? I'm not ready to hear them preach to me. I'll wait and invite them to the wedding. I may invite Tasha to the wedding."

"Tasha?"

He hunched his shoulders as his face went lifeless. "She gave me life, although she stole life from me." He wiped his eyes.

His sorrow yanked at my stern demeanor, and I eased off my baby brother. Tre had suffered a lot in his life, and he didn't need me adding to his misery; therefore, I gave him a check for fifty thousand.

"Weak" SUV Malik

APRIL WAS THE BEST MONTH OF my life, as the San Diego Chargers declared their beliefs in my skills. Moving back to California was a no-brainer. I shook my head twice. The speed I displayed on the field was magnificent. Atlanta wants me to play on the practice squad, but San Diego offered me a roster spot.

"Jesus, I cannot believe the opportunity you placed before me. Father God, I'm ready to train in Hawaii and San Diego until August's pre-season. Can you allow the appointment tomorrow with Dr. Allen to benefit me?" I prayed while waiting for my manager, Kyle.

Kyle patted me on the back to alert me of his presence. "They have to make some changes to the deal, and once Dr. Allen gives you the all-clear, you will be a San Diego Charger!"

"Please give moms the courtesy of viewing the final draft. You know how she can be about her baby. I mean her oldest."

Kyle chuckled. "I faxed it over to her and the lawyers already."

I was planning to spend the day getting reacquainted with my old stomping grounds when my mother called. I figured I would leave San Diego and stay the night with my parents before heading to Los Angeles.

I called Kyle to explain my plans, and an hour later, he knocked on my door with the keys to a rental truck. Kyle was an honorable manager, a characteristic rarely found in this business. He could have dropped me after my injury but never counted me out. He knew I would make it back onto the field. He carried faith and vision when I struggled to find mine. The only thing missing in my world was my Vegas sunshine.

As I drew closer to the freeway, something drew me to the Starbucks in the Stonecrest Plaza. The pull in my gut was massive, even though I was not a coffee drinker. Instead of getting on the freeway, I followed my intuition and turned into the parking lot.

Starbucks was a smorgasbord of beautiful black people. Most of the men were preying on the women. The woman I hungered for was not in this room. I loved this woman so much that I could smell her ambrosial scent drifting in the ambiance.

While waiting in line to order a dark black coffee and something sweet, a group of women passed me, giggling. I continued to canvass the room. The same group of ladies stepped into my sight, and I turned away.

They chatted and giggled among themselves—one eyeballed me. I turned my head to the right to avoid her gaze. I felt a tap on my shoulder. I slowly turned around, hoping it was not one of the ladies.

"Hi, my name is Kathy."

I smiled while contemplating whether I wanted to give my government name or not.

"Nice to meet you, Kathy," I replied.

"I cannot believe your girlfriend let you come out without her on your arm." I nodded, and she continued to speak. "I love your dreadlocks." Without notice, she shuffled her hand through the tips of my locs.

She resembled the R&B sensation and actress Aaliyah. I'm sure most men are mesmerized by her beauty and would fall to her feet, but I wasn't interested. My heart belonged to another.

"Kathy, it was nice talking to you. I am currently not accepting applications for new friends."

She roared with laughter at my response, then slid her hand over my chest.

I scanned the room to see if people had observed our exchange when I heard her. Gently pushing Kathy out of the way, I listened intently.

"Upside down caramel Frappuccino with a shot of espresso for Miya," the barista announced.

I watched my Vegas mystery woman approach the counter.

Her name rolled off my tongue like silk. She headed towards the exit while Kathy gripped my hand. Pushing her away, I had to go before my future escaped my grasp.

I left the rental car in the parking lot and followed her on foot. A gentle, warm breeze swept through her hair, sailing her scent up my nostrils. The intoxicating aroma almost blew me off my feet.

Pausing at the door, I watched Miya walk into the Hilton Garden Inn toward the kitchen area to grab napkins. She placed her items on the table, wiping the coffee she spilled on herself.

Time slowed down as I approached her. I walked beside her without an open invitation and laced my fingers around hers. She whipped her head to the left, her protest stopping short, landing her sneer on her bold intruder.

A smile slowly glided across her honey-brown face, and I wanted to kiss the curl in the corner of her mouth.

"I've missed you," I proclaimed, then kissed the back of her hand.

"You barely know me," she hummed sensually.

Time paused as I sketched a picture of her angelic face on my heart.

"I knew you before we even knew of ourselves."

A cute wrinkle formed on her nose, causing all my favorite love songs to play in my heart as I imagined our lives together. In her crystal honey brown eyes, I foresaw the unity of eternity.

"Do you hear that?"

"Hear what?" she asked, stepping closer to me. The dark mystery of her eyes enthralled me.

"Our hearts were beating as one, my love."

She pulled her hand from mine, stepping back and chuckling. "We have to stop running into each other like this—yea, we need to stop."

"We were always destined to reconnect." I wrapped my arms around her waist, and she placed her hands flat on my chest.

I traced her lush lips with my thumb, then glided my hand along her cheekbone to her ear. I opened my palm, running the silky strands of her hair through my fingers before massaging her scalp.

She purred in pleasure.

When the tension became unbearable, I guided her lips to mine, locking them in an enthusiastic kiss.

She pulled away short-winded. My dreadlocks swayed backward as she wafted her sweet breath all over me. She suggested we go to my room. Which forced me to admit I didn't have a room.

"I spotted you at Starbucks and followed you."

"Ok, stalker, so my room."

She possessed the power to make me follow her into a den of lions, then fight for her honor.

I wanted to take her to her room and make love to her from dusk to dawn. I resisted. I needed to ensure our attraction went beyond physical passion. "How about we go to your room and change, then go out on the town? A little dinner and dancing, and then I can have you for dessert."

"Deal," she shouted, then planted a kiss on my lips. The fiery ache in my bones ceased the second I felt the fleshy warmth of her mouth.

While she was getting dressed, I called Kyle and my parents. Kyle informed me that Dr. Allen must perform an emergency surgery tomorrow and see me on Saturday. The universe was smiling upon me. I could spend all tomorrow getting to know Miya.

She emerged from the bedroom, and I was struck speechless. "Are you ready to spoil me?" she teased.

"Yes, I am, my love. The car is already downstairs waiting on us."

My face hurt from smiling so much by the time we made it to the moonlit dinner cruise.

According to Miya, she was here on business for three days. While driving back to LA, something drew her to the Hilton Garden Inn instead of getting on the freeway. She decided not to fight the urge since she didn't have to work on Friday.

My only complaint was that she still refused to tell me anything personal. I didn't push her for her name because I knew it. I also discovered she has an assistant named Eva because she called her during the date. We talked about everything and nothing throughout the day and night. Our conversations flowed like smooth Jazz.

Her heart resting against my chest was as welcoming as sunshine on a stormy day. She planted a kiss on my lips. "I had a wonderful day."

"Me too," I admitted, then climbed into the car. She coiled in my arms and slept. I gently shook her and almost called her by her name to wake her. "We are back at the hotel, baby."

She purred like a kitten, then uncoiled. "Stay with me tonight, sir, and I'll tell you my first name in the morning." I quickly agreed.

Once we entered her suite, she went from a gentle kitten to a lioness. Clothes vanished before we reached the bed. I started with her manicured toes and slowly worked up her elongated legs. I rotated between my moist tongue and wet kisses until I reached her sweet equator.

Thoughts of another man sharing in the nectar that I considered mine drove me insane. My tongue slammed long aggressive strokes across her rosebud. My fingertips sank deep into her inner thighs while I feasted on her sweet nectar. I was never allowing her to get away from me again.

Her pleas sliced through contemplations. "Baby, take me now!"

I flipped her over and then pulled her onto her knees. I slithered between her honey thighs, gripped them, and pulled her downward. I was not ready to merge my juices with hers. I was determined to make her river flow one more time under my mouth before bringing ours together.

Submerged in arousal, passion, and love, Marvin Gaye's "Sexual Healing" reverberated in my head. Her moans chimed like a sexual cello. My tongue gently played her center-like strumming piano strokes.

I slid her jaded body down my physique. I wondered if we should stop, but Miya's roaming hands diminished that thought.

I nibbled on her earlobe, then sang the words in my head. She hummed the song's lyrics with me. I plunged inside her sweet nectar.

My body tingled from the top of my head to the tip of my toes. This woman was invoking emotions I had never felt before. Her womb felt like climbing into a warm bed on a frosty winter night.

I love you dangled on the tip of my tongue, then slipped from my lips.

Time slowed and stopped as depletion ripped through our bodies four times that night.

"Sweet Lady"
Tyrese
Miya

TOSSED AND TURNED ALL NIGHT, RECALLING the words that slipped from his succulent lips. I've read enough books to understand that men say things they do not mean in the heat of passion. I needed to escape from my Vegas lover's grip before I mistook lust for love. However, each time I pulled away, he gripped me tighter around my waist. He was holding my body hostage. I finally reassured him that I couldn't go anywhere and would be here when he opened his eyes to a new sunrise.

I stretched out in the bed and rolled over to kiss my mystery man, but his side of the bed was empty.

I could smell sweet bread and fruit. I slipped into the sitting room, kissed him, then sprinted back into the bathroom—the steamy water sparking memories of last night's lovemaking.

I smiled at my reflection in the mirror, recited my daily mantra, and reminded myself that today would be a good day. Before my subconscious could reply, I cut my thoughts off and recollected in my heart and mind about the bet. I believe he would be an excellent husband.

I jumped back, startled by my Vegas lover's presence by the bathroom door. "We are too high up for me to jump out of the invisible window," I joked, pointing to the bathroom's wall.

"I was going to come in and join you, but you locked the door."

I smiled. "Old habit. It will never happen again."

He licked his luscious lips and tugged at my towel. "I am starving, and I need something to eat."

"You can order room service."

He pulled me close. "I did. I tried the melon, and it was not sweeter than you." He licked his fingers. "I need you to feed me some sweet nectar, baby." His whisper removed his deep baritone. Yet, the sultry masculinity screamed out to me, and my nipples hardened. His eyes dropped below my waist. "Can I taste it before we go?"

I blushed. He glided his left hand along my thigh until he reached my sweet spot. He drew his bottom lip into his mouth, and my bath towel hit the floor. I intertwined my hands through his dreads. A smirk glided across my face. It felt as if we were making love for the first time.

"I missed your gentle touch."

He responded with a hearty growl.

He raked his fingers across my back, and my back arched under his touch. Sparks hopscotched across my skin as his soft hands seductively explored my body. He parted my lips and our tongues danced. The sweet taste on his tongue and the warmth of his heart weakened me at the knees.

His enormous hands clenched both sides of my waist as he lifted me off my feet. I tried to wrap my legs around his waist. He lifted me above his chest and rested my thighs on his shoulder. My body stiffened until I felt the wall grace my back.

I ran my hand across the softness of his neck. The warmth of his tongue had me smitten. He connected to my soul like Luther Vandross's lyrical skills in "If Only for One Night."

Both body and soul were suspended in a place where nothing mattered, and time stood still. I savored each drop of his essence as I yielded to our fate. Wisdom flooded my mind. In him was a home filled with love.

Tormented by pleasure, I bucked against the wall. He lowered me until my backside rested on his chest. I shivered as he blew passionate wafts of warm air across my love button.

I arched my back, and my body melted into the crisp white sheets. I ran my palm across his unyielding abdomen. "I love your teardrop breast," he mumbled while saturating the narrow top of my breast with kisses and then ravishing the bottom of my rounded breast.

I traced his shoulder blade, collarbone, and broad neck with damp kisses. Overwhelmed by his tempo and the emotions forming in me, my hips rose and collided with his.

His eyes rolled skyward. His white fleshy veiled expressive eyes made him appear possessed. My eyes crossed in euphoria as my body transcended to the same realm of pleasure.

I matched his movement until our rhythm united into one solid beat. Our hearts pounded like a tribal drum as we both hit high notes of ecstasy. His body jerked as he filled my sugary canal with life.

I eased out of bed and went into the sitting room to eat. "Baby, someone will knock on the door soon with everything I need for today." He stepped out of the room, then back into the room, and watched me.

"What's wrong with you?" He sighed, nibbling on his bottom lip. "You can tell me anything, lover."

"Baby, will you be here when I get out of the shower?"

I smiled brightly. "I planned on being here until you finish showering." He smiled back at me, garnishing his pearly whites. "Can I move to answer the door and get your stuff?"

He winked. Before I could place the melon in my mouth, he was on top of me, tickling me.

"Stop! I'm ticklish," I hollered.

"I was hoping you were." He kissed me on the tip of my nose, and my body shivered with delight.

A knock on the door interrupted me as I answered my emails and nibbled on the warm fruit.

I opened the door, and two slender women stood in the hallway holding garment bags and a tote bag. "Are you Mrs. Walker?" I nodded. "These items are for Mr. Walker." They followed me into the bedroom, hung the bags in the closet, and handed me the tote.

Who the hell is Mr. Walker, I thought to myself?

"Honey, was that the door?" He called from the bathroom as I placed the tote on the bed.

"Baby, can you bring me my toiletries?" he asked as I poked my head in the door. I returned to the tote bag, unzipped it, and got the requested items.

I sighted the clock out the corner of my eye and jumped in the shower with him. "Honey, can you apply some cream to my back?" His fiery breath made my body tremble. I ran my hand across his collarbone, then kissed it. It was the sweetest kiss ever until he kissed me on my forehead. Electricity soared through my entire body. My mind screamed, and I forgot about the art walk as our bodies sailed the waves of hot ecstasy. I hurried out of the shower before we devoted the entire day to making love.

He grabbed his phone and called for a car. "Both of us have a car," I reminded him.

He gripped me around my waist and pulled me close. "If I'm driving, I won't be able to study every curve on your sexy body." He licked his lips. "I love this sundress." He kissed the crown of my breast.

I blushed. "Do you think I'm sexy?"

Instead of answering me, he pulled me into his powerful arms, holding me tight. He placed kisses on my forehead and head. "Honey, you are sexy. If I was in a room with you and a million supermodels and somebody asked, 'How many sexy supermodels are in here?'" He kissed the tip of my nose. "I would reply, 'Only one.' Baby, ever since we met, all I see is you."

My heart, body, and soul craved this type of intimacy and love. "If you relax and let go, we can make magic together." I unraveled at his comment.

Mr. Walker spoiled me the entire day. I wanted to ask him personal questions, but I was again afraid he would tell me he was married. Maybe he had a fiancée, or he and his wife had an understanding. I knew Mrs. Walker existed because the ladies said as much this morning.

They say ignorance is bliss. If I don't know the truth, I can't stress or feel the guilt behind my actions.

We visited five murals on our Ocean Beach walking tour. Time and nature destroyed some of the walls. He promised to bring me back to the OB Street Fair when they painted the Union Bank of California sidewall on 1858 Cable Street in June.

I checked my watch, and it was almost two o'clock. All this walking had made me hungry.

"We have to get on the road, Love." I wondered where we were going.

I fell asleep in his arms as we kissed. When I woke up, I let down the window a bit, and all I could see were grapevines perfectly lined in rows going further than I could see.

The day and evening breezed by as we enjoyed wine and lunch at a couple of wineries. Heading back to San Diego, he dragged me across his body.

I planted kisses on his clean-shaven chiseled face.

I jumped when his thick fingers slipped past my sheer panties. His shallow breaths hopped down my back. "Baby, you are smoldering and soaking wet," he growled hotly in my ear.

I nuzzled my head under his neck. I bit and sucked on his Adam's apple as his finger hurried. Gentle moans escaped my body. I was grateful for the privacy window. I locked my legs tightly. He took my tongue into his mouth and savored my juices. I eased my legs back open and buried my head in his chest. "I cannot wait to get you to the room."

I purred loudly, trying to speak as my shaky voice failed me. My bottom lip trembled once the rhythm of his hand increased. I latched onto his neck, blowing rapidly as my body shuttered in his arms. I screamed into his nape, his arms holding me tightly as I bucked in his lap. Depleted, I slumped and leaned back against the door. He pulled my dress down, and I coiled in his lap as he gently rocked me off to sleep.

Gentle kisses stirred me from my slumber. "Do you want to get food at a restaurant or take food back to the room, sleepyhead?"

Mr. Walker was surprised that lunch had filled me, and I had no room for dinner. He rubbed his abdominal muscles because the boy had no ounce of fat in his midsection. "I'm hungry, and you will be too once you fully wake up." My heavy eyelids shuttered close as the warm touch of his lips touched my forehead.

I stirred. Mr. Walker instructed the driver to keep circling the block until he spotted him at the light. Then, he leaped out of the car into traffic and dashed into a restaurant. I tried to locate where he went. But my blurry eyes danced in the darkness. The driver and I made the block four times before spotting my lover. I screamed, "There he is." The driver maneuvered fast and pulled over to the light.

I advised the driver that he didn't have to get out. I swung the door open and bobbled out of the backseat. I was fighting Mr. Walker for the bags in his arms.

"Are you going to eat all of this food?" I questioned.

"Most of it. I ordered you some tacos. These are the best tacos in San Diego. You will be hungry once you smell them, but I don't know if I want to share mine," he joked through snickers.

The driver had to help carry our treats upstairs. We had a ton of food and the wine we bought at two of the wineries we visited. The second he opened the bag, a whiff of carne asada and grilled chicken invaded my nostrils. I was hungry, but I wasn't hungry—hungry.

I eased my hand into the bag and snacked on some chips. Mr. Walker placed four tacos in front of me. I ate two street tacos and all the guacamole and chips. He continued to eat, and I snuggled next to him. I wondered where all that food was going. Gluttony was cute on a man, not a woman.

I rolled over in bed the following day, ready to greet Mr. Walker with a warm treat. However, his side of the bed was empty. I hopped from the bed and combed the small suite in a panic. He was gone.

I unlocked the bathroom door, hoping he would join me in the shower or watch the soapy bubbles glide down my body. I slammed my eyes shut and navigated through the pain.

The room was empty.

Tears drenched my cheeks, and my reflection mocked me.

He wined and dined me, and then we made scorching love. I could not comprehend why he ghosted me. Was he trying to pay me back for Las Vegas?

His Casper rendition massively hit my heart with agony because I fell in love with him, and the sex was an absolute bonus.

My eyes blazed like torches, and my tears refused to cool them off.

"(Lay Your Head On My) Pillow"
Tony! Toni! Toné!
Malik

Y OVERWHELMING DELIGHT WAS MASKED BY fatigue. I rested my back against the elevator's dark wood-paneled wall. Reminiscing about the beautiful angel waiting for me in the room. God was raining blessings down on me. Fear of losing these blessings makes an attempt to slip into my heart.

"This time, I won't let anybody steal my miracles," I mumbled.

Kyle called me at six in the morning and instructed me to report to the team doctor's office within forty-five minutes. I tried to wake Miya, but she refused to get up. I left a note telling her to stay put until I returned. I took her keycard and left one garment bag hanging in the closet. However, when I returned to the room, she ghosted me again.

Since Dr. Allen cleared me, the team doctor said I was ready for training camp and the season. I asked him several times if he was allowing me to play. He merely laughed at my redundancy.

I struggled to maintain my cheerful demeanor because I missed Miya tremendously.

My phone buzzed. I couldn't answer the call. The elevator door opened, and I bounced out. I dialed Kyle back. "What's the word?"

"Once I receive the contract with the revisions, I'll swing by your hotel to get your signature." Tears streamed down my face. I was back. "Man, both doctors cleared you."

April was indeed the best month of my life. I was about to become a San Diego Charger. I spent two days with Miya, the love of my life. I replayed the entire week in my head.

I scoffed.

"What a mighty God I serve!" I told Kyle, disconnecting our call.

I leaned against the sizable, picturesque window at the end of the hallway. I cast my eyes upward and prayed. "Father God, I will train hard in Hawaii and San Diego. I will give you all the glory and praise each time I walk on the field. I only ask for your protection and no more career-ending injuries. Big G, thank you again for favoring a sinner like me. Amen!"

At that moment, I realized how my mother could shout and praise the Lord anywhere because I was there. I did a quick two-step of thanks to the man above, not caring who saw me. He deserved all the praise I had in me and some I did not know I possessed.

I scanned the room numbers before realizing I was on the wrong floor. I strolled back to the elevator. Where am I going to stay in San Diego? Should I commute from my parents' house? What am I going to do with my Atlanta mansion? Question after question slammed against my cranium.

The elevator door opened, and a group of guys stepped inside. One of them addressed me.

"Are you going down, bruh?"

I scanned the buttons, then realized I had never slipped my key in the security slot to access my floor.

"I am going to the fifteenth floor," I replied.

"This elevator is going to the first floor, so you're riding down with us," the smallest guy noted. Then they all chuckled. I noticed one guy, but his name continued to avoid my tongue. I recalled he was a senior in college and was supposed to be one of the MLB 2008 top ten draft picks in June. People were saying the LA Quakes were looking to draft him.

I silently uttered, "God, I promise not to take this new opportunity for granted. You will be the only thing I put before this second chance. Amen!"

Then I prayed that the rookie was in town getting great news concerning his future, and he wouldn't allow anything to get between him and his dreams.

The door opened on the first floor, and I wondered how I had missed all the people in the lobby. It appeared the hotel was hosting multiple events this weekend. I decided that if I got bored, I would crash one of these parties tonight.

While the door was closing, I heard a familiar voice yelling, "Hold the door, please!"

I reached for the door in a zombie state, but it closed. My keycard bounced in my hand and then collided with the floor. I tried to pry the doors open with my hands.

I took the elevator back down and searched for Miya. I knew I heard her voice. After hanging out at the bar in the pool cabana and walking around for four hours, I decided to throw in the towel.

I briefly wondered if she was the manager of the hotel. She couldn't be a regular employee because she has an assistant. Then it hit me like a ton of bricks. She had to be a guest. I could ask the front desk for Miya's room. However, I still didn't know her last name. Feeling defeated, I went back to my room.

My phone buzzed in my pocket the moment I walked through the door. "This is Malik," I greeted the caller.

"I wanted to call you and tell you your ring is ready, and it will be delivered this evening," Jay Rock, my jeweler, informed me. "I can have my assistant bring it to Temecula."

"Outstanding, but I am not in Temecula. I am at the Four Seasons in Beverly Hills. I will text you the room number."

"Dawg, I'll head back to the shop and grab your ring. I have another client who made some last-minute changes to his jewelry. I'm delivering it myself to him at the Four Seasons in Beverly Hills. His event starts in two hours. I'm cutting it close by turning back with evening traffic, but I got you. I must find him the second I arrive. He may want me to stay for drinks and shake some hands. He loves passing customers my way."

"Give me three and a half hours. Then, we can link up if it is okay with you. I have some cigars my uncle brought back from the Islands. I think you may love it. If you have plans, my bodyguard, Rick, can bring the ring to you when I get there."

"Jay, get your money, dawg. I'll be in my room. Could you bring it to me when you're finished, then we can puff on those cigars? I know you'll keep my shit safe."

"Bet! If I get too busy, my bodyguard Rick got you. What floor are you on?"

"I'm on the fifteenth floor." After the call, I went to the wellness center to pump some iron. I needed to work off some of this sexual frustration. Two hours later, I headed back to my room to shower. I lay on the bed, waiting for room service, and nodded off.

The constant beeping of my phone woke me from my nap. A woozy haze sailed over me as my body demanded rest. The first message was from Tre asking if he could come to get the ring from me. I shot him a quick text message updating him on the ring's status and informing him I had changed the design. I couldn't give his fiancée Sabrina's old ring. The other text came from Jay Rock, telling me he was onsite.

I opened my room door, hoping to find food there. My stomach rumbled as I gazed at the carpet, willing my dinner to appear.

I dialed room service and inquired about my meal. "The server knocked, sir, but no one answered. So, he brought the order back to the kitchen. We called the room three times, and no one answered. I can have the food remade and brought to you," she said politely. "It may take forty minutes to remake your order. The kitchen is a bit behind on orders."

"No need. I'll go to the Cabana restaurant."

The door opened on the first floor. I licked my lips at the most magnificent sight I had ever seen. Miya was standing there, hugging herself.

"Baby, tell your man who did it," I swooned, arms wide open.

She blinked a couple of times at me, then rushed into my arms. My heart pounded rapidly, and I struggled to breathe. I drummed my fingers against her spine. At that moment, I realized we had missed each other equally.

She nuzzled her head under my neck and kissed my Adam's apple. Memories of San Diego flooded my mind. "We have to stop meeting at hotels," she teased.

I was struggling with the emotions looming in the atmosphere. I gripped her tightly until she patted me on my back. I released her from my embrace, and she gulped for air.

I tapped my keycard against the security pad and pressed the button for the fifteenth floor. She leveled a glowering look.

I held my breath, hoping she wouldn't protest.

"Spend My Life With You"
Eric Benét
Malik

I OPENED THE DOOR TO MY ROOM and stepped aside, allowing her space to walk in. I watched her ample bottom bounce to the beat of my heart. Cutting through the thickening silence, Miya pushed me against the wall, kissing me deeply before the room door closed. Astounded by her assertive behavior, I struggled to maintain her pace as she yanked my shirt apart, sending a flurry of buttons scattering in multiple directions across the floor. She kissed and gently bit my chest, capturing a nipple between her teeth. I had created a monster.

I lifted her off her feet, loving how her elongated legs felt wrapped around my waist. I carried her to the beige and gray loveseat and plopped down. I tried to kiss her, only for her to lean back and shove me in the chest. I licked my lips, flashing her my bad boy grin.

She pressed down on my broad shoulders and elevated herself on the sofa until she was hovering over me, and the familiar aroma of a sweet summer's day swept through my nostrils. I leaned my head back and allowed my eyes to savor her beauty. I ran my hand under her skirt and squeezed her naked backside.

"Where are your panties, young lady?" She pointed to a spot by the front door.

Passion sprung in her eyes, and her body bloomed like chrysanthemums on a warm autumn day. She leaned forward until I feasted my eyes on her yoni. I kissed her slowly on her stomach and then kissed her lower. I traced around her rosebud with the tip of my tongue. Her legs quivered, and she laced her hands behind my head.

I gripped her ample butt while my tongue slowly danced with her rosebud. Letting go of my head, she steadied her hands on the wall. Her juices were raining on my tongue. I gulped hungrily, determined not to allow one drop of her nectar to slip past my lips.

She squatted in my lap. In a racy whisper, she asked, "Am I ready yet?"

I kissed her on the neck, watching as she threw her head backward. I slipped her shirt off and then unfastened her bra, cupping her teardrop breasts in my hands, trying to smother myself.

She chirped. "I presume that's a no."

I smacked her on her ample bottom, and she playfully shoved me back. Sniggering, her teardrop breasts bounced in my face, and my strength grew until it poked her, demanding attention.

She looked at my lap, pointing at the bulge, fighting my zipper. I sheepishly smiled. She moved in closer, and her sweet aroma made me grow harder.

She pecked my lips. "You may think I'm not ready, but he is," she informed me, licking her lips. She continued to make her point. "I think you should free your anaconda."

I didn't protest when Miya unbuckled my belt and unfastened my jeans. Flashing a mischievous smirk as her warm hands caressed my shaft. My eyes widened with pleasure the moment she replaced her hand with the warm wetness of her mouth.

A deep feral growl escaped my throat.

She stood abruptly, walking further into the suite, and I followed like a lost puppy leaving a trail of clothes. She laid on the comforter. Her radiant honey skin contrasting against the pure white bedding drove me insane. She slowly raised her legs in the air, then parted them. I went to taste her again, and she slammed her legs close.

"I am ready now, sir."

I bit my bottom lip and then flicked the tip of my nose. Miya's presence pulled on my heartstrings, igniting love ballots from my soul.

"Your wish is my command, baby." She slithered her legs apart. I braced myself on my hands and toes across her body, preparing to do push-ups. "Are you sure you are ready for this curve?" She rolled her eyes and twisted her lips. She opened her legs until they rested against mine.

"Pick a number."

Her eyelashes fluttered, and her eyes turned big and round as saucers in confusion. I licked my lips and then traced her lips with the tip of my tongue. I repeated the question in a light whisper against her ear. I tugged on her earlobe with my closed lips. She blushed in anticipation of my sex game.

"We are on the fifteenth floor, so fifteen, sir," she cockily replied.

Balancing on my hands, I moved my legs inside of hers. "One," I counted as my curved strength latched onto the sugary entrance of her yoni. Her nails dug deep into my back, tugging at my warm flesh, trying to fuse our heat. I balanced myself on my left hand, slapping her hand away with my right. Her pouty lips were turning me on.

"The only contact is my penis and your yoni. Now, I believe we have fourteen more push-ups to go. Each time I'll go deeper and deeper." She moaned as I did another push-up. My strength rested at the entry of her canal as I lowered myself again.

She squealed, "Fourteen." She thrust her hips upward, trying to force me deeper inside her. I pulled my body up into an upside-down V and then came down on my knees and sailed deep inside her.

"Fuck! Fifteen," she hollered.

I leaned back on my knees, sat on my thighs, and then dragged her into my lap. I clamped my hands around her waist and rocked her hips back and forth until she found her rhythm. She pulled at my back. She eased onto her feet and playfully bounced up and down as I struggled to pull her down harder on me. A deep growl escaped my throat when she captured my earlobe with her teeth.

I seized her waist, then dipped deep, emptying all my seeds of love in her womb.

Surprised, she could bounce on my strength; I wanted to ask her if she had been with another man since Las Vegas, but I knew I had no right. She was not my woman. Maybe it was the hopefulness of my heart speaking, but my penis fit her love canal like a glove. I snickered at myself.

Can a man tell if he is genuinely the only driver of his woman's body?

As we lay locked in each other's arms, my phone rang. I didn't want to leave my baby's side, but what if it was Jay Rock calling?

"Baby, I need to get my phone." It was my jeweler telling me his bodyguard would bring me the ring.

I slowly eased her off my chest, grabbed my phone, and turned on "You Put A Move on My Heart" by Quincy Jones & Tamia.

"Baby, I have to run downstairs. I will be right back and freshen up. I'll join you in the shower in a few. We can order room service, then make love again if you like." I kissed her forehead, grabbed my keycard, and rushed out the door.

The elevator door opened, and Jay Rocks' bodyguard stood before me.

"How did you access my floor?" I questioned Rick.

"Some dudes held the elevator for me, using their keycard. They went to the sixteenth floor. I pushed fifteen, but it didn't light up, then the door opened, and you were standing in front of me," Rick stated.

He stepped off the elevator, and we walked back to my room. "P.Y.T" by Michael Jackson was playing. I adjusted the music volume. Rick was eying Miya's ripped panties on the floor. I kicked her panties out of the way.

"Thanks for bringing the ring, Rick." He held the box open before me, and I examined it.

"Jay Rock did his thing on this ring."

Shit, the way I felt, I was ready to propose to Miya the second she stepped out of the shower.

"He used every diamond from the last ring to make this new one," Rick confirmed without me asking. "He also sent you these cigars."

I took his contents and sat them on top of my bag in the bedroom. "You didn't have to walk me back."

"Rick, you need the keycard to access the floors." Rick scratched at his head, pondering my comment.

I trekked back to the room, wondering if I should present Miya with this engagement ring. Would she marry me or laugh hysterically, then call me insane? I wanted to call RB, but he would encourage me to slow down.

I recognize we had only spent four nights and two days together, yet that was all it took for me to fall head over heels in love with this woman. Hell, I could run to the mall and buy Tre's girlfriend another ring. No, I promised

Tre Sabrina's engagement ring. I'll take Miya to my jeweler to design her engagement ring. She deserves better than Sabrina's leftovers.

I entered the room, and the music was off. Miya was still in the bathroom. I twisted the knob on the bathroom door, but she had locked me out. I gently tapped on the door.

"Come in," she demanded, stepping back from the entrance. I approached her for a kiss, and she turned her head.

"Baby, we need to make a quick run early in the morning, then attend brunch with my family. I promise we will only have those two detours, then I am all yours, and you are all mine. I promise that tomorrow will be a day neither of us will ever forget."

"Oh, okay, hurry up and take a shower. I'm tired."

"Okay, now you're one and done," I joshed, but her lips did not curl. Something in her tone and body language was off, but I shook it off. I wasn't about to let the enemy trick me and ruin tonight or tomorrow.

Tomorrow would go down in the history books because I will ask this queen to grant me the honor of changing her last name. Hell, Pamela Anderson and Tommy Lee were married ninety-six hours after meeting.

My only issue was Tre getting upset at me for proposing the same day as him. But I cannot allow Miya to walk away when my heart knows she is my rib. Those days in San Diego were the happiest days of my life.

I leaned against the shower wall, imagining her facial expression when I popped the question.

"All Around the World"
Lisa Stansfield
Malik

STRODE OUT OF THE SHOWER, FULL of passion. I walked into the room, and she was not there. I swallowed hard and shuffled my feet on the carpet. I perked up when I saw her ripped panties on the floor. I scanned the room for her purse but couldn't find it. She could not go down the elevator without a keycard. I checked the dresser, and mine was resting where I dropped it.

"She must be a guest here," I tried to convince myself. What if she went to freshen up in her room or get us food in one of the restaurants?

I sat in the armchair and scrutinized the door of my room. After an hour, I paced the floor. She ghosted me for the third time. I know they say three strikes, and you're out, but I could not let go of hope. I could feel it in my heart. I was going to see her again.

My eyes squinted at the clock that revealed it was almost midnight. I went to the lobby and walked around the hotel, searching for Miya. I sat in the lobby and watched people walk in and out of the hotel entrance.

"Sir, you cannot sleep in the lobby," a security guard warned me.

"I'm a guest," I informed the stocky white security guard, flashing him my room key.

"Thank you for being a guest at the Four Seasons; however, you cannot sleep in the lobby. Can I assist you back to your room?"

I sprung to my feet, pouring my heart out to the security guard.

"Sir, I will keep an eye out for your girlfriend. I'm sure she will return after she calms down," he assures me.

As I was stepping onto the elevator, I spotted Tre. I placed my arm between the doors, and they retracted.

"Tre," I yelled. I slowly approached him.

The short, thick woman he was with greeted me with a welcoming grin. "Is this?"

Tre cut me off. "I'm escorting this young lady to her car." The girl peered at him strangely. He placed his index finger on her lips as she was about to speak.

Suspiciously, I eyed my brother as I stepped onto the elevator, hoping he was not up to his old schemes. By the time I reached the fifteenth floor, my mind was back on Miya.

She had disappeared again! I couldn't believe this woman had made love to my mind, body, and soul to leave without a word for the third time.

I gazed at the Los Angeles skyline from my balcony; my thoughts focused on her smile and warmth. My baby was out there, and I needed to find her to confess my love. Defeated, I walked back into the room and looked at my buzzing phone. My brother asked if he could spend the night in my room. When I replied sure, he replied, never mind. I could not deal with Tre tonight. I opted to ignore his texts for the rest of the evening.

I lay in bed, watching television as I whiffed the sweet floral scent on the pillows and sheets. My nose twitched, and a burning sensation formed inside my nostrils. I was about to cry. "Pull it together, Malik." I got out of bed and took three of my pain pills. My body may not have been in pain, but my heart was aching.

As the morning sun kissed my forehead, I jumped out of bed, reaching for my beeping phone, hoping it was Miya. Sarcasm filled the fleeting laughter as the realization hit me. She didn't have my number, nor did I have hers. I hit the message icon on my phone. Most of them were from Tre. He wanted the damned ring, so I instructed him to meet me in the lobby in fifteen minutes.

Observing his interactions with some girl who worked at the hotel, I approached Tre from behind.

"Are you being good, baby bro?"

His hands shot into the air, protesting his innocence.

"I was asking the hotel employee what time Sunday brunch ends," he confessed, telling me his actual plans. "I texted and called you last night to come down to the party. I know your meetings didn't take all day."

I shook my head. I saw Tre last night, and he didn't mention any of this. I was not in the mood for one of his you failed to protect me or weren't there when I needed my big brother. He used these outbursts to gain access to my wallet. I wasn't fond of his spoiled little brother's tirades.

"Tre, whatever the fuck I was doing was my motherfucking business. All you wanted is this damn ring, and you have it now!" I snapped, shoving the ring into his chest.

"Damn, bruh. Did you sleep badly or something? Did momma dig in your ass again?" he questioned, frowning the entire time.

"I argued with my baby, and she ghosted me while I showered. I didn't get a chance to tell her my good news or apologize for upsetting her."

"Now I see why you looked crazy last night. I was trying to bunk with you."

"I said, sure. You said, never mind. Baby bro, keep it one hundred! You were trying to use me. You thought I was going to offer to get you a room. You should have booked yourself a damn room! Shit, you told me to book a room at this hotel."

"Shit, I hope your girl calls you back soon because you have a shitty attitude. I can't recall a time when you cursed like this."

I flared my nostrils.

"I have been calling my girl all morning, but she's not answering me either. We argued last night about sex. She was upset that her cousin got engaged before us. I tried to tell her sex could not fill a void. It only feeds a habit," Tre voiced, trying to change the subject.

I softened my demeanor because it was not Tre's fault that Miya ghosted me. I patted him on the back.

"I'm proud of you, baby bro."

"Mimi needs to get here soon. Brunch ends at 2:00 pm. Mom and Dad will be here at 11:00 am. I hope you're coming to brunch to see me propose. I invited Tasha, Shanice, Eboni, and Aaliyah."

I zoned Tre out as I scanned the lobby. I knew that checkout was at noon, so I planned to search for Miya until I left for the airport.

"I'm not in the mood to sit around a table chatting with her family or ours,"

I honestly admitted. "Text me after she arrives, and I will join you guys. I won't miss your proposal."

"Damn, bruh. Are you in love with this Rudy bitch?"

"Who?" I bit on my bottom lip and tugged on my dreadlocks.

"The bitch you met in Vegas." My chest reacted to his words, rising as my stance widened. "…Um…down, boy!" My brother placed his hand on my chest, patting me lightly.

My ears rang when I slapped his hand away.

"You may not want to admit it, but…. but…. yo' ass in love." Before I could respond, he walked away.

Time passed as I sat in the lobby, people watching. I hadn't blinked until my father texted me around noon to join them for brunch. I sent a quick reply explaining I wasn't hungry. I recommended that they text me once Tre's girlfriend arrived. I walked around the pool area, searching for Miya. I went back to my room and started packing when Tre texted me. I called him back. I was not in the mood to text.

After I ended the call, I went downstairs to greet my parents. Momma was kissing Tre goodbye when I stepped off the elevator.

I approached my parents, embracing them tightly.

"I do not think Tre should be getting married," Pops blurted before properly greeting me.

"Tre is a grown man, and he and his girlfriend mixed their wires up. That is all, my King," Momma told my Pops with a kiss on his cheek.

Momma was always making excuses for Tre. Pops wrapped his arms around her and hummed in her ear.

Why can't I find this, God? Am I not worthy of this type of love or better?

I closed my eyes as my heart cried out to my heavenly father.

Pops addressed her directly. "Single life is the preferred life."

"God prefers marriage," Momma countered.

"1 Corinthians 7: 32 –35 says, '*I would like you to be free from concern. An unmarried man is concerned about the Lord's affairs—how he can please the Lord. But a married man is concerned about the affairs of this world—how he can please his wife— and his interests are divided. An unmarried woman or virgin is concerned about the Lord's affairs: her aim is to be devoted to the Lord in both body and spirit. But a married woman is concerned about the affairs of this world–how she can please her husband. I am saying this for your good not to restrict you but that you may live in a right way in undivided devotion to the Lord.'*"

Pops recited the scripture as if he were reading it directly from the bible. Momma's face creased with the makings of a frown.

My father inhaled deeply. "Our son needs to read the remaining verses and examine his soul. 'If anyone is worried that he might not be acting honorably towards the virgin, he is engaged to, and if his passions are too strong and he feels he ought to marry, he should do as he wants. He is not sinning. They should get married. But the man who has settled the matter in his mind who is under no compulsion but has control over his own will and who has decided not to marry the virgin—this man also does the right thing. So he who marries the virgin does right, but he who does not marry her does better'" (1 Corinthians 7:36-38)—Pops smiled at Momma.

I wondered if that scripture was for Tre or me.

"Mark, I know you know the word and can quote scripture verbatim. However, can you support our son?"

Pops kissed Momma on the cheek. "Queen, the scripture fell on my heart, and I needed to recite it. Both of us know Tre is selfish. If he struggles with his relationship with God, how can he be selfless and serve God and his mate?"

"Because he has praying parents who will help him be a fabulous husband. Kings raise kings!"

Pops skeptically grinned at his queen as she eased onto the tip of her toes and kissed him on his forehead.

I gazed off into space, wondering if God gave Pops that scripture just for me. Miya was a virgin, and I wished to marry her. According to the scripture that ministered to my soul, my heart would align with the word. I merely needed God to bring her back my way.

"Are you okay, Malik?" Momma probed, pulling me into her arms.

Tears flowed from my eyes onto my mother's shoulder as my emotions erupted. She held me, inspected me, then wiped the tears away. "Son, what is it? I can count the times you have cried."

"I am waiting on Kyle to bring the contracts for me to sign. They are adding in the stuff you suggested." Deciding to tell my mother and father that Dr. Allen had cleared me was better than saying the real reason for my demeanor was Miya.

Overjoyed by my news, Momma praised God as if we were not in the lobby of the Four Seasons. Pops patted me on the back and hugged me.

"Son, are you sure nothing else is bothering you? You have a hint of sadness in your eyes. The news you just told us is joyous."

I bit the interior of my cheeks. My shoulder sagged, spine dithering in defeat.

"Pray on it, son, and God will give you guidance."

My pain cradled my faith.

"We're going to head out to Tre's proposal dinner, then head back to Temecula," Momma announced. "Are you coming to the BBQ place?"

"I Can Love You"
Mary J. Blige
Miya

 AVESDROPPING, I LISTENED INTENTLY TO
MR. Walker talking to his jeweler about an engagement
ring. I paced the floor in the bathroom, wondering what
I should do. I was barely visible as I peeked my head out the bathroom door.
Silence greeted me.

Tiptoeing into the room, I turned off the music playing in the background,
stealthily looking around the corner to see if they were by the door. The little
black box perched on the top of his bag caught my attention, halting my
beating heart. Staring at it, I examined his luggage for a name. No name on
the tag; it boasted an Atlanta address.

The suite door opened the moment I drummed up the courage to open
the box. I pushed the little black box back into his bag, tossing the cigars on
top before running back into the bathroom.

Hot tears stung my torching cheeks, my heart racing as the devastation
of what I heard and saw sunk in. I tossed icy water on my face. I imagined

confronting Mr. Walker, then realized he was not my man; he belonged to Mrs. Walker after all.

The sound of his knocking echoed through the confined quarters of the bathroom. I invited him in, leaning backward as he came in for a kiss. I knew if he touched me, I would start crying and plead for him to stay in Los Angeles. Falling in love with him was unintentional and caught me off guard. I was scared I might even beg him to leave her and marry me instead. I knew I could love him better than any woman breathing.

I exited the bathroom, sat on the bed, and stood several times. My mind echoed as the war in my soul incited, "Go!" My heart rang, "Stay!"

The second I heard the shower, I dashed out of Mr. Walker's room. I stood in the elevator, willing it to move while digging in my pockets, searching for Tamia's keycard. I contemplated going to Tamia's room, but she would want to know where I had been. I decided going for a drive would be my best bet. I roamed the highway for a couple of hours, debating if I should go back to Mr. Walker's room and confess I could love him better than this Atlanta chick. I wondered if she was prettier than me.

My mind drifted back to my and Imani's conversation concerning love and lust. Did I represent lust or love? Could he be in love with both of us? I hoped he was in love with me because I loved him. In the pit of my gut, I knew I was a fatality of his sexual desires, which made me represent lust.

I wanted to cry out to God, but I had no right. I wanted to be his always and forever, but that was crazy. Right? I didn't know this man, but my heart did. I wondered if this was the defragmentation of my life due to my one-night stand? Question after question blurred my vision as tears streaked my cheeks. I struggled to see the road. My eyes were dancing in the dense darkness.

After driving for what seemed like a lifetime, I decided to go home to the man who loved me. On the drive there, I had decided I would tell Tre I missed him so much that I had to return home at two in the morning.

To my surprise, I walked into an empty bedroom.

I could have sworn he planned to go to the house after Paxton's party. The last time he came home this late, he walked in, reeking of a cheap bitch. I believed he was at the bar after Tamia assured me he had been with her.

Well, Tamia was at the Four Seasons, so where the fuck was my man? More tears welled in my eyes as I dived into our bed and curled in the fetal position.

The sound of my phone ringing woke me. Used Kleenex was scattered on the bed and gathered in my right-hand palm. As the tears returned and pooled in my right ear, I curled in the fetal position.

Silly of me to think me and— "Fuck!" I yelled. All this time, I still didn't know his first name. I knew he lived in Atlanta and came to LA to purchase an engagement ring for his girlfriend. He couldn't resist the urge to make love to me again.

I hopped off the bed and went to the bathroom mirror. Pointing at my reflection, I corrected my heart. "No bitch! It was not lovemaking. He screwed you, and you assumed that was love as you allowed a stranger to enter us raw."

Dread took over my body as I paced the bathroom floor. What if he gave me something? I attempted to laugh the notion off. It momentarily worked, then sobs replaced my giggles.

"Get your ass off the damn floor," my reflection yelled at me. "Didn't I ring the alarm in San Diego warning you Mr. Walker had a wife … a whole damn wife or was in a fucking situation? Yet you continued this no-name or personal information game to avoid the truth I tossed in your lap and face.

"The same way you have created me to deal with your emotional issues. It's easier for you to ignore situations than deal with them. We both know you do not love Tre. You love Mr. Walker!"

I tapped the reflection staring back at me.

"He's… he's going back to Atlanta to make love to his new fiancée. You will remove any notion regarding leaving Tre and be grateful for your blessing. He is a good man."

"Stop pointing your finger at me and turn it on yourself. I think this bet has you making poor decisions. We should walk away from Tre and Mr. Walker."

My phone rang again, interrupting my tirade with my inner consciousness. I ran into the room, yanking my phone off the bed.

"What?" I yelled at the caller without saying hello or looking at the screen.

"Mimi, where are you?" Tre asked.

"I'm at home. Where the fuck are you?" I tapped my foot on the floor, waiting for his reply. "You were supposed to come home last night!" Anger brewing, I walked into the empty kitchen, and rage engulfed my aura.

"I stayed in Santa Monica at Tamia's. I wanted to be close. I planned to eat breakfast with you and the girls at the Four Seasons. When did you get home? I thought you spent the night with Tamia in the hotel."

"As you can see, I did not. I am at home," I barked. "Now, where the fuck are you?"

The line went silent for a while.

"Brunch ends at two o'clock. Can you drive to LA?" he mumbled.

"Drive where," I snapped.

Flopping onto the bed, I listened to him whimper.

"You know what? It doesn't matter because I cannot drive to LA or anywhere else. You need to make your way home," I demanded.

He blew a cyclone of air into the phone.

"Anything else?"

"You don't have to drive to LA. I'm craving barbecue. Can you meet us at Lucille's Smokehouse?" Tamia asked.

"Who is everyone else?" I questioned Tamia.

"All of the BAEs. Oh, and Tre," she added.

"Ok, I will start getting dressed. I could never leave my BAEs hanging. Does he have to come?" I whined. Tamia giggled, then disconnected the call.

Three hours later, I pulled into the parking lot. I drove around for two hours after I left the house. The pain rattling in my chest was unbearable.

I walked into Lucille's Smokehouse. I didn't see one BAE. All I saw was Tre, waving for me to join him. He told me how much he loved me.

All my heart heard was, *Blah, blah, blah.*

"Tre, I must make love to you," I bluntly told him as he spoke. It was more of a necessity than a desire. I had to make sure he and I shared the same magical connection as Mr. Walker and me.

Was Tre able to ease all my fears with a single kiss or pull joy from my pussy with each stroke of his cock? The happiness Mr. Walker rained upon my life had faded away when I spotted the ring box sitting on top of his bag. Lexi getting engaged before me meant she would be married first. Those facts alone were a gut punch.

Paxton's MLB gathering was supposed to be a celebration party, not an engagement party. When we walked into the room, red roses and candles filled the space. 3D white words decorated the floor, spelling out "Will You Marry Me, Lexi?"

Disappointment washed over my body, and I felt miserable.

I was on the verge of losing the bet to Lexi. I begged Tre right then and there to reserve a room and make love to me. If he had done what I asked of him, I would have never slept with Mr. Walker again.

Tre snapped his fingers in my face, breaking me out of my thoughts. "Baby, we have discussed this already. This is not the place to discuss it again."

I rolled my eyes and smacked my lips. I understand I was acting like a brat, but damn! I wanted to feel good.

"Yeah, yeah, yeah. It's all good." I pouted like a little child.

I was tired of hearing, "You descended from heaven for me." This bullshit was not working anymore. How many blessings did he need from God? I am sure God was not giving him extra points because we didn't have sex before marriage. All I wanted to hear was "Ride me all night long," "How do you like it?" or "Daddy is going to beat it up all night." Shit, I would even settle for "Whose is it?"

"Ugh," I mumbled in frustration.

"Trust me, Miya. Our wedding night will not disappoint you, and I promise to rock your world. I have destroyed many relationships by basing it all on sex, and I desire more than sex from you. Good or bad pussy, I'm not going anywhere. You descended from heaven to marry me. I love you," he alleged.

Regardless of what Tre's mouth may have been saying, I sat there furious at the world. I have never heard of a man who was not a virgin restraining from sex if he didn't have to. I needed him to sex the pain away. I wondered if he was sleeping with other women.

I looked at him, smacking my lips, and rolled my eyes.

"Miya, I love you. Marry me, and this issue will no longer be important to either of us," he noted, sliding out of the booth. Kneeling on one knee, he presented me with a ring box. A blue light illuminated the ring. Awesomeness was the only way to describe the large platinum diamond engagement ring.

"Can I change your last name to Young?"

I searched my mind for an answer when I heard Tamia's voice. "Fuck, your rock is phat!"

Slowly turning around, I was greeted by my parents, Lexi, Tamia, Naja, Imani, and Tre's family. Their tables circled ours. I pondered how I could not have noticed them when I arrived.

"Say, yes!" Tamia urged, pushing me in the back.

I tugged at the choker I was wearing. Overwhelmed by this entire day, I replied in a jittery tone. "Yes, I will marry you."

The tables had turned. Tre and I will get married as soon as possible then I can finally stand in the spotlight by myself without my cousin eclipsing my shine.

The wrinkles in his brow deepened as he sighed. "You don't look happy to be marrying me."

"I am happy, although I have two things bothering me. The first being you haven't introduced me to your family. I don't know any of them. Second, I'm sorry for my behavior, and promise me you will never break my heart or cheat on me."

"Apology accepted." Tre stared deep into my eyes. His joyful expression disappeared, and a disturbing glare replaced it. "Miya, divorce is not an option. You need to be sure you want this. I will always fight for our marriage. Will you do the same?"

"I promise," I replied, then hugged him.

"I promise never to hurt you on purpose, divorce you, and I vow always to rock your muthafuckin' world," he discreetly moaned into my ear before kissing my earlobe.

"Break that shit up," Tamia yelled at us.

Pulling her off to the side, I wanted to ask if she helped him pick out this ring.

Tre gripped my wrist and yanked me back. I eased my wrist from him and massaged it.

"You guys can't have her yet," he whispered.

He slid the engagement ring on my ring finger, and I stumbled until I flopped into my seat. I meticulously examined the sparkling diamond ring, hoping he would rock my world because Mr. Walker made my world stop a couple of times.

"He'll be fine, Miya. God sent you this man," I mumbled to myself.

Even though I was hoping God sent me Mr. Walker instead. I secretly hoped Tre would make me forget all about him. I wanted to cry as I realized I was in love with another man.

I love an out-of-towner headed back home to propose to his girlfriend. I wondered if he loved me or settled for her the way I was with Tre. If I could not have Mr. Walker, I would beat Lexi and the other BAEs to the altar.

"Did you ask God if he was your husband?" My mother asked me while patting me on the back. "Tre is a good boyfriend, but will he be a fabulous husband? You look unsure."

I could never hide anything from my mom.

"I do not think he's your husband. He is not the man I would have picked for you." My mother looked into my eyes and sighed heavily. "There is something broken in him that needs fixing. I can sense it."

I rolled my eyes.

"Why haven't you met his family before today? His parents told us they only live forty minutes away. Tre has been around your family and the BAEs."

I opened my mouth to lie.

"Don't lie to your mother," my aunt interjected.

Wedged uncomfortably between my mother and aunt, they leaned back and whispered amongst themselves.

"Mark my words… she will regret this later," my mother said to my aunt. I wondered if they believed I could not hear them belittling my decision to marry Tre.

I pulled my mother away from my aunt and whined in her native tongue. She frowned. I started to question her decision to stay with my father. The entire world knows my father cheated on her throughout their marriage, but I wasn't brave enough to speak those words.

"Dang, Mama! Can you be happy for me? I'm the first BAE to get married, and Tre loves me. I won."

"What did you win?"

"Nothing, Mom. I'm first." I examined Lexi, and she appeared unmoved by my engagement. I smiled mischievously; the last will finally be first. I tried to reassure myself as thoughts of Mr. Walker invaded my mind. I wondered how he felt when he walked out of the restroom and found me gone.

Tre introduced me to his biological mother and the couple who raised him. I mimicked his joyous appearance and pretended to be as happy and sure about marrying him as he was.

"You kids need to read 1 Corinthians 7: 32-38 before you set a date," Tre's foster father announced.

Tre rested his head on his foster mother's shoulder and whined in her ear while creasing a tight brow at his foster father. Her husband hunched his shoulders and kissed her forehead as she silently chastised him.

My heart melted because Mr. Walker kissed me on my forehead similarly. I watched Tre's foster parents interact. My soul acknowledged that Tre and I would never share a bond that deep. I could feel the love, respect, and admiration circulating between them. Each time they referred to themselves as king and queen, a goofy smile graced my face.

He pulled me towards the booths on the other side, interrupting my view of a perfect love scene, and introducing me to two of his four siblings. It was strange hearing him call his biological mother, Tasha, and the woman who raised him, Momma. His father and my mother had the same concerned facial expressions.

I excused myself to the bathroom and Googled 1 Corinthians 7: 32–38.

"For You I Will"
Monica
Miya

I CAN TRACK MY LIFE THROUGH SONGS. Gospel music helped me get through the death of my uncle. Each time a listener requested "Missing You" from the soundtrack "Set It Off," I had to take a bathroom break to release a few tears. I didn't have a song to describe my current conduct. My heart was singing Mary MacGregor's song "Torn Between Two Lovers." which was inappropriate for a newly engaged woman. I needed to get my shit together.

Every hour of my day, my thoughts tortured me with visions of Mr. Walker proposing to his fiancée and how she enjoyed his touch. My assistant, Eva, was more excited about my upcoming nuptials than I had been.

Love songs became my tormentor. I wonder what love sons he played while proposing, envisioning how he set the stage. Did she say yes, as I would have?

Mr. Walker and I are kindred musical spirits. I created an engagement playlist for Mr. Walker and me the other night, and I know our list would be the same had we compared them.

I wondered if he allowed the songs to express his emotions, then eased down on one knee and asked those four famous words.

My mind spun like a rumitone. *Fuck! Did she say, "yes?"*

Slamming my body against the buttery soft seat in my Lexus, I waited for the BAEs to arrive. I removed my makeup, dreading getting it on these pricey dresses. I glanced at my fresh-faced reflection and smiled. I honestly loved being natural. I even refrained from putting on perfume, which was a massive battle.

I was grateful for Eva. She booked my dress fitting appointment and has been the point of contact in planning this destination wedding. She was the maid of honor for her sister's ceremony a month ago, so she has all the insights on the do's and don'ts. I will nominate her in September when the BAEs have open enrollment.

I heard a knock on my SUV window and whipped my head to the right.

Imani was always the one I could count on to be on time. I popped the lock for her to get in, hoping we could talk awhile before the other BAEs arrived. She gestured for me to get out, and I turned my head to the left, hearing the distinct sounds of taps on the passenger side of my luxury vehicle. Naja was smiling from ear to ear with her hands against my window, mouthing, "Open, open."

I giggled. Hugging Naja and Imani, we walked over to the bridal boutique entrance. Lexi and Tamia crept behind us as we approached the shop door.

"Why didn't you invite my aunt and my mother?" Lexi questioned before even greeting me or hugging me.

"I already have to deal with four mothers. I do not need to deal with two more who always have a negative opinion on everything," I informed my cousin.

"I do not act like a mother," Naja stated. "You heifers are grown."

We all nodded in agreement. Naja stared at Tamia, then at the glass carafe in her hand.

Tamia smacked her lips before explaining herself. "I mixed us some bomb margaritas. Don't nobody want no damn champagne," she insisted as she held the container in Naja's face.

Naja shook her head. She may not be a mother hen, but she is that no-nonsense auntie who controls everybody in the family, young and old alike, with just one glance.

We all stood there waiting for my consultant to come out and greet us.

"Hi, my name is Melinda," she greeted us, glancing at the group. "Who is Miya?"

I raised my hand and stepped forward.

"Who did you bring with you today?" Melinda questioned.

"I have my BAEs," I proudly sang. Naja passed out black signs which read "yes" on one side and "no" on the back.

"It seems like we are about to have some fun," Melinda announced, escorting us into a room with a runway. A tall girl brought out two chairs. "Where is the wedding?"

Lexi answered before I could. "She has no idea."

Little did Lexi know, Tre and I inked the date last night.

"More than likely, it will be at someone else's event," Imani said sarcastically. "It seems to be Tre's MO."

"We're getting married on July 4th in St. Thomas," I retorted. "I was going to tell you guys today at lunch."

Melinda's eyes bucked. "That's only nine weeks away! Why did you wait so late to get your dress?"

All the girls chuckled.

"He popped the question last weekend," Tamia enlightened the hostess. "Melinda, can you give us a few minutes?" Melinda nodded at her, pausing briefly to hear Tamia's departing request. "Can you also bring some glasses and a bottle of champagne when you get back?"

The second Melinda stepped away, Lexi went off. "I thought you would be in the Caribbean broadcasting live from June 27th - July 3rd? Do you think it's wise to mix business and pleasure?"

Imani added her piece, pointing out the obvious. "I knew it would be around somebody else's event." She peered at Lexi and rolled her eyes.

"Tre is a cheapskate. Your job is flying you out and paying for the hotel. What is he doing?" Lexi asked.

"I don't know! We haven't worked out all the kinks yet. He suggested we get married on the fourth a couple of nights ago."

I wanted to tell the girls that I agreed with them. I observed Tre being a cheapskate and an opportunist on several occasions. The boy loves to save his money and spends everyone else's. Therefore, I informed Tre that our wedding event should be separate from my work events. However, he ignored me and had Eva hook him up with one of the co-hosts. They insisted they host a pajama bachelorette party for me on Tuesday night.

"Don't allow him to fuck off your coins," Naja integrated.

I nodded my head. As Melinda approached, I became ecstatic.

Melinda spun around the room. "Miya, are you ready to try on some dresses? What is your price point?"

"Under three thousand?" I mumbled, bracing myself for all the comments the BAEs would toss in my direction.

"With a ring that enormous, he only gave you a three grand budget?" Melinda questioned.

I felt judged by this heffa, and she worked in a dress shop. She didn't understand me or my struggles. It was enough to have the BAEs cast judgment, dammit!

Following Melinda, we searched through dresses. I saw nothing that spoke to me. I wanted to be spicy on my wedding day, and everything she showed me was traditionally dull. Melinda held up two more dresses.

"I want people to call me sexy on my wedding day," I informed her, frowning at the disappointment that washed over me.

She pulled three more dresses. I agreed in defeat.

None of the ladies uttered a word as I walked onto the catwalk from the dressing room. Naja stared at all the ladies, and they all flashed the "no" side of their signs in unison. We repeated this cycle three more times, and as I walked back into the dressing rooms, I could hear the girls chattering.

"Tell me about your fiancé?" Melinda suggested as we waited on her manager to pull me more options.

"He is handsome, works in finance, is frugal, has no baby mothers, and has no drama in his life. Has his own home, and he wants us to abstain from sex until we are married?"

"Does he have any siblings?" Damn, Melinda was nosey as hell.

"Yes, he has four siblings. I have only met two of them. We haven't had the time to meet each other's families. Our courtship is moving fast. We met in March at church." I told her how Tre and I met and the location to halt her investigation.

Melinda stepped out, closing the door behind her. She walked back in with four sexy dresses.

Stepping onto the runway, I looked at the girls, and they nodded at the dress, but no deep emotions ignited within them or me. I loved the top of the dress, but its bottom resembled napkins stitched together. The second option was a blinged-out mermaid dress with a plunging neckline. The material hugged all my curves; nevertheless, it lacked the wow factor. The third dress was a two-piece with a high slit on both sides.

"So, this is a hoochie wedding," Imani bellowed the second I stepped onto the catwalk.

Instead of defending the dress, I turned and walked back to the dressing room. I peeped around the corner and saw Lexi speaking to Melinda. Lexi's face contorted at every dress I put on.

While waiting for them to bring more options, I wanted a question answered.

"Melinda, what did my cousin tell you?"

She appeared to be on the verge of tears, her face flushed as she placed her hand against her chest and took a breath.

"She told me not to be concerned about the cost of the dress. Her exact words were, "Make my cousin resemble a sexy princess no matter the cost."

My eyes widened.

"Damn, your cousin loves you! She told me, you're like sisters. I don't have any family. My parents died, and I have no siblings. I had nobody to help me get through their death. Your cousin-sister told me her dad died, and if it were not for you, she would have never made it through the whole ordeal. I wish I had a precious bond with someone like you two."

Sadness sailed across Melinda's face, and I pulled her into a hug.

My heart dropped, and sorrow stirred in me. Failing, I tried to control the tears that welled in my eyes. My lip trembled as they flowed. I never knew Lexi credited me for helping her get through Uncle Steve's death. She didn't grasp that I felt like both of us lost a father. Her dad was more of a father to me than my own. My father, Gerald, spent all his time chasing money and ass.

Tears fell from Lexi's eyes when I stepped onto the runway, and I knew I had found my dress. Nothing could stop the tears as they rolled down my cheeks. My heart instantly melted at my cousin's compliment. "Miya, you make all these dresses beautiful, but this one has a wow factor. You look sexy and drop-dead gorgeous!"

I glanced at the other BAEs reading their signs, which all said 'yes.' It felt like this was my dress in my heart and soul; I knew this wasn't a show, but I smiled, yelling out, "I am saying yes to the dress!"

All of us laughed, hugged, and cried with each other. Who knew weddings and wedding dress shopping could bond us closer?

I grabbed a glass of bubbly and raised it in the air. "To the BAEs!"

"Soon as I Get Home"
Faith Evans
Malik

MY DAY ONE WAS THROWING ME a going-away party in his penthouse overlooking midtown. I wanted to forget certain things about Atlanta; my friendship with RB was not one.

Cognac in my right hand and a stogie in the other, I raised my glass to RB. He patted me on the back. I followed him outside onto the balcony, joining a group of girls lounging on the white circular sofa next to the small wet bar. I hoped RB was not trying to hook me up with anybody.

"Can we get the space, ladies?" RB shouted to all the women sprawled around his balcony.

They all marched inside. I watched as he walked over to the rail and leaned back against it, puffing on a cigar.

"I cannot believe you'll be in San Diego on Thursday. I envisioned you on May 1st on Atlanta's practice field, not San Diego. Damn, you're a San Diego Charger, dawg."

I scratched my head in disbelief. It was still surreal. I tried to focus on God's new blessings over my life. I could not shake the feeling that Miya was God's other blessing and would be a part of my new journey.

"How does it feel?" RB asked, interrupting my thoughts.

Similar to draft day. Except I'm wiser and understand it can all be over in the blink of an eye. I am grateful for this second chance. I will allow no one to destroy my opportunity, not even Miya."

I stopped talking once I realized what I had said.

"Who is Miya, Bruh? You do look a little lovesick. Did this bitch cheat or run out on you?"

Something about the way he phrased his question hit me the wrong way. Miya was nothing like Sabrina.

RB shook his head and shot me a displeasing stare. "Is this the woman from Vegas?" I pulled hard on my cigar.

Chuckling at my non-verbal response, he kept interrogating me. "Have you been fixating over this woman since March?"

"Have you been fixated on your island dream?"

RB waved, and I looked behind me, staring at the group of people. "We can talk later. People want to come outside."

"This is my house. Fuck what people want to do. I've thought about my island dream every day. If God ever gives me another try with her. I will change her name to Mrs. Brooks. Bruh, loving someone is risky because you give them the power to hurt you. I'm willing to take that chance and be broken a million times for one unforgettable moment of her blooming embrace."

"Damn, dawg."

"Fate brought us together, but fear and lies ripped us apart," RB told Malik. "Don't allow pride to cheat you out of unconditional love."

"How the hell do you recognize unconditional love?"

"Love can be a beacon of light or a hot flame that consumes your soul. The root of love is joy, patience, and kindness. It becomes unconditional and undeniable love if you pull them all together."

This time, RB pulled hard on his cigar, swiped his right hand over his face, and smiled brightly. "Stop holding your breath—Excel in life. Love won't always be bittersweet. I would not turn back my time on the island."

I nodded at RB's remark. My mind, heart, and soul couldn't foresee a happy ending for my love life. I trusted God in every inch of my life except there.

"Now tell me everything about Miya, Mr. Fool in Love."

I bowed my head and spilled my guts. I told RB about her ghosting me in Vegas, San Diego, and LA. I even told him I was ready to propose to her.

I thought my brother from another mother would go off. Instead, he surprised me when he spoke in an investigative tone.

RB gestured with his hands as he spoke. "Miya may not have seen your note in San Diego. She probably thought you ghosted her to pay her back for Vegas. I say this because the Vegas girl seemed happy to see you in LA, from what you're saying. Do you believe she overheard the conversation with Rick and thought the ring was for your woman? Maybe, just maybe, she thought you planned to propose to another female."

A light bulb went off over my head. RB was making sense. That would explain the switch up in her mood after returning from the elevator.

"Before Turks and Caicos, all women were gold diggers and cheaters, so my advice was tainted. I view you like a baby brother, so I'm overprotective, but real talk, Bruh, I was in your life before Sabrina, during, and after. I saw how she destroyed your world. I don't want you to go through the same shit again."

I dipped my head in admiration.

RB honestly admitted, "I constantly pray for you. I need the young kid I met back in college to return. God is restoring your life. Don't waste this second chance on a fickle woman."

I closed my eyes and reflected on how far I had come. Besides my parents, RB had been the only other person I confided in these last six years. Shit, he was a present friend before the NFL contract and encouraged me even though I thought I had lost it all. RB has been a better brother to me than Tre.

"RB, you have been a great brother. I was ecstatic when I landed in Atlanta because I already had a friend and mentor dominating the field." RB popped his imaginary collar. "Now I am leaving with a brother."

"Real talk, stay focused on this opportunity, Bruh. God is giving you a second chance. Show Him daily how much you appreciate this opportunity. If you and this Vegas chick are meant to be together, you will be once God is ready. God will allow your paths to cross with no effort from you."

All I could think was, *yeah those words are for him and me because RB continuously prays that God will allow his Summer Paradise to cross his path.*

"Amen! I received that, Bruh."

"Man, I have been hanging out with yo' ass too much. That shit was too deep for me, and my soul received it also."

I gave RB a bro hug. "I appreciate you, dawg. Real talk," I confessed, pulling my vibrating phone out of my pocket.

Tre // 10:00 pm: I am getting married on the 4ᵗʰ of July.

Me // 10:05 pm: Cool.

Tre // 10:05 pm: Are you going to be my best man & RB a groomsman?

I frowned as I read my brother's text messages. This boy was getting married in nine weeks. "Tre wants you to be a groomsman at his wedding?" I informed RB.

RB scoffs before chuckling. "I am not Tre's friend. I see his ass. Why can't any of his friends attend the wedding?"

This time I chuckled. "Tre has no friends. He always fucks his friends' girlfriends and wives." I hunched my shoulders at the thought of my brother's actions. "He hasn't had sex with the girl he's marrying. He swears he's a changed man."

RB swiped his face with his hand. "I feel bad for the girl. Tre is a sex addict, and they don't change easily. If he isn't fucking her, he is fucking some other chick. Mark my words."

"They live together. Shit, I hope she won't marry him if he is cheating."

"No disrespect. Tre isn't shit! He leeches off you and uses his past to use you and your parents. I hate to see what Tre is doing to his fiancée. I hope he isn't fucking her friends. Do you remember the time Tre was fucking the daughter and mother? He would leave the daughter's bedroom and sneak into the mother's bed, smashing both in one night. Yo' boy took me out when he joined them for breakfast. Not to mention the random hookups and the money he spends on call girls and porn sites. The boy has a sex problem, and you're always throwing money at his predicament. Your money will not heal him," RB testified as if I were not paying for his sex addiction therapy.

"I can only pray that he has changed. I went to a family session, and his therapist said he's making progress."

RB roared with laughter. "The therapist he's fucking?"

I wanted to laugh, but I knew this was serious, and my brother could not help himself. His therapist shared with us that Tre's issue stemmed from his childhood. My parents blamed themselves, and I could have done more to help protect Tre.

"No, I found him a new therapist," I informed RB. "She's elderly, and I hope Tre is not fucking that old woman."

"Bruh, I cannot commit to being his groomsman. What I can commit to is helping you sell your house."

I swooned at his announcement. "Damn, dawg, you're relieving a ton of my stress right now."

"Raven has been my assistant off and on for years along with Kris, her girlfriend."

"Okay," I responded, wondering where this conversation was going.

RB patted me on the back. "Let me talk to Raven and see if she will come to San Diego and find you a house. Raven is still wearing Kris's promise ring, but they are taking a break.

"I think they need space right now, and you need help. I know she'll keep you from giving Tre your life savings. Raven is mean as hell." I laughed. People's perception of Raven was sweet and wholesome. Although she was drop-dead gorgeous, she was also blunt.

"You are on the verge of being swamped, and stuff will get hectic. You will require assistance. Allow everything to pass through Raven. There's nothing she can't handle. Baby sis looks at you like a brother, so she'll block gold diggers and users as she does for me," RB stated, popping his collar.

"Shit, I've seen how Raven and her girls handle things. The events she'd planned were magnificent, and the way she dealt with the Sabrina incident meant the world to me."

"Then, it is settled. Raven can stay in my San Diego penthouse until she gets you all set up," RB finalized.

"I suppose we need to ask her first?" RB pulled out his cell phone; moments later, Raven tapped on the glass door. RB gestured for her to step out.

"Raven, do you want to go to San Diego and find Malik a house as his assistant and block all those gold diggers from his soft ass?"

She tried not to laugh, but I heard a slight snicker. Raven smiled widely. "Can I block him from his brother too?"

My mind shouted, *Oh damn, does anybody like Tre?*

"Especially his leech of a brother," RB insisted. "Do not forget he is family. It's okay to show him some tough love."

Raven nodded her head.

"Don't allow this fool to pay for Tre's wedding. All requests come through you."

"When and where is the wedding?" Raven inquired.

Me // 10:35 pm: Where is the wedding?

Tre // 10:36 pm: St. Thomas. Are you and RB renting a jet?

Me // 10:37 pm: RB can't commit yet. Run all the details of the wedding past my assistant, Raven. She will make sure I am there.

Tre // 10:37 pm: What? Can I get some money?

Me // 10:37 pm: Contact Raven. 678-555-5555

I looked at the screen a couple of times. Tre makes good money, and I already gave him a check for the wedding. His selfish spirit makes him hold onto his shit and spend everyone else's money. I took a deep breath and braced myself for RB's comments.

"Fourth of July in St. Thomas. He will contact you, Raven, from here on out regarding everything. When he texts, please text back on my behalf. I don't want to be bothered while in Hawaii and San Diego training."

"Okay," Raven responded.

RB doubled over laughing. "Not okay! Tre is ridiculous. I see his trickery. He thinks I will rent a jet to fly us to St. Thomas and hope Malik pays for everything else."

Damn, RB knows Tre better than me. I opened my mouth to confess I had already given Tre fifty racks, then decided against it. Some facts needed to stay between my brother and me.

"This fool is getting married in nine weeks and wants to do it in St. Thomas," RB announced again, sounding more bewildered.

Raven shook her head at me and RB.

"The girls are going to St. Thomas for some radio show Caribbean getaway the same week," Raven informed us.

"Damn, your brother is using somebody else's event to host his wedding? Leech!"

Raven bubbled with excitement about our move to San Diego. "What day are we leaving, Malik?"

"This Thursday. I have to be at practice on May 1st."

Raven threw her hands in the air. "I better leave and go pack. I have a lot to do in a couple of days. Are you keeping the house here?" RB answered her before I could. She nodded, then instructed that she would take care of everything. "I'll see you tomorrow at your house. I'll get you all packed." Before I could say anything, Raven walked away.

"Baby sis will get you together," RB informed me. "It's like having a wife without drama. I don't have to worry about you going crazy over Raven.

She would rather die before she sleeps with a man. She is the safest woman besides your mother to have in your lovestruck life," RB jokes.

We both chuckled. Real talk, Raven was the only woman I needed in my life right now.

"Let's Get Married (Remix)"
Jagged Edge
Miya

CLUTCHING MY ARMS ACROSS MY CHEST in a vain attempt to ease my trembling hands, I stare into the mirror, detached. "Girl, check and see if my feet are as cold as the brides," Tamia jokes.

Disheartened by her comment and the scowl on my face, my mother demanded that everyone leave my dressing room.

It was hard to ignore the disappointment slowly nibbling away in the pit of my stomach. These past nine weeks have been hellish. First, Naja told me that Dakari couldn't attend the ceremony.

Soon after, Imani called, saying, "Winten couldn't participate in the wedding because he couldn't find the money for the event in his budget." I was baffled because Winten's father has generational wealth.

At that point, all I could do was scoff and laugh—disappointment gnawing harder in my gut.

When I informed Tre about Dakari and Winten, his behavior insinuated that their nonappearance was my fault. He demanded that I pay for Winten's flight and his biological mother and sisters' accommodations. Ranting on and on about how my ring set him back financially, I agreed to pay for everyone's expenses. I was relieved when his foster brother footed the tab for himself and his parents.

When Lexi found out I was paying for Winten, she flipped out on Imani. Paxton and Lexi decided to pay for Winten, Imani, Tamia, and my aunt. I asked Lexi for one more favor. I wanted Paxton and Tre to get better acquainted. Tre had already hung out with Winten. He met Dakari when he came to town, but I needed Paxton and Tre to form a closer bond since they would be family soon.

Lexi arranged for Tre to meet with Paxton and his friends at two bachelor parties. When Tre came back from Big Bear, he was standoffish. I questioned him about the party. After what seemed like pulling teeth, he finally shared, "Paxton threw Davis a bomb bachelor party." He shut down when I pushed for more info, so I left it alone.

Lexi placed Tre on Paxton's friend Antonio's bachelor party guest list. Tre refused to go. It took me four days to convince him he needed to get familiarized with my family. Once Tre returned, he bragged about Paxton's yacht, his friends, how much money they blew, and who was investing with him. Every time I turned around, Paxton was calling Tre. They made plans to hang out whenever Paxton was free.

A week ago, Lexi informed me Paxton could not attend the wedding. He had a game. I wondered how they were getting married on the 4th of July if Paxton had a baseball game? It was mind-blowing how Paxton couldn't fly in for the wedding or Tre's bachelor party, yet he could fly in for one day to celebrate his wealthy friend's soon-to-be marriage. Paxton thinks he's better than Tre, as Lexi considers herself better than me.

Planning this wedding and producing a radio show in the Caribbean has been stressful. I would have lost my damn mind if it were not for my assistant, Eva. She and the BAEs made my wedding elegant, glamorous, and sophisticated.

Tre did four things for the entire wedding: picking the date, instructing me on spending my coins, choosing the men's attire, and showing up. He wanted to keep the groomsmen's outfits a secret. This was a damn wedding, not a surprise birthday party.

Lexi forced Tamia to tell her what the men were wearing. Tre styled them with a standard white tuxedo complemented by a champagne vest and a lavender tie.

Standing in the long-length mirror, I scrutinized myself as the photographer snapped photos. Instead of basking in the splendor of my big day, I kept asking myself if I was ready to get married because Tre doesn't give me butterflies in my tummy. When he hugs me, I wring my eyes exceedingly tight, hoping to feel the same utopia of peace and tranquility I felt in Mr. Walker's enchanting embrace. Hell, these days, I would settle for a downpour of safety because I have yet to experience the richness of completion I felt in San Diego with Mr. Walker.

"Stop it, Miya," I murmured. I needed to focus on my good man and not someone else's man.

I spun around, allowing the photographer to capture the dress's front. I adjusted the thigh-high slit.

Oh God! I thought to myself. *Was I too sexy? Was the slit too high?*

The BAEs saw the original gown at the bridal store, but have yet to see the alterations.

I refrained from showing my mother and aunt my dress because I didn't need the negativity. They were not on board with me marrying Tre. After the dent this wedding placed on my savings account, I was marrying somebody today.

"God, did Mr. Walker marry his fiancée? Has he been thinking about me?" Scoffing, I continued. "Lord, it would be crazy if he were getting married today." I stood there quiet as a church mouse, waiting for God to answer my questions or snicker at my corny wit.

I giggled after a couple of minutes at my silliness. Rocking my head from side to side, I swung those ridiculous thoughts from my mind.

My pride yelled, *you should be ecstatic you won the damn bet. You made it to the altar before Lexi.*

After almost five months of dating, I was the first BAE to be a bride. All the BAE's predictions were wrong. Lexi may have received her ring first, but the proposal didn't count, only the first wedding. Still, dark clouds hung over me.

"Can you get some pictures of the wedding party and the guest?" I asked the photographer. "My cheeks hurt from smiling."

"I'll make my rounds. I'll come in and out, snapping pictures. You won't even know I'm here," the photographer reassured me before leaving the room.

I looked out the window and stared at the turquoise waters.

"Lord, your baby is getting married today. Why am I not happier, Father God? Today is my big day."

I ran my fingertips over the Swarovski crystals beads and sequins, which I had hand-stitched into the corset.

Startled by a presence in the room, I spun around. Imani's lovely smile greeted me. She was radiant in the lavender tulle A-line dress Lexi had picked out for them.

I broke the silence hovering between us with a warm hug. "One moment I think I am ready, then the next I'm unsure," I secretly admitted to Imani. Drawing close to her ear, I whispered, "Hypothetically speaking, would you marry Winten if you had a deep sexual connection with somebody else?"

"You can have sex with anybody, Miya. Would you want to spend your last hours with Tre or somebody else if the world ended today? If you say somebody else, then you are not ready."

I hunched my shoulders. In my heart, I wanted to say somebody else. I would have loved to spend it with Mr. Walker. However, I knew it was not possible. He already has a fiancée. They were somewhere planning their wedding.

"Wait! Are you saying you are no longer a virgin?" Imani raised a judgmental brow. I retreated.

"Tre will be my first," I mumbled with my eyes downcast.

Eyeing Imani, I bit my inner cheek as I played with a strain of my hair. "What are your thoughts about Tre and me?"

"Only you know what you are ready for and whom you want to spend the rest of your life loving. Regardless of what any of the BAEs' opinions may be," Imani indicated, "all I can say is trust your heart."

"I love you to pieces, and I value your opinion." Embracing each other in a tight hug, we rocked back and forth. "I pray I am making the right choice. There is an ominous feeling in my soul."

"Maybe you should stop complaining and enjoy the moment," Tamia snapped.

Imani and I gawked at each other, then turned towards Tamia. I wondered where she came from and how long she had been standing there listening to Imani and me.

"Not all of us can meet a man and have him sweep us off our feet in a couple of months."

I couldn't tell if Tamia was joking based on her facial expressions. I raised my brow, and she started giggling.

"You are stunning, Tamia," I gushed, making her twirl for me. Tamia was stunning in her satin ankle-length lavender pantsuit with three-inch diamond-studded heels. Her attire was shitting on the men's tuxedos.

"You are the most glamorous groom's girl I have ever seen!" Imani bobbed her head in agreement.

Tre demanded Tamia stand at his side. I forced myself to smile, although I was disappointed she wasn't a bridesmaid. Tre didn't have enough groomsmen to offset the BAEs. He desperately wanted his best friend at his wedding party.

I extended my arms towards Imani, reaching for one more hug. When Lexi and Naja walked into the room, she instantly turned away from me, finding a seat in the corner. I wondered if they were still upset over the Winten ordeal.

"Heifer, are you ready to do the damn thang?" Lexi inquired as she fluffed my decorative veil hanging on the mirror.

"I believe I am," I replied. Forcing a fake smile upon my face as my cousin primed my dress. I swayed as a dizzy haze circled my head. Tamia reached for my hands; I eased back. I clapped my hands, rubbing them together until I felt a surge of heat in my palms. Lexi smacked my hands away before I could run them over my dress.

"You are going to rub oil on your dress. Stop tripping. Today is your day. All the money you spent on this St. Thomas wedding is about to pay off, so you better know you are ready. Your co-workers are out there. Don't be the talk of the office by becoming a runaway bride."

The girls giggled as I fidgeted, tugging at the spaghetti straps on my dress.

"I am," I lied. "Can you stop calling me a heifer just for today? It is my wedding day. Hence my day!"

Waving her hand in the air, Lexi stared at me and then shouted, "Heffa, please! You know I keep it real. Now, stop tripping. You are my favorite cousin."

"I am your only cousin," I clarified, shaking my head and rolling my eyes at her.

"Mrs. Heifer," Lexi said, "you are my sister." Lexi kissed me on the cheek and gazed over at Imani. She mouthed, "Sorry."

I was thrilled to witness my BAE bury the hatchet as Imani smiled.

"Who was the tall chocolate glass of milk screaming trifling three in the house with you and Tre?" Naja asked Tamia.

"I saw him earlier. If I weren't with Winten, I would wrap these long chocolate legs around his waist."

Shocked, we all turned towards Imani and placed our hands over our mouths.

"Girl, leave that fool Chocolate Ty alone. He will leave your coochie sore and your pockets light."

Imani licked her lips. "Chocolate, Ty. He is fine, but his name sounds like a stripper."

"Imani and I are going to check on Tre and the guys." Lexi winked at Imani. "The last time I looked, Tre's brother was still MIA," Lexi informed me. Halfway out the door, she glanced back and winked at me. Relief soothed my frayed nerves; my cousin was not mad at me for beating her to the altar.

"Damn, Miya, that dress looks stunning on you. I see you had them raise the slit," Naja pointed out, walking over to the garment bag hanging on the wardrobe door. Glancing in the bag, she pulled the lace short set out. "Are you wearing this tonight?" Her eyes widened, holding the tiny pieces of fabric with the tips of her fingers. "Ma'am, your ass cheeks will be fighting the fabric."

A mischievous smile glided across my face.

Tamia looked at Naja and smacked her lips, adding her thoughts. "She will look like she is ready for some dick."

"Oh my." We all turned our heads towards the voice coming from the doorway—Tre's three sisters. I smiled warmly, motioning for the ladies to join us.

"I'm glad your dresses fit. You all look stunning."

Before they could respond to my compliment, Lexi stormed into the room.

"I think we're going to go find our grandmother and Mama Walker," one of Tre's sisters noted, backing out of the room as suddenly as they appeared.

"Tre's brother is not here yet. His girlfriend has a major attitude problem. I had to walk away before we destroyed your wedding space." Lexi rants, walking in circles. "I asked for her boyfriend's estimated arrival time and why they didn't travel together. Then out of nowhere, the bitch snapped. Tre's mother tried to explain the situation and calm his brother's girlfriend down. If it were not your wedding day, I would have molly whopped her ass."

"His fiancée flew in from Los Angeles yesterday. He is flying in today from Hawaii," Imani commented. "He's training there or something like that. His mother attempted to explain over Lexi and his wife-to-be squeals."

Lexi continued to pace the floor. Naja followed behind her, rubbing her bareback.

"Lexi, you must admit that the rock on her hand was blinding. It was the heart-shaped engagement ring you wanted," Imani interjected.

"Yes, I did," Lexi answered. "It was a canary yellow heart diamond trimmed in white diamonds. Tre's brother has a bit of dough. But she was still a bitch!"

Naja started cackling, her infectious laughter spreading as we all joined in.

"Nothing like diamonds to calm a woman," Naja effused. "They are a woman's best friend."

We sat around, reminiscing over the bet, trying to tally how much money I would get out of the bank account. I was waiting for Lexi and Imani to renege on giving me the twelve thousand. Instead, they mentioned I'll have access to the money once back in Los Angeles. Then they went on to predict who would be next.

"Are we going to bet on how long this marriage lasts?" Tamia asked.

We all stopped talking and stared at her.

"Go be with the men, Petty Patty," Naja insisted. "You are the best girl after all."

Tamia walked away. Naja rolled her eyes. Lexi cut Tamia off the moment she turned around to speak.

"Heifer, stop asking so many questions."

I knew it was time to walk down the aisle when my mother and father walked in. Lexi gave me my bouquet and fluffed my train and gown out again. My BAEs and I carried snow-white calla lilies. The off-white satin ribbon and white pearl pins decorating each flower's center made my arrangement classy and breathtaking.

I walked over to my mother and father and hugged my father. He was dressed handsomely in his all-white tuxedo paired with a lavender vest nicely complimented by a white and lavender tie. My mother modeled her form-fitted lavender paisley dress with a cape that hugged her figure.

"Turn this way a little," the photographer's voice startles me. I chuckled nervously.

He was right. I didn't hear him come in and was unsure how often he had been in my space. "The best pictures are the natural ones. I need a good picture of you and your parents. I'm finding it hard to get your father to face the camera."

"He hates pictures. You truly have to catch him off guard."

We all chuckled.

My father and I got into position. I was ecstatic that he finally agreed to get on a plane for my wedding.

"Do you have to go to the bathroom?" he asked.

I shook my head. "Dad, you look good," I chirped, pecking his cheek.

"And so, do you, darling," he replied. "I'm glad I came." He kissed me on the cheek. "Every father dreams of the day his baby gets married. I am proud of you. Are you happy, baby?"

I blushed, then scanned my dress.

Lexi fixed my dress and train for the last time. As the music started to play, we all got into formation. Doubt crept into my mind. I shook it off, humming to motivate myself. I was about to be the first BAE married.

Our entire party walked down the aisle separately because I had six bridesmaids. He only had three groomsmen and a groom's girl.

Tre decided he would walk the aisle instead of walking in with the Preacher. He was the first person in line. I tried to peep around the girls. I could see nothing beyond Naja's or Imani's elegant ebony frames.

Before coasting down the aisle to reach my happy and enthusiastic groom, I drew a deep breath. My stomach was doing flips the entire time.

Suddenly, my mind cut to the gorgeous dreadlock gentleman who stole my heart away in Las Vegas and San Diego. Visions of Mr. Walker standing at the altar waiting on me appeared. I blinked my eyes rapidly, jerking my father backward.

"My Love"
Jill Scott

Malik

ADRENALINE SURGED THROUGH MY HEART AS I raced directly to the ceremony from the airport. The wedding party had already walked down the aisle. I quickly took my position next to Tre, straightening the lavender and gray pastel tie and smoothing my platinum gray suit sleeves. I glanced at my mother. She shot me a smile and waved. I patted my brother on his back and stood straight as everyone rose for the bride.

Ooh's and ah's mixed impeccably with the melodic sound of Charlie Wilson's "You Are."

My mouth flew open, and an unfathomable glare penetrated my eyes. I held my abdomen, hoping to keep my stomach's contents under wraps. Despondency nipped at my soul like a vicious wind as I gazed in astonishment, then slammed my eyes shut to pray, but I could not conjure a single word. My inner fears were manifesting themselves in my dreams. I pinched my hand to wake up.

"Are you ok, Malik?" Tre smiled. "I refused to get married until you made it."

143

I went to smile, but my bottom lip trembled.

My nightmare was becoming a reality.

I searched the crowd for Raven. She drew a smile across her lips with her index finger reminding me to smile. I peered at the bride, willing her to feel my presence—a tear rolled down my cheek. I could hear distant chatter, then all sound disappeared. My lashes clung together. The more I blinked, the less I could see.

Taking the back of my hands, I wiped the water from my eyes, opening them to see the bride had fixed her gaze on me.

Her tear-streaked face tugged at my heartstrings.

Breaking our gaze, I gawked at Raven, pleading with my eyes, mouthing the words, "Stop the wedding. I love her."

Raven hunched, shaking her head in confusion. My heart sank.

I turned to face the bride, whose gaze was cast on Raven. She peeked at me, and I winked. She swiped a tear from her face. I passed Tre my handkerchief so he could clear her tear-stricken face.

He dabbed at his non-existing tears.

Pulling the handkerchief from his hands, I passed it to the bride. An electric current shot through my body when our fingers touched. She drew back rapidly.

I scratched my head as my entire body burst into itchy irritation. Welts formed on my skin as my thoughts reflected on my heart.

My heart song cried, *if she wants us, she will not go through with this.*

Didn't she know that my love was a hundred times better than Tre's? My pride questioned my heart.

Time stood still as my heart pleaded its case silently. My ego had finally consented to my heart. I opened my mouth to contest the marriage.

"You may now kiss your bride," the preacher announced, trapping my words in my throat.

My mind didn't recall the moment she said, "I do," or the preacher asking, "If anyone here knows why these two should not be joined together in holy matrimony."

I took a step to leave as they kissed. Miya had lost the greatest king. My ego declared until Tre's groom's girl pulled me back by the hand, hindering my wounded heart's retreat.

"We walk out behind them," she whispered. I didn't want to be rude, so I eased my hand from her grip, nodding at her words. I exited the stage right when the newlyweds had made it halfway down the aisle, cutting off any protest with a baneful glare.

I could hear Raven screaming my name from behind. I stopped and wiped my eyes with my tuxedo jacket sleeve. Everything RB said replayed in my mind; maybe he was right. I am too soft. I was in love with a woman who ghosted me three times.

Most people love being loved. Evidently, my device was to be loved by the people who never loved me in return.

Raven placed her hand on my shoulders. "Are you okay, Bossman?"

"Raven, would you fall for a guy like me? I mean wholeheartedly, love me?" She folded her hands across her chest, and a hint of sadness graced her warm tan face.

She blinked her thin almond eyes at me. "If I weren't a lesbian, I would date you. However, I am already in love. I love Kris to death, but she wants to be in a poly relationship. I'm not down with sharing my lady. Either she wants me and only me, or she needs to step off."

A tear rolled down her cheek. She composed herself and then apologized for ranting about her relationship.

I pulled her into my arms and squeezed her tightly. She rested her head on my chest. I kissed her on the top of her head.

"Everything will work out according to God's plan," I assured her. Although I did not believe that pertained to my situation.

"You know you can call me Malik or brother. You do not have to call me Bossman. We are so much more than that."

She looked up at me, her grin illuminating the night. "You have been a positive influence on RB and me. The stories I could tell you about RB's wild years. Your beliefs and the fact that you're not always trying to smash bitches have changed him. You have a good heart, bruh-bruh. I have witnessed it in action. RB was torn up by what Sabrina did to you and your injury. He and I are two peas in a pod. I feel what my brother feels for you. What I am trying to say is I love you." She smiled. A hint of admiration sparked in her honey brown eyes.

"By the way, I call you Bossman, so I do not get my roles confused. I can respect you, check you, and protest your actions because you are my brother. I can only defend and respect my Bossman." We laughed.

"Well, Raven, sometimes, I may need you to check me as my employee.

I usually follow my heart. Tonight, I allowed my pride to lead me. I made a huge mistake."

"Tre's late brother, we need you for pictures," a tall woman shrieked.

"Ugh," Raven griped, distorting her face and cracking her neck. "This bitch gets on my last damn nerves. If I were with RB, I would have beaten her butt. I'm only holding back because I know you don't play, Bossman."

I kissed Raven on the head and released her from my embrace. I waved my index finger in her face. "If I have to play nice, so do you." She slapped my hand away.

"Is this one of those moments where I can check you?"

"Nope!" I rapidly reply, pointing towards the group of people huddled in front of a water fountain. "March, young lady." Like a bit of a kid, Raven stomped her feet and marched in front of me.

A gut-wrenching roar escaped my belly.

I spotted my mother, Tasha, and Tre taking pictures in front of the water fountain.

"Damn, big bro, where have you been? Come, take some photos with the most handsome groom on this damn island."

People chuckled at Tre's antics. Raven spun me around and analyzed me. I pulled back and squinted my eyes when she noted, "Your eyes look crusty." Raising an eyebrow at her as she continued to groom me. "I think mine are two. It is all your fault. Had us out there crying and having heart-filled moments." She playfully punched me in the side of the gut. Then she pulled some wipes from her bag and cleaned my face before saturating it with oil. Lastly, she applied oil to my locks' tip.

"Did you do this stuff for RB?"

A mischievous smile graced her face as she opened her bag to me. "The only thing in here is my credit card, lip gloss, money, and the rest is your stuff. If you stay ready, you don't have to get ready."

I rocked my head back and forth in her face. "I see you, baby girl." She tugged my locks. We giggled. I appreciated Raven. I needed these small bursts of happiness.

"Bruh, stop playing with your girl and come on," Tre yelled at me.

I stood there as Raven twisted my locks away from my face. She smiled and bounced her head in approval.

Turning around, I walked to Tre and spotted the love of my life standing off to the side, surrounded by three women. I smiled.

"Mimi," Tre called out. All the ladies moved aside, and my lover walked through.

"My Miya…" I hissed under my breath.

"Mimi, this is my brother, Malik."

Tears ran down her cheeks. I wondered if they were for the loss of us or the joyous union.

"Here," I heard Raven's voice, but I could not move.

My feet were rooted in the ground.

Raven stepped around me and passed Miya some tissue, but one of her bridesmaids snatched it from Miya's hand. She gently shoved her bridesmaid aside.

Miya reached her hand out for me, but I still could not recall the command to demand my body to move. I adjusted my imaginary glasses to focus on the woman I loved who had become my brother's wife.

Miya's smile recoiled from her face as she retracted her hand.

Tre caressed her back. My heart stopped as words glided from her lovely lips.

"Nice to meet you—Malik Walker—Tre's brother."

"Untitled (How Does It Feel)"
D'Angelo
Miya

THE MORNING SUN CREPT THROUGH A slit in the Venetian blinds. I turned over and placed sweet kisses on my husband's neck. I promised myself that I would fulfill my matrimonial obligations during our reception no matter how dreadful Tre was in bed.

On our wedding night, I recited additional vows to my husband, pledging to choose him every day and love him in words and deeds. He asked me to swear, 'I would never withhold sex, love his flaws, and never stop fighting for us.' Reluctantly I did.

Shit, he fought for my hand, not Malik Walker.

Rolling out of bed, I eased into my fluffy pink slippers and stumbled off to the bathroom. The sight before me was unbelievably sticky grape jelly tangled in my hair.

Last night Tre and I played refrigerator love. At first, he refused to play until I reminded him that he agreed to a thirty-day sex challenge to enhance our sexual bond and love. The article I read declared that earthshattering sex would be imminent as the more in-depth partners trekked into the thirty-day sex challenge. I hoped these facts were accurate.

We only had a couple of days left in our thirty-day experiment. I still didn't feel our carnal connection. Desperate, I searched the internet and found an article regarding rule-breaking sex. The thrill of being caught or seen was supposed to be exhilarating. Having intercourse outside and nontraditional areas ranked high. The next night we had sex on the front porch at 3 am. Tre behaved as if this was normal conduct for him and lacked the same enthusiasm as me.

A week ago, I fantasized about Malik inducing an orgasm. I've indulged in numerous imaginations since. Technically it's not cheating since it isn't real. Right? Feeling terrible, I declared I would stop until I heard it was widespread practice for women to imagine making love to Idris Elba, Denzel Washington, Henry Cavill, or Morris Chestnut to sail the waves of euphoria.

The game last night had two simple rules. You and your mate sit together in front of the refrigerator naked and only use items in the fridge to stimulate each other into orgasmic bliss. Tre was finally excited. It was fun, but no bombs or fireworks burst in the air.

I didn't expect countless things to change after we were married. Before we married, Tre and I painted the Los Angeles streets. Our kisses were passionate. I felt lust radiating from his pores when he held me in his arms. Now we only peck each other on the lips. There is no sexual chemistry. When we go out dancing, he rides a chair, and people watch. He used to dance until he couldn't breathe. The other day we went to the movies, and he complained non-stop. Nothing about the theater had changed except we were a married couple attending the show.

Let's not even mention the sex. Two weeks after my wedding night, sex became a rapid and rough chore. Most of all, it tended to feel a little one-sided. He makes love to himself. I'm merely the vessel he needs to achieve his orgasmic goal. He could care less about me having an orgasm. Our marriage lacked the fire and desire I shared with Malik.

My nana would say, "Whatever you did to get your mate is the same thing you need to do to keep your mate." I have recited this to him every day. I thought about admitting defeat. Then I heard Nana's voice say, "You made this bed. Now lay in it!"

I read every book and article I could get my hand on about marriage, sex, and communication. I was determined to give my union a shot. I took comfort in knowing I was not the only lost soul struggling in her marital bed. There wouldn't be tons of books written on the subject matter if I were.

Besides, what would the BAEs think if I announced I was getting a divorce before our first anniversary? I would be the butt of every joke for the next five years.

Warm lips adorned the side of my neck. I jumped.

"Morning, why are you so jumpy?"

Turning around, I looked into the gorgeous brown eyes that belonged to my husband. I tried to kiss him passionately. He avoided my kiss and pecked me gently on the lips, stepping away from me.

"Am I sexy to you? Am I the most beautiful woman, you know?"

"Damn, Mimi! What is up with the interrogation this morning?"

My bruised pride did not respond. I picked up my toothbrush and freshened up, dabbing my mouth with the washcloth. I spun around and decided to reset the moment. "Good morning to you."

Tre hovered above me, kissing my chest before alerting me of my appearance.

"You have a cherry stuck to your... I mean, my breast."

I turned to the mirror, laughing with him as I plucked more cherries off my body.

"You have an undercover sexy vibe."

Before asking what he meant, Tre pulled me by my waist back into the bedroom, pushing me onto the bed.

"No, I have to go," I protested, glancing at the clock on the dresser. Today was my mother's birthday. I took off from work to spoil her rotten. I planned a whole itinerary: brunch, spa, and shopping. Time was of the essence today; I could not afford to waste any of it on a quickie. Quickies always messed me over. They were about him, not about us.

He pushed me down on the bed. Laying down next to me, he turned his head, kissing me on the tip of my nose, then my forehead, before he rolled onto his back. "Momma, get yo' fine ass up there and RIIIIIIDE," he sang, pointing at his erect penis.

He slapped me on the thigh. "Come on, Mimi, slide that warm pussy on daddy's dick." He stroked his thick shaft, then licked his lips. "You know you want it! Grab a condom and hurry up."

I did what he said and straddled my husband backward, bucking and riding him like no tomorrow.

"Get on your feet. Daddy wants you to bounce on this dick, right," he commanded.

Like always, I obeyed. I slid off my husband's penis, pulling him around to the side of the bed, pushed the mattress over, placed my feet on the box spring, and mounted him backward. He loved this position because it allowed me to spring off his dick like an acrobat. I loved this position because I could also stimulate myself. Let's say my thighs stay tight and right. Sex is the best workout in the world.

I could swear I touched the ceiling as I bounced on his dick at one point. I pulled his hand around my waist so he could flick my pearl. Instead, he pulled away. I slowed my pace so I could stimulate myself.

I moaned in pleasure.

"Mimi, stop playing with yourself. I'll top you off after you fuck daddy the right way."

He slapped my ass hard.

"What the fuck" I yelled, punching him in the leg.

"Ride me, right!"

'Smack!'

His hands stung the fleshy curve of my butt, instructing me once more. I pushed back the tears welling in my eyes as I convinced myself our passion made him behave like an idiot. I closed my eyes tightly as I popped, locked, and dropped my warm goodness, forsaking my satisfaction.

"I'm about to bust!" He screamed, filling the condom. I reclined back onto his chest, waiting for round two. He kissed me, fondled my breasts then pushed me off him.

I lay there wondering how the hell I allowed this to happen again. He played me for the umpteenth time.

Smiling brightly as he lingered over my limp body. "I thought you had to go and spoil your mother."

I wanted to slap that silly grin right off his smug face. "This is why I didn't want to have sex with you. You are a selfish lover."

He yanked me off the bed to my feet. "It is only sex, Mimi."

"Tre," I calmly said, "this is the umpteenth time you have left your wife unfulfilled. I never let you walk out of this house unsatisfied. Why would you allow me to go out into the world full of disgruntled wolves?" I cleared my throat. "Some women become cheaters when they feel sexually mistreated."

"Mimi, don't get fucked up," he uttered.

"Love Is Blind"
Eve
Miya

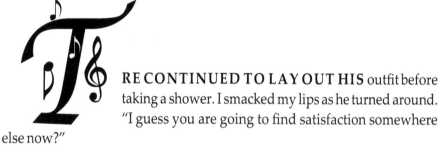

RE CONTINUED TO LAY OUT HIS outfit before taking a shower. I smacked my lips as he turned around. "I guess you are going to find satisfaction somewhere else now?"

I rolled my eyes. "Do not put words in my mouth. In every book I've read, the storyline begins with neglect or selfishness, then the marital conflicts start, and the marriage ends."

He huffed as he tapped on the door rail of the bathroom.

"People become too comfortable and forget to satisfy their partners. Why would a cat look for milk elsewhere if she gets enough milk at home?"

He shrugged. "Please yourself," he barked, "but remember it will cost you."

I contemplated playing with myself, but he hated it when I did. His jealous ass would get mad and refuse to go down on me for days.

I expelled a long gust of air.

Tre peeped out the bathroom door. "Should I come to taste, Mrs. Kitty?" He shook his head and chuckled. "Naw!"

I bet Malik would nibble, lick, suck, slurp, gulp, devour Ms. Kitty, then do twenty-five pushups inside her. A slight grin skipped across my face, then vanished.

Damn it! Thinking about Malik was making me wetter and hornier.

Stay focused, Miya. Do not bring Malik back into your bedroom.

"Bitch did he ever leave," my subconscious retorted.

"Why did you lie back down? Get up! Your mother is waiting for you. You need to take a long, cold shower."

"I didn't have an orgasm. You exploded too fast, sharpshooter!" I snapped at him.

"Oh, poor baby," he taunts me some more.

"Yes, poor me."

"My baby wants to have an orgasm this morning, even though she climaxed over a dozen times last night. Oh, she is dreadfully neglected." I nodded in agreement. "You want to achieve an orgasm?"

I nodded and playfully allowed my bottom lip to slip. He strolled over to me, yanked my legs apart, and flicked my clit twice with the tip of his tongue. I moaned in pleasure. I laid there anticipating his next touch, but I felt nothing.

I sat on the bed and gawked at him in disbelief as he groomed himself in the bathroom mirror. If I treated him in this manner, he would whine like a little bitch.

He glanced over at me. "Next time, concentrate on climaxing. You shouldn't need my hand, your hand, or my mouth to get off. Learn how to position yourself to have an orgasm. Hell, you were riding. You could have played with yourself. Pleasing yourself is allowed when we are making love. By yourself, it is not, ma'am."

I sneered at his remark. "I normally do because you don't! Besides, you told me to stop!"

"I appreciate your obedience. I'm glad you know how to listen. Sex can't always be about you, right?"

Instead of responding, I rolled my eyes. He continued to shape up his goatee. "If you roll them again, you will make me slap them straight."

"I wish you would, you fucking asshole!"

"Let's end this convo. Stop pushing my buttons. You might not like my reaction." He kicked the door close.

What should I do? Aunt Geraldine always told Lexi and me, 'Nip bullshit in the bud when it first happens, or it will continue to happen.' However, my mother would say, 'Respect your husband and do whatever he says. He is the king of his castle. It is your job to support all his decisions no matter how you feel about them.'

Vaulting off the bed, I rushed into the bathroom. Staring at the misty shower door, I mulled over my next move. I eased open the shower door and stepped in. Tre was standing under the showerhead with his hands planted on the wall.

I kissed him on the back. He shoved me back with one arm.

"Mimi!" he harshly hissed at me.

I frowned.

"Stop smothering me. I have a critical meeting this morning. I cannot be late. You just put me in the right mindset, which helped your hubby relax." He pleaded in a faint tone. "Please don't take that from me with your bullshit."

"Fine, I won't," I responded, disappointment trickling into my voice.

"We can't all take off work when we desire to. Some of us have responsibilities," Tre snapped.

I noticed he could be a bit of a bully when things don't go his way. He either tries to belittle my family, criticize my role as a wife, or make me feel bad for him. I despise emotional bullies!

"What the fuck does that mean?" I barked.

He swiftly turned around, his right hand slapping me across the chest. He gazed at me with this uncompromising stare. "I hit you 'cause you're too close. Give me some damn space." The burning pain and the darkness in his eyes sent a cold shiver up my spine, and I decided to drop the subject.

"I would love some warm water," I said meekly. He stepped aside as I moved in front of him, removing the showerhead. I wanted to run some hot water over my entire body.

A loud sound reverberated off the walls. I whipped around.

"What the fuck are you doing? Put the showerhead back before I spank yo' ass again," he demanded.

"Why hit me that hard?" I queried, twitching my burning nose as tears threatened to spill down my cheeks. "I'm just trying to run some water over my back to warm me up."

"I bet, bitch. You are trying to fuck the showerhead. I told you later! You can have an orgasm when I allow it. Now, wait until I give your spoiled ass one."

Stepping one leg out of the shower, I whined, "I'll take a shower later."

My heart thought a lion had walked into the bathroom as Tre yanked my hair through the shower cap, causing my right leg to slide. My arms clamored frantically for non-existent rails as my head smacked against the shower door. Pain ripped through my body as I tried to straighten my pretzeled core. Grunting through the pain, I eased back against the bathroom wall.

"Get the fuck up. You didn't fall that damn hard."

"Have you lost your fucking mind?" I screamed at him, observing my red nail beds. "We talked about you putting your hands on me. You promised they were accidents, and you never meant to be rough. But this is abuse."

"Nope, my mind is good," he replied nonchalantly. "You like when I chastise yo' ass. That's the only time you listen and fall the fuck back."

"I could have broken my damn neck, my motherfucking neck, Tre! Or fell through the glass door, you motherfucking punk!"

"Watch your damn mouth in my house! I am not your fucking child," he replied, pointing his finger in my face.

I slapped his hand away. My head collided with the wall. A waterfall of tears drenched my face.

"You are not going to keep talking to me like I'm your fucking kid. I am a man. Yo' ass will respect me! Now stop fucking crying. I didn't smack you with my open palm; I used my fingers."

"Then act like a fucking man… and not some insecure punk! Real men don't hit on women."

His arm went up as if he were about to slap fire from me.

"I am not a fucking punk," he growled. "You will take a shower right now with your freaky ass. Yo' ass is trying to double back and fuck the showerhead. You wait until I decide to give yo' ass some of this dick," he snarled, jiggling his dick in my face.

"Oh my God, who… who did I? Who did I marry?" I wailed.

I leaned my head against the shower door. The right side of my body was red. I could not believe this fool didn't even try to catch me. I touched my hair. "Dammit!" I barked.

"Shower, then get out of the bathroom," he demanded. "Stop pulling on your hair and wash your ass. See what happens when you play too much? Now you have to get your hair done because I'm not trying to look at you in a fucking ponytail all week."

My bottom lip quivered as my heart broke. My heart screamed out to God. *Who did I marry?* I placed my hands over my eyes to hide my tears. When I removed my hands, he was standing in front of me.

"You know what? Come here. I'll wash you up." He clutched me by one arm, yanking me back into the shower. My soaking wet hair whacked my face as he jerked me to my feet under the showerhead.

Lathering a towel, he smacked me on the ass and gently kneaded my stinging flesh. My body jerked at the sound, but I refused to utter a word. Trembling like a leaf caught in a hurricane, tears cascaded down my face. "Open up your legs so I can clean my pussy." When I did not move, he slapped me on the ass harder. Pride wounded and body aching, I did as instructed, allowing him to wash me clean.

Stepping out of the shower, he slammed me against the wall, tucking his arms under my legs. He eased me up the wall, burying his face between my legs.

I punched his shoulders and pushed at his head.

Suckling viciously, he bit on my clit, rippling pain shocked my soul, and my body went limp.

I concentrated on the pain I felt when Uncle Steve died. Willing my body to deny itself any pleasure, refusing to feel the sweet release of jubilation.

His tongue swirled around my clit like a tornado. Pain turned into pleasure, and I erupted. The familiar feeling of disappointment nipped at my soul like it did on my wedding day.

"Say thank you, hubby," he insisted, trying to kiss me.

"For abusing me or genital mutilation?"

"You know what, crybaby? Fuck your spoiled ass!" he shouted, then stormed out of the shower. He stomped out of the bathroom, slamming the door behind him.

I leaned against the shower wall as sharp pains ripped through my right leg, examining it only to see black-and-blue spots forming on my sore skin. Tears streamed down my face. I could not believe the way he treated me. Were these the early signs of a violent man?

No! The first time he manhandled you was.

I wanted to tell the BAEs about his frequent mood swings, but I was embarrassed. They'll say I rushed into my marriage to win a bet. A part of me knew it was the truth.

The bathroom door flung open. "Mimi, stop acting crazy and get out of the fucking shower."

Stepping out of the shower, I plugged in my blow dryer and flat irons, deciding to spend my day doing my hair and lounging around the house.

"I thought you had to leave. You're mad at me, not your mother. You promised her today. You are a fantastic daughter," he noted. His tone dripped in sarcasm.

I turned on the blow dryer to drown him out.

"Do not mistreat my mother the way you mistreat yours," he hissed.

I rolled my eyes as my inner bitch emerged. "Which one? The one who didn't want you or the one that felt sorry for your ass?" I barked.

His hand flew up in the air. I braced myself for the impact. I knew the last time he hit me wasn't the last.

"Put all this shit up and go get your fucking hair done with your mother," he demanded, yanking my hair.

"Don't you need to get to work?" I asked. "I thought you had an important meeting."

"Whateva!" Tre said, then tried to kiss me. I leaned away from him.

"You are evil, Mimi," he joked, a big Kool-Aid smile spreading on his face.

Looking at his stupid grin was pissing me the fuck off.

"Damn, I made you rain like a waterfall. Ease up on a brother. You got what you wanted."

Why did he think any of this was ok?

"Kiss me mean girl."

I looked at him and smacked my lips. I was not kissing his ass. I would not reward him after the shit he did to me.

"I could have broken my neck this morning. I am not a puppet. You will not get rewarded for treating me like shit," I assured. "I hope you call my mother to tell her happy birthday. Do not mistreat my mother because I do not mistreat yours."

He chuckled.

"Kudos. Now stop acting like the victim. Baby, I did not hurt you." He pulled my left cheek to his lips.

"How did we get here?" I asked the reflection in the window as Tre walked away.

How did you get here? She responded with an attitude and then turned her back to me.

Staring wide-eyed at my reflection in the mirror, I observed the glimmer in my eyes slowly fade away.

"Treat Her Like a Lady"
Joe
Miya

I **FRANTICALLY STUMBLED AROUND THE YELLOW AND** cream modern kitchen, trying to prepare dinner while entertaining Naja.

In the last three weeks, Tre's complaints were endless. He ranted about my food being too salty or bland. I don't want sex enough, or I crave sex too much. He whines about me not talking to him, yet every time I attempt a conversation, he gets pissed because he is either trying to rest or watch television. I didn't know what to do besides talking during sex or while he was on the toilet.

I was sick of arguing. My mother, father, auntie, and uncle never bickered every day, so this behavior was unfamiliar. It seemed Tre craved the drama. The one consistent factor around his ranting was that our discussions always ended with him going for a drive or hanging out at a bar with Tamia.

Last weekend we went to the zoo. The sweltering heat was my fault. Next, the long lines to get food were also my fault since I did not know what to eat.

I have seen my parents disagree and my auntie and uncle, but they never argued and disrespected each other in public. They would always wait until they were away from Lexi and me before they hashed out their drama. Not Tre. He did not care who was around or what he said to me. Sometimes I thought about responding to his behavior, but I didn't want to add to my embarrassment.

He perpetuates the stereotype that all Black people are loud, ghetto, and don't know how to conduct themselves publicly.

Each day I motivated myself to stay in my marriage. I was trying to pour all into my marriage to honor my vows to God. Once I walk away, I can say I have exhausted all possibilities.

We will see Mint Condition this weekend at the Yoshi in San Francisco. I wanted us to have an enjoyable day. I will be an angel tonight, so I can have a peaceful weekend, which means biting my tongue until I savor the salty taste of red crimson.

"Miya, can you talk to me for a minute?" Naja asked, grabbing me by the forearm, halting my thoughts and steps.

I wiped the sweat from my brow. "I'm sorry. You came over here to talk to me, not watch me cook," I noted.

Naja patted the seat next to her at the bar. "I wanted to apologize. Dakari surprised me and you at the wedding. He never told me he was going to make it. The last thing I wanted to do was steal your spotlight."

"I realize you would never. You are not Lexi."

Naja eyed me questionably. "Miya! Lexi loves you to death. She would never do anything to cause you harm or agony."

I shrug without conviction.

"Lexi threatened everybody at your wedding. She ensured we all did what we were supposed to and that the location had everything according to your specifications. She wanted it to be a day you would never forget."

Dammit! I felt like shit, hearing Naja ramble concerning Lexi. I was pissed about so many things on my wedding day. I was mad that Malik was Tre's foster brother. Disappointed, I was marrying Tre instead of Malik. When Dakari showed up with a wedding band, I was ready to kill him.

Dakari quickly announced that he and Naja were married the prior month. I was pissed when I found out Naja beat me to the altar and even more furious that I was not at her wedding.

I wondered if I would have married Tre after Naja revealed she was first to the altar?

I pulled Naja's hands into mine. "I am not mad because you won the bet. I am upset because you were married, and not one BAE was present. We love you. We are supposed to experience everything together. BAEs for life!"

A tear rolled down Naja's face as she confessed. "At least you are showing me affection. My parents haven't talked to me since we eloped. One minute we were debating, crying, then laughing. The next second we were saying, 'I do.'"

"Your mother has been waiting for you to be married since you were a little girl. Grant her time to get over the shock. Maybe you and Dakari should still have a big wedding to please your parents." I said while passing her some tissues.

Tears flowed liberally as I cried with her. "Naja, I married a man I do not recognize nine out of ten days. He is bad with managing money and viol…."

I stopped talking with slumped shoulders and an ironclad fist, clutching tightly to my pinned-up secrets. Too embarrassed to divulge, Tre was physically and mentally abusive at times. I poured Naja a glass of white wine.

"He is a stranger to me. I thought he managed money for a living, but."

"I didn't want to mention anything unless you approached the subject first."

"Do you still have the bank account we opened in college to pay our rent?"

"Yes," I responded. "I still put one-third of my paycheck in the account." I shrugged. "It's for rainy days."

"Did you have a downpour?"

"No, I am financially sound. Naja, you are a straight shooter. Do not be coy now."

"The bank has been emailing me with low balance alerts."

I frowned as I calculated how much money was in that account. "Impossible! That account should have at least sixty thousand in there." I pulled out my cell phone to check the account balance.

My mouth dropped open the second I saw the balance. The account had only one hundred dollars. I checked my other two bank accounts.

I recalled Tre asking me to add him to the account when we planned the wedding. I never knew he would take all my money out of the bank account.

I huffed, thinking about the text I sent him this afternoon. I noted I would cook dinner and end the night with the three B's (bubble bath, blowjob, and back rub). He didn't deserve any of those things!

A lonely tear slid down my cheek. I sniffled.

"Miya, are you okay?"

"I am okay. I was reading Tre's text. He canceled our plans tonight because he is bringing his foster brother home for dinner."

Naja passed me an envelope full of money. I blinked in confusion. "It's my portion of the bet money."

I smiled widely. "Keep it. You won it fair and square. I am not hurting for money. It was more about getting to the altar before Lexi, not the coins," I honestly admitted.

Naja expelled a long stream of stifling air. "Allow me to adjust your crown before I go, Sis. I know Tre is behind your money issues."

Resting the muscles in my face, I struggled to shield the truth. Naja raised her hand when my lips parted.

"Stop competing with Lexi because she is not competing with you. If Lexi knew Tre was taking money from you without your consent, she would kill him. Husband or not. Whenever Tamia teases you, Lexi always checks her ass. Lexi loves you. Your competitive behavior towards her blinds your vision. Trust me. You are focusing on the wrong issues. It's causing you to make poor decisions."

I wanted to tell my friend Tre was one of those bad choices. Instead, I smiled.

"Be on your best behavior, don't act a damn fool tonight," I mumbled, rereading Tre's laundry list of preparations for his foster brother.

Tre and Malik needed to learn a lesson about hurting me. I chuckled to myself. "I'll take a fool for one thousand, Mr. Trebek!"

"My My My"

Johnny Gill

Miya

RE WAS DUE TO ARRIVE AT 6:30 pm with his foster brother. I set the table and prepared dinner as instructed. I glanced at the microwave clock that flashed 5:00 pm. I dashed into the bathroom to freshen up.

After cleaning the tub, I prepared Tre an ultra-hot bath, laid his silk pajama bottoms across the bed, then slipped on a sexy sheer stretch black halter mini dress with red thong panties and matching bra before stepping into my black, three-inch fuck me pumps.

The tantalizing aroma of garlic bread wafted throughout the house, demanding my presence in the kitchen. I made all of Tre's favorite dishes: steamed crab legs with a spicy butter sauce, roasted garlic vegetables, seafood pasta, my famous cheesy garlic bread, and embarrassment for dessert.

I heard Tre walk through the front door. I leaned over and placed my elbows on the kitchen island, eager to arouse Tre and Malik with my sexually enticing pose. I knew Malik's little tomboyish fiancée was not dressing like this for him.

I ignored Tre as he called out for me, knowing he would come straight to the kitchen to get a beer. Swaying my hips from side to side, I could feel the dress gliding upward until it reached my plump derriere. I inhaled deeply and arched my back.

"What the fuck?"

Bouncing my butt in the air, I eased away from the kitchen island, bent over, and touched my toes.

"Yeah! All of this is for you."

"Mimi," he hollered — pure frustration lingering on his tongue. I struggled to suppress my glee.

"What!"

"Stand the fuck up and turn around."

I gradually turned towards him for dramatic effect, striking a pose as Malik undressed me with his bedroom eyes. A huge mischievous grin ran across his foster brother's face.

Tre's lips tightened into thin lines until they disappeared. Eyes narrowing, a vein bulged in the center of his forehead. I should have felt immensely ashamed, except both of their facial expressions were better than I could have ever imagined. "Mimi stop posing and put on some fucking clothes," Tre demanded.

Forehead and brow slanted in solid disapproval; Malik yelled Tre's name.

"Mimi, do not piss me off. Take yo' triflin' ass upstairs and put on some fucking clothes before I slap yo' ass silly."

Malik's eyes narrowed, crinkling into slits. "Before you slap her, what?"

Tre shrugged. I scoffed. I finally found the one person my dumbass hubby feared.

"You don't have to talk to her like that," Malik reprimanded Tre.

I smiled inwardly but frowned to mask my excitement.

"She had no idea you were bringing me home. She is trying to be a good wife. If my wife did this, I would appreciate her." His words rendered me speechless. Twirling my red thong in his direction invaded my psyche.

I bit down on my index finger. "I am sorry, king! Please forgive me," I expressed regret, prying my eyes off Malik's robust biceps.

Thoughts of his fiancée pulled me back from the ledge of fantasy. He caused my heart to leak sorrow, flaunting his fiancé at my damn wedding. She was beautiful, but she did not ooze sex appeal. During the reception, I feared he would divulge our secret love affair. I presumed he was trying to shield his secret from his fiancée because he never uttered a word.

I swung my hips from side to side, reminding Malik of our past encounters. His eyes locked on the swerve he composed in my hips, knowing he would never die between them again. I plastered my eyes on Malik. "I didn't know you were bringing somebody home."

Malik smirked.

I rolled my eyes.

I slowly swayed my torso and tilted my head from left to right. In my mind, the act was captivating. The glare on Tre's face revealed it was not.

The three of us stood in utter silence for a couple of minutes, staring back and forth. The reality of being close to Malik was driving me crazy. Downcasting my eyes, I reminisced about the last time we made love. I could feel moisture forming between my thighs. My attentions were to torture Tre and Malik, yet I was the one in anguish.

"What did I tell you, Mimi?" My eyes swung up, glaring at Tre wildly.

"We always hold our heads high," Malik noted proudly.

I stood straight with confidence.

Tre yanked me by the arm. "Stop looking at us dumbfounded and go put on some clothes." He eyed Malik, then mumbled, "Please."

I rubbed my body against Malik, easing between him and Tre.

Tre walked into the room and smacked me on the ass. "What in the hell were you wearing?"

I twirled. "This was a little fuck me outfit for you. I sent you a text message about tonight. I didn't realize you were coming home with someone. I mean, your foster brother."

"I didn't come home with somebody. I came home with my brother, Malik. Also, stop saying, 'foster brother.' We are brothers. No foster needed, understood?"

I smacked my lips. Reminding myself that they were not blood brothers helped me feel less guilty about falling in love with Malik and sleeping with them.

"Mimi, what did your text message say?"

I hunched my shoulders and then walked away.

"Slide on some jeans and a shirt and go entertain Malik. I am going to take my bath. Is my water ready?"

Liar, I thought. If he didn't get my text, why would he expect to have a hot bath waiting on him?

"Yes, hubby," I replied.

I had embarrassed him enough. I was not giving Tre any reason to back out of our San Francisco trip to see Mint Condition.

I sat on the bed. I did not want to go back into the living room with Malik alone. He had already made me wet once tonight. I giggled as their facial expressions replayed in my head.

Tre emerged from the bathroom, barking, "What in the hell is so fucking funny?" I looked at Tre. Rolling my eyes, I stretched across the bed. "Don't lay yo' ass down. Go entertain my fucking brother."

I blinked owlishly. "Trust me. You do not want me to amuse Malik."

"I want you guys to get acquainted."

Trust! Malik is familiarized with every inch of my frame. He and Ms. Kitty are on a first-name basis. Shit, I think he knows me better than you do. I wanted to say but wasn't brave enough.

"Helloooooooo! Stop daydreaming and get yo' ass downstairs now!"

I peeped into the living room at Malik. He was shooting pool with his shirt off. His all-embracing biceps glistened in the dim light, his six-pack looking like a plastic surgeon chiseled them just for his frame. A surge of sexual desire rushed through my veins.

I swallowed the thick ball of sexual frustration that coiled in my throat. Drooling from the mouth the second he cast those smoky gray eyes upon me, revealing his million-dollar smile.

"Can I um… get you something to drink," I sputtered.

"I would love some of you."

Ms. Kitty tingled.

I twisted a string of hair around my index finger. "Excuse me. What did you say?"

"I would love some sangria if you have some."

"Tell Me"
Dru Hill
Malik

MY EYES HADN'T LAID UPON MIYA'S adorable face since her wedding reception. Watching her dance cheek to cheek with my brother at their wedding annihilated my heart. Whenever I attempted to leave the reception, my mother or Raven pleaded that I stay for Tre's sake. My father and I were ready to bounce. When Miya and her girls sashayed onto the dance floor to perform a dance routine, I damn near had a heart attack. The revealing outfit was alluring as the one she had on tonight.

People should only reveal certain things in the privacy of their bedroom, not in public.

When I rose from my seat to yank her off the dance floor and drape my jacket around her half-naked body, my father gripped my hand, pulling me back down. "If her husband is okay with her costume, then so are we," he voiced. I was thrilled that my father disagreed with her attire as I did.

Miya drew my attention towards the room's corner as she placed glasses of sangria on a round glass bistro table before she grabbed a pool stick.

"Fuck!" I mumbled, slightly above a whisper. I knew coming here was a terrible idea, but Tre kept bugging me. I gave in after he threatened to call our mother. I didn't want to explain my reasoning for avoiding her baby boy's wife.

One day I will reveal my feelings for Miya to my parents because I keep hankering for their prayers and guidance.

Miya leaned on the table to take a shot, and my rod saluted her plump backside. I spun, placing my hand on my strength, trying to push it down.

Glancing at the entrance before I dared to utter a word. In a whispered beat, I divulged. "I never knew you and Tre were together. Had I known, I would have never taken advantage of you." I intended to tell her I would have never fallen in love, but what would confessing my love change?

"Tre and I had only been together a month. Please know I felt something for you," she admitted as she knocked a ball in the right corner pocket. "Something residing in me demanded you be my first lover. The lyrics flowing between us were genuine. We are musical and sensual soulmates. San Diego was our destiny. You know that, right?"

Her statement and question hung in my mind like a catchy hook.

I smiled. Before I could answer, she swatted the air between us. "Forgive me. I don't know what I am saying." She snickered, scratching the table while attempting to sink a ball.

As I analyzed the striped balls on the billiard table, she exclaimed, "I imagine you are happy and making arrangements."

I was happy with my career but tormented because I allowed my wife to slip between my fingers. That thought repeated twice, but I was too afraid to speak those words verbally.

To lighten the mood and fill the silence, she bashfully smiled. I couldn't stop the corners of my lips from curling upward. My damn heart missed this woman. I hadn't seen her in several weeks, but it felt like a lifetime.

"Stay focused on your career," I grunted.

"Did you say something to me?" She asked as she slowly approached.

I could swear she was trying to seduce me or drive me crazy with desire for a second. It made me wonder if the kitchen seduction was for Tre or me. I wanted to grab her by the hips, place her on the kitchen island, and taste her luscious folds when she seductively swayed from side to side.

I looked towards the stairs and prayed Tre would come down the steps before I did something that would have me on my knees, repenting.

Miya stepped close to me until our bodies touched and moaned, "I wish—"

"What do you wish for?" Tre asked, strolling into the game room.

"I wish you would hurry. However, here you are. I don't need to wish anymore," Miya replied rapidly.

I stood there in shock. My heart was pounding as if a lion had walked into the room.

I rushed to my brother's side and demanded we go outside to talk. I needed to put some distance between his gorgeous wife and myself.

Tre looked back at Miya before stepping through the glass sliding door. "When we come back in, have the table prepared." I wanted to check his tone and rudeness. But I didn't know if I was overreacting. I was jealous because he had what I ached for and mistreated her by being a jackass.

We sat under the gazebo. Tre reached inside the small fridge and retrieved two beers. "Damn big bro, I thought I would see you more since you moved back."

I took a sip of my beer, placing it on the bar before speaking. "Tre, I have been in training camp. I'm only here now because we have two days off."

"You can stay with me on your off days since you haven't had time to find a house."

"Raven has a place for me to stay when I'm off. It took her a while, but she found the perfect house. She shows me designs, and I pick the ones I like." I guffawed quietly to myself. I was genuinely trusting Raven with every part of my life. "I haven't seen the house's interior since I bought it. I have no clue what it looks like at this point. However, according to Raven, the renovations are almost complete."

Tre peeked at the sliding door. "Where did you find Raven? Bro, she is drop-dead gorgeous. She sounds like the best wifey assistant any man would dream of having."

I cleared my throat before speaking. "Raven is RB's sister. You have met her before."

"Maybe she wasn't fine before. Her body is banging. I would smash."

Anger grew inside me. He had the most striking woman globally in his bed and arms, yet he was eyeballing Raven. "She is not your type," I expressed brazenly. "Focus on your marriage."

Tre tilted his head and sucked on his teeth, then exclaimed, "I get it. She's a lesbian, but every woman is my type, and I am theirs." He clapped his hands together. "Ain't no man hit that pussy right. If I hit it, she would sing my praises. You saw Mimi's outfit when we walked in, right?"

I ignored his ignorance, remained silent, and sipped on my beer. "That's because I hit that virgin pussy right! When Mimi acts up, I put her on oral timeout. If I'm mad, she gets no dick for days."

I balled up my fist and punched myself in the thigh. I could feel my chest inflating higher and higher the more Tre bragged about his bedroom skills.

"One rookie on my team was at Paxton's friend's yacht party," I said, switching the topic. "He tried showing me some footage from that night." The expression on my brother's face let me know he was guilty of cheating. I placed my face in my hand, attempting to ease my anger.

Even though the indiscretion happened during their engagement, I wanted to march into the house and tell Miya so she would divorce him. The other part knew my mother would blow a gasket if I destroyed Tre's marriage without helping him.

I knew I had to allow his marriage to run its course and do whatever I could to support my brother. If he lost Miya, it would result from his wayward activities. I needed Miya to choose me because she loves me, not because Tre was a philanderer or because I was a football player. For once, I wanted to be the chosen one.

A huge part of me wondered how Miya could have fallen for Tre and me. We are polar opposites. Did she see his flaws and kiss them away? Then I recalled my pastor's sermon on the "Audition Chair." He said, 'Most people are too busy pretending to be something they are not while courting. Because they are auditioning for the perfect mate, they will pretend to be everything you said you desired in a partner. They don't show their true colors until after they say I do or get tired of pretending because being fake takes tons of energy.'

Tre hasn't shown her his authentic self. I rationalized with myself.

"Did he say he had a good time?" Tre questioned, invading my thoughts?

I took another sip of beer and continued my story. "As I handed the rookie his phone, you flashed across the screen. You are back to your old ways." I peered deep into his eyes, waiting for him to break.

"I only slept with one person that night. I was only fifty percent naughty," he admitted as if that justified his cheating.

"I hope you wore a condom when you cheated."

Instead of answering my question, he paused, then spouted. "Miya insisted I go to those parties. Things may have gotten a bit out of hand."

I raised a skeptical brow.

"I'm behaving, Superintendent. Yes, I wore a condom. I am wearing one with Miya as well."

"I can't imagine Miya forcing you to be at a wild party with alcohol, strippers, and drugs if she knows of your obsession with sex," I retorted. "You told me she is aware of your addiction, and you guys went to therapy before you were married. Why are you wearing a condom with your wife if you are not cheating?"

He sighed, pretending to be hurt by my assertiveness. "Mom told me to wait on telling her."

His stutter confirmed he was lying. I slammed my hand on the bar. "Our mother would never tell you to deceive or lie to a woman. Bullshit!"

"Calm down, Malik. Tasha gave me advice."

"Since we were kids, you have never called Tasha mom. I suggest you tell your wife the truth. If you are still cheating, fucking stop! Your check-up was negative for all diseases before you were married. Keep it that way for your wife's sake."

"I will! My wife and I don't fuck unless I am wrapped up! I will never fuck her without one because I know how to care for my wife. She is my wife. Mine. Mine. Not yours!"

I stood to my feet, challenging his tone.

Tre sat his beer on the bar before tilting in my direction. "Why should I tell my wife about women who don't mean shit to me? I'm sure she knows I was not at those parties all night, twiddling my damn thumbs. If or when she asks about other women, I will tell her the truth, big bro."

I slapped his hand away when he patted my shoulder. He jumped back as I stepped around the barstool.

"Hey guys, the food is getting cold," Miya shrieked from the sliding door.

"Fuck! Then warm the shit up. Do I have to tell yo' silly ass how to do every damn thing?"

Hearing Tre belittling the woman I love in a disrespectful tone provoked something dark inside me. I snapped, grabbing him by his collar, pulling him so close that our noses touched. "Motherfucker, never let me hear you talk to her like that again. You're mad at me for calling you out on your bullshit, not her." I released him with a rough shove. His body collided with the built-in BBQ grill.

I waited for him to say something. Instead, he tucked his tail and walked towards the house. He paused steps from the glass sliding door. "I'm calling mom and telling her how you hurt my back, Malik."

Pacing laps around the bean-shaped pool calmed the monster brewing in me. When I turned around to go in, I bumped into Miya.

"Tre asked me to give you a hug and bring you in."

Her angelic smile deflated the beast. I tried not to smile, but I loved her to death.

"You know my body is not ready to be that close to you, love."

She blushed at my truth.

"He wanted you to calm me down. Well, your smile has accomplished that goal. You lead; I will follow."

I walked behind Miya and knew I was sinning because my eyes stayed plastered on her hips and backside. Man, I was hungry, but not for food!

The night was going well. Tre's demeanor towards Miya had tempered. He loved her the way my father would have adored my mother. My heart ached because I was not the one making her smile or cuddling with her every night.

Tre whispered something in Miya's ear. She shook her head, no, then whispered in his ear.

Tre's eyes tightened before he exclaimed, "He isn't married yet!"

"So, is it okay to be with other women until you say I do? Does being engaged mean nothing to men?"

Tre looked at Miya in disbelief. I cleared my throat to remind them I was at the table, and whispering was rude. He whispered in her ear again. She shoved him away with her shoulder.

When He leaned in to whisper again, Miya looked at him and shouted, "Hell no! I do not think Malik and Tamia would make a good couple."

Frantically, I nodded my head in agreement.

"Why?" Tre barked, gazing at me.

He kissed Miya on the cheek and softly said, "Tamia is cool; she is my best friend. I think she and my brother would hit it off marvelously. His wifey assistant would not mind."

Miya grunted at Tre. I wished he would stop calling Raven my wifey assistant. It was bad enough that she insisted on calling me Bossman.

"I guess we will see tomorrow," Tre responded.

"Tre, I thought we would hang out with mom and dad in San Francisco this weekend?" I interject, attempting to ease the tension in the room.

The only woman I wanted was Miya. The thought of me and her friend would never happen. When she jerked me by the hand at the wedding, her behavior confirmed she was not my type.

"We have to get an early start since you insisted on not flying," I reminded my little brother.

Miya rolled her eyes at me.

I elevated my right brow at her, and she whisked her head away. I must admit I enjoyed the jealousy on her face.

"Tre, I thought this was our weekend? Did you forget the Mint Condition concert at the Yoshi? You promised to take me this weekend."

Tre looked at me, smiling brightly. "Do you care to explain?" I insisted, grimacing. "You told me, your wife, and our parents three versions of this weekend's events. I only care about our parents. You told them you booked a concert and dinner for them and their boys. Did you do that, or should I?"

"I did not lie to anyone. We are doing it all," Tre announced.

"Fuck," I grunted. The last thing I needed was to be stuck in a car inhaling Miya's sweet summer aroma for a six-hour drive. I peered down at my lap, hoping my strength would hibernate the entire ride.

"Ring the Alarm"
Beyoncé
Miya

KNOTS FORMED IN MY BELLY WHEN Tre insisted Malik spend the night—petrified that he might hear me moan in my sleep or call out his brother's name. Tossing and turning all night, I woke up each time my dreams drifted to Malik. I wanted to give myself climatic relief, but it terrified me that Tre might wake up and show his ass.

I yawned as the tantalizing aroma of flapjacks, bacon, grits, and scrambled eggs forced me out of bed in the morning, preparing for the day with what felt like thirty minutes of sleep.

I freshened up and eased into the kitchen.

"We cooked," Tre sang.

I bet Malik did all the cooking. He just gave out instructions.

I didn't say a word as they packed my platinum Infiniti QX56 after breakfast. I thought we were taking the BMW coupe. Embarrassed by my behavior yesterday and my thoughts about Malik last night, I tried my best not to speak or be in the same vicinity as Tre and Malik.

Tre kissed me on the lips as he held the door open for me to get into the SUV. Once Malik got in, Tre still didn't pull out of the driveway. Malik hit the back of the seat twice, yet Tre did not move. Wanting this ride to be stress-free, I refused to say a word.

"Tre, are you waiting for something?" Malik queried, mirroring my thoughts.

Tre was about to speak when Tamia's car pulled into my driveway.

"Hey, you guys," she greeted us, strolling to the car with an overnight bag in her hand.

"Surprise," Tre hollered. "All of us are driving to San Francisco together. Then, we will hook up with my parents for dinner and the concert tomorrow."

I was livid inside with firm composure. I smiled.

If Malik is half the man I think he is, Tamia is not his type. She was my girl, but she could never replace me.

The ride to San Francisco was going to be long and stressful. I knew I couldn't stomach seeing Tamia hang all over my man.

A speck of cheer hit me. Tamia is known for sleeping with married men or deacons. The last time I checked, Malik had a fiancée, but that wouldn't stop her. However, a rule we BAEs have in place asserted that once one of us smashed a man, he was off-limits forever. That was girl code. I raised a skeptical brow at my thoughts. The problem was that Tamia didn't know I had climbed that rocky mountain, and his hook belonged to me.

I slammed my head against the headrest. Tamia's behavior was driving me crazy. She was overly laughing, smiling, and touching on Malik's dreadlocks, overdoing it as always in the backseat.

"Girl, stop acting like yo' ass ain't never seen dreadlocks before."

"Leave them alone," Tre demanded.

Tamia timidly rubbed Malik's chest or legs every chance she could. That bitch didn't talk with her hands; Imani did. Tamia was behaving like a desperate woman. She was in the backseat seducing the man of my dreams, literally.

I was ready to leap in the backseat and beat her ass. I went to sleep to avoid awkward conversation and control the anger simmering in my gut.

"Are you going to sleep?" Tre asked.

"Yes," I snapped.

"Hey, wake up, sleepyhead. Do you want to stop and get something to eat," Malik questioned?

"No, we just ate breakfast. By the time we make it to San Francisco, it will be one or two o'clock. I'll be hungry. I can wait," I replied.

I turned to look out of the window. "Why is it dark outside?"

"We stopped to get food and play some games since you were sleeping. We left you in the car. We are a little behind schedule, but we will see the show tomorrow," Malik promised, smiling at me, revealing his flawless pearly whites.

"Where is Tre? Wait a minute! You mean to tell me you guys left me in the car by myself while you all were eating and playing games," I inquired in a state of confusion.

"He's asleep in the back seat, wrapped in Tamia's arms. I gave them sleeping pills. I needed some alone time with you," he retorted as though this was all normal.

"Are you okay with being alone with me? We need to talk about your sweet nectar and when I'm going to taste it again."

I swallowed hard. Was this man going crazy or what? "We are not alone. Your foster brother and my girl are in the back seat sleeping."

I inched towards the car door as far as I could go. The last thing I needed was for Tre to wake up and accuse me of seducing his brother or popping me upside the head. "He and Tamia are not waking up soon. Watch this."

I glanced back at Tre and Tamia, startled when Malik screeched at the top of his lungs, bellowing Tre's name. Malik was coming off a little unstable, bewildered by the entire situation. I sat there silently.

"Are you okay being alone with me?"

"I'm fine," I stammered nervously. "Why don't we address the big pink elephant sitting in the car? Did you tell Tre about Los Angeles?"

"Yes! I told him I had reconnected with my Vegas lover. She ghosted me before I woke for the second time. I also told him that I would make her mine if I saw her again," he confessed with a devilish grin.

I blushed. "I'm sorry. I never meant to hurt your feelings. I don't know the protocol of a second one-night stand," I sincerely replied, "I even prayed that God let us meet again. I did not think it would have been under these circumstances."

He smirked. "Yeah, God has a funny sense of humor. I asked God for the same thing. I imagined you being single, us getting married, and sipping on your fountain of youth every night."

I moaned in pleasure, thinking about him making love to me every day. The idea of waking up with his head between my thighs made me moist. I gazed in the back seat to see if Tre and Malik were setting me up.

I nervously shuffled through songs. The silence in the car was annoying me. "May I pick the song?" Malik asked.

"Sure."

"Can you plug my phone into the charger," he asked, "then select my Miya playlist?"

I glanced at the phone resting in his lap. I slowly reached for his phone. Feeling his bulging manhood, I blushed.

"I have some lyrics that have been waiting to caress your frame."

Goosebumps hopscotched across my skin when he glided his fingertips up my left thigh.

"I Can't Help It"
Michael Jackson
Miya

NURSING MY BOTTOM LIP LIKE A pacifier, I blinked with feigned innocence when Malik smiled. My chest heaved. The first song on his playlist was Keri Hilson's "Turnin' Me On."

Malik's sexual energy engulfed me. If I were not married and my husband was not in the back, I would have demanded he pull over to feel his life immerse my womb. I would have his ass screaming like Lil Wayne. However, he would howl, Ms. Tasty Nectar babbbby.

"Get it together. You control your cookie. Your yoni does not control you," I mumbled to myself.

I slammed my head against the headrest, closing my eyes, doing the breathing technique Malik taught me in Vegas.

"Oh, Lawd," I moaned, gawking at my lap. Malik had his hand under my sundress, rubbing the thin fabric on my panties.

I could not believe how my rosebud instantly reacted to his sensual touch. My yoni repeatedly jolted before drowning herself.

"I want you right now," Malik admitted.

I bit my bottom lip, shifting in my seat to recheck the backseat. Tre was snoring, and Tamia was drooling on his chest.

Malik moved his hand back to my thigh and massaged it. I opened my legs wider, arching my back and plunging my head backward. He pulled my panties to the side.

"Shit, she's already soaking wet," he grunted.

I moaned and groaned in sweet agony. He polished my rosebud twice with his middle finger. I know I should have told him to stop! Instead, I opened my legs wider.

Turning my head towards him, I tried to ask him to stop, yet I could not say those words. He pulled his fingers out of my nectar and slid them into my mouth. I suckled on his fingers until he started shifting in his seat.

"Suck 'em, baby."

He pulled off the road before getting out and strolling to my side. He opened my door, swinging my legs out of the vehicle. I glanced in the back seat to find Tre and Tamia still asleep.

Malik fell to his knees and ripped my panties off, burying his head between my legs. I fought his shoulders, but the sweet torment building between my legs was more substantial than my will to stop him.

Leaning back, I threw my legs on his shoulders. He dipped two fingers in my sopping wet pussy, gently sucking and nibbling on my rosebud. "Ah," I moan as the pleasure built.

"Do you want me to stop?"

"No," I hissed, half out of breath. I was excited! I was unsure if it was Malik's skills or the thrill of Tre and Tamia catching us that ignited my body with hunger.

"Ooooh shit, Malik," I hooted as my juices flowed across his fingers and tongue. He backed away from me. "No! Stop playing! I was about to explode again."

My entire body was pulsating. Once my breathing subsided, Malik blew cool breezes across my clitoris. I frantically wiggled, trying to make him taste my sweet nectar again.

"I need your strength to satisfy me," I bellowed.

"Stop getting furious. You will explode in ecstasy tonight," he promised.

Pulling me out of the car, he cradled me in his arms. I glanced toward Tre and Tamia once more to confirm they were asleep. "I gave them sleeping pills," Malik whispered in my ear. He turned my face to his and planted a peck on my lips. "They are not going to wake up," he guaranteed.

He placed me back in the car.

I pulled him close to me and freed his penis. "Mmhmm. It still tastes like sweet chocolate." I licked, slurped, gulped, and devoured every inch of his chocolaty treat.

Reaching for my purse sitting on the floor, I paused briefly, sliding Malik's dick out of my mouth, popping a few Altoids, then deepthroated his shaft.

"Oh shit! Is this how you are going to do me? Are you trying to make me lose my mind and kill Tre so I can have you all to myself?"

Incentivized to be his, I sucked his penis harder.

"Yes… yes. I am falling in love with you, Miya," he declared through moans.

I worked the hell out of his penis, triggering him to yell at the top of his lungs. He pulled away from me.

"No, no, no," he chanted, "I am not ready for this to end."

His damn games were always killing my vibes.

He lifted me out of the car. I wrapped my legs around his waist, then slid down his rock-hard pole, bouncing up and down as if my life depended on it. Sucking on my tongue, he carried me to the car's hood.

"Nibble on my breasts," I instructed, guiding him to my pleasure points.

He lifted my dress over my head, devouring my breasts before kissing me on my belly. My heartbeat hiccuped when he eased towards my sweet spot.

"I cannot stop tasting her; she is so damn delicious," he muttered, licking and sucking me into a deeper state of euphoric delight.

A scream of euphoria cultivated in me. Poking out my bottom lip, tugging Malik's dreadlocks, I demanded, "Make love to me."

He laid me on the hood of the car. The chilly night breeze and the warmth from the engine ignited a sexual rage in my core as he plunged deeper into my pulsating honeypot.

I gazed at the moon until my eyes were ogling at my optic nerves. I hollered like a lovestruck she-wolf. His ego explored parts of my yoni Tre could never reach.

"Baby, I'm about to explode."

"Me too! Me too," I howled with him as a bright light flashed in my face, interrupting my orgasm.

***

"Miya, wake up. Miya," I heard a deep baritone voice say .

Slowly, I opened my eyes to find Malik glaring at me from the driver's seat. Looking in the back seat, I noticed Tre and Tamia were missing.

"What did you do with Tre and Tamia?" I queried, my voice barely above a whisper. "Please say you didn't kill them."

Amused by my question, he chuckled. "They went into the restaurant to get a table. Are you okay? Do you want some food?"

I rubbed my eyes, trying to focus. I glanced around, struggling to identify my surroundings.

"Tre wanted to leave you in the car and let you sleep, but I didn't think it was safe," he finally concedes.

Puzzled, I mumble incoherently. "I thought you gave them sleeping pills. They were not supposed to wake up."

A confused and distressed look replaced his warm, inviting smile.

Attempting to block the sun beating against my brow, I guarded my face with my hands. "Did we see the show already?"

"Are you okay, Miya?" Malik asked again. "You need to get out and eat."

We walked into the restaurant. I spotted Tre and Tamia at a table laughing.

"Mimi, didn't you get enough sleep last night?" Tre questioned. "You slept for three hours straight. Tamia was starving, so we stopped."

Before I could respond, Tamia jumped out of her seat and pulled me off to the restroom, trying to gossip about Malik.

I slammed the bathroom stall in her face and checked to see if I was wearing panties. I recalled Malik ripping them off. Yet here they were soaking wet, clinging to my flesh.

I stumbled out of the stall and splashed some water on my face. "Miya, I like Malik. I can tell he wants me," Tamia babbled with glee. "I could be the next BAE to win the bet."

I scoffed in exasperation. Malik would never marry her.

I gazed at Tamia with empty eyes. "Tamia, think twice before you get married. This shit is hard. Men do not show their true colors until they say, 'I do.' He already has a fiancée."

"Fuck that bitch. He's single until he walks down the aisle."

Tamia slid into the booth until she was sitting damn near on Maliks' lap. She played with one of his golden dreadlocks. "How many times a day do you exercise," she asked, rubbing his stomach.

"Baby, did you sleep well," Tre asked.

I rolled my eyes before staring blankly at Tre. He wrinkled the ridge of his nose at me.

"I slept fine. I'm glad you and my girl left me in the car alone," I snapped. "Damn, with friends like you two, who needs enemies."

"Miya, what the fuck is wrong with you?" Tre probed with attitude. "I think the sun and lack of food got you delusional."

Malik cleared his throat.

"I am mad because my husband left me in a hot ass car by myself, baking in the blistering sun, and my BAE unwisely agreed. If it weren't for Malik, I would still be outside while you enjoyed the air-conditioned restaurant."

I shoved the condiments on the table towards Tre's lap.

"Now, do you have any more stupid ass questions?" An eerie silence smothered the table as Tamia and Malik gawked at their menus. Tre gaped at me in disbelief.

Tre gazed at Malik before speaking, "You are right, baby. I should have never left you in the car."

Tears rolled down my face. Tre attempted to comfort me by patting me on the back. "I am not a baby that requires burping," I emphasized, shifting out of his reach. The more I realized the lovemaking between Malik and me was a damn dream, the harder I sobbed.

"We are all sorry," Malik replied.

I wanted to snap at him as I had done Tre and Tamia, but his smile halted my tongue.

I sat at the table, mean-mugging Tamia as she continued to touch Malik's firm chest, bulging biceps, and muscular thighs.

Dream or no dream! Married or not! There is no way I am about to let her be with the man I love.

Fuck! I'm not crushing on Malik. Shit, my heart screamed. *I'm madly in love with him!*

"Fuck me," I squealed.

Everyone at the table laid their baffled eyes upon me.

"Breakin' My Heart (Pretty Brown Eyes)"
Mint Condition

Malik

STEPPING OFF THE ELEVATOR, I WONDERED what the hell Tre was thinking. There was no way I would share a room with Tamia, even if we had separate queen beds. I would never place myself in a situation that would hurt Miya by sleeping in the same space with one of her best friends. Miya can pretend I mean nothing to her if she wants to, but I saw jealousy in those cocoa eyes each time Tamia touched me or played with my locs.

I rounded the corner, spotting Tamia and Tre laughing at the bar. Scanning the room for Miya to find she was nowhere in sight. An uncanny feeling twisted in my belly as I observed their interactions. I sneered as Tamia ran her hand across Tre's head as he kneaded her thigh.

I walked towards Tre, and Tamia quickly withdrew her hand. Placing my hand on his shoulder blade, I squeezed hard until he squealed in pain.

One heavy brow slanted in solid disapproval, I asked, "Where is your wife?"

He hunched his shoulders. I smacked them back down, and then I spun his chair around. Tre picked up his glass and took a sip.

Please buck, lil bro. Please.

I scoffed because I knew he was putting on a show for Tamia. I shot him a disgusted glance. Tre knew I didn't play regarding any woman's wellbeing. My feelings towards Miya intensified my stance.

I cleared my throat. My patience was growing thin.

I was about to place my hands on Tre when he bellowed. "She's upstairs. She doesn't feel good. I told Mimi to lie her ass down until she felt better. Shit, Tamia is hungry. What am I supposed to do? Starve Tamia and me. Hell no! We are going to get a bite to eat. Miya will still be sick when we return."

I ran my hand over my face. Was my baby brother serious? Did he not learn anything from our father? He showed both of us how to love our wives the right way. I placed both hands on the top of my head and bit my bottom lip until the skin broke.

"What, Mr. Perfect? Did I fuck up again?" he asked, sarcastically throwing his hands in the air.

Before I knew it, I smacked Tre upside his head. I was angry. He was married to the woman I loved and didn't know how to treat her. "What the fuck, Malik!"

He gawked at me; I slapped my open hands against my thighs, hoping he would buck.

Tamia snickered. He whipped his head in her direction, and she ceased instantly.

Tre shoved his room key in my chest. "If you are so worried about Mimi, go check on her. I told her to take something. Shit, I ain't no damn doctor. What the fuck do you want me to do?"

My nostrils flared. "You're no kind of husband either. Go get your wife some crackers and ginger ale!"

"Sounds like a plan. You got the key. Take your sister-in-law all that shit!"

Tre and Tamia chuckled.

My chest rose, punching me in the chin. Tre patted me on the arm, and I slapped his hand away.

"Maybe you can get her to join us. We're going downtown to Sotto Mare. Tamia and I will reserve a seat for four. See you soon." I watched as my brother and Tamia leisurely walked out of the hotel without a care in the world.

The elevator slowly climbed to our floor, giving me time to think. I had convinced myself that Miya needed to know how I felt about her on the way up. I was ready for my love to care only about our happiness and say fuck everything else.

Pulling out my phone, I created a Mint Condition playlist. I wanted the lyrics to convey my feelings about Miya since my mind could not conjure the appropriate words.

I knocked on Miya and Tre's door, but she didn't answer. Using the keycard, I granted myself entry.

The sound of her sobs filled the space the moment I stepped in. She was lying on her right side in the king-size bed, peering out the window.

I strolled over, sat at the bottom of the bed, and placed a warm hand on her leg. She slowly eased her knee up.

"Are you feeling ok?"

She gazed down at me and didn't speak. Her honey eyes were puffy and red. I wanted to wrap her in my arms until she laughed and hummed with happiness.

"Mint Condition is your favorite group, right?"

I retrieved a glass from the bar, dropping my phone inside. The glass amplified the lyrical notes of "Breakin' My Heart" by Mint Condition.

She curled tighter in a ball. Her head bobbed around the room as if she could see the lyrics prancing on the walls. Tugging at her clothes, she shoved me away, grabbed a fluffy white pillow behind her, and cradled it to her chest. My heart broke at the sight of her anguish. My presence was instigating her pain. I didn't want to hurt her, but my affection for her blinded my vision.

"You Don't Have to Hurt No More" bounced around the room, shot through my soul, and struck her in the heart.

"Please, Malik," she begged, "why are you hurting me?"

I squatted before her, gazing over the pillow until our eyes connected. "I never meant to hurt you."

"You keep hurting me. I lost you and the bet on the same night."

"What bet, baby?" I ask softly, assuring her that I would always be here for her and that she could reveal anything and everything.

She sat cross-legged in the bed, never removing the pillow from her chest.

"You made love to me in San Diego and Los Angeles when you knew you were proposing to your girlfriend. I saw the ring box in LA. Then you brought the same girl to my wedding. Now here you are, flirting with Tamia. Where is your fiancée?"

I reached my hand out to her, and she inched back. I did not care. I stood on my knees and reached for her until I touched her knee, caressing it. Waves of electricity shot through my arm to my heart. Her love was the music that played in my heart. I thought that song had been abandoned.

"Cat has your tongue now?"

Rubbing my brow with my free hand, I contemplated if I should tell her the truth or merely ignore her questions.

"If life is a song, what's our ballad, Malik?" She tossed a pillow at me. "I know. "One Night Affair," that's it.

I skeptically blinked. "I didn't ask God if my last girlfriend was my wife, but I prayed, and I thought He confirmed you were my wife in San Diego, then you married my brother."

I raised my hand in the air cutting off her comment. "Since you selected the O'Jays, I'll do the same. My song would be "Forever Mine" At least, I thought that was our song.

"Fucking jackass!"

"Miya, please don't insult me."

"You have no idea what I've endured."

"Tell me."

"The truth is some women you fuck, and others you wife. We both know what category you placed me in."

"Enough. It's funny how you are trying to sound hurt and wounded. Pointing out what I did. What about what you did?"

She stifled a chuckle.

"You should have added, " Nothing Left to Say" to your playlist. What is left to say? Oh, I saw you at the wedding kissing her on the forehead. I know those sweet kisses you give out."

I scoffed in anger.

"Don't look at me with your brows twisted. You know those kisses make women weak at the damn knees. You ripped my heart out, playing and laughing with her in front of me. Did you have to bring her?"

I should have asked her whether she had to marry my brother. But I couldn't. Thinking those words wounded my pride, so saying them may destroy my faith in love.

I eased off the floor and sat next to her on the bed. Pushing my wounded pride aside, I leveled a compassionate stare and tried to speak with an assured tone. "Miya, Raven is my assistant and play sister. I kissed her on the top of her head, not the forehead. And the ring…."

She held her hand in my face. "You buy all of your wifey assistant's engagement rings? Tre told me all about your wifey assistant."

A shaky chuckle escaped my lips, and her brow twitched.

"Evidently, they have graduated from the title of sideline ho." She sighed.

I touched her hand, and she drew it back. I ran my hand over my face in frustration. "Tre misinformed you...."

A belly rumbling grunt escaped her body as she slammed her face into the pillow. When she raised her head, her eyes appeared red and glowing. "Tre told me you were smashing her. You didn't deny it at dinner when Tre called her your wifey assistant, nor did you speak up about not wanting to smash Tamia before you get married. Everyone knows she is your fiancée. So please stop lying," she insisted.

"I would never lie to you, Miya."

"All men are liars, abusers, and dogs!"

She covered her face with both hands, bawling like a newborn baby. I eased closer to her and embraced her tightly. She laid her head on my heart. It skipped a beat. In this woman's presence, all reason and common sense eluded me.

I placed my finger under her chin and pulled her mouth towards mine. My strength grew as our tongues danced in each other's mouths. She pushed me away and leaped from the bed, heading for the door.

She pulled the door open and demanded I leave. I placed my index finger against the door and pushed it close.

"I wish you could swim through my heart. Even if dementia seized my mind, I might occasionally forget my name, but my heart will never forget your love and touch. You're the perfect hook over my favorite beat, and it's not just true love that I feel. It's earth-shattering unconditional galactic love. No affliction, person, or entity can ever change this fact."

Mint Condition's "If You Love Me" played right on cue. I sang the beginning of the song in her ear.

Her stiff body melted between the door and my powerful physique.

I kissed her on the neck, caressing her breasts. My breath slowed with deliberate exhales and inhales, waiting to see if she would stop me or resist. I eased my hand below her waist until my finger felt her moisture. My hand held her hostage as I gently stroked the spot I once called my beautiful rosebud.

I captured her pearl between my index and middle finger, rotating my hand. She moaned in pleasure, her body leaning against the door. I seized her earlobe with my lips, French kissing her ear canal.

"I am sorry, Miya. I did not mean to hurt you."

Tears rolled from my eyes and struck her shoulder blade, gliding over her collarbone. I imagined my tongue traveling in the same direction, but I would not stop until my mouth reached her sweet spot.

"End Of The Road"
Boyz II Men
Malik

MIYA ENTANGLED HER LEFT HAND IN my dreadlocks and purred. I pulled her body firmly against mine, taking a shallow breath, imploring my heart to slow its pace.

"When we first met in the club, beams of lights ripped through the room, but there was a spotlight illuminating you. I thought it was the club's theatrics, but your spirit drew my heart to yours. The first time you laid your head on my heart, I fell in love with you. My soul surrendered when those honey brown eyes kissed it."

She intertwined her right hand around my dreadlocks, pulling my head onto her shoulder. I traced her shoulder blade with the tip of my tongue.

"The second time we met in San Diego, I was ready to place a ring on your hand. I was going to ask you to marry me in Los Angeles, but you ghosted me yet again. I was going to tell you I was moving to San Diego to join the Chargers."

She tugged at my hair, turning her face to kiss me as her juices saturated my hand. Her lips tasted of confusion, desire, and passion, leaving a lingering question mark. Yet, her eyes blazed with a torch of love. My body shivered when she placed wet kisses on my neck.

I embraced what if as a myth. In her eyes, only possibilities resided within me.

"I... I am sorry, baby, this is all my fault. I sat in the lobby looking for you until I had to leave for the airport. If I had gone to Tre's proposal dinner, I would have interrupted his proposal and proclaimed my love for you. My pride wouldn't allow me to stop the wedding. I felt that if you loved me, you would have chosen me and never married my brother. I needed somebody to choose me for once," I rambled.

She yanked my hair, causing my neck to jerk. Bumping me back, she spun around and shoved me in the chest. I raised my hands in surrender, unsure of what I had done.

I slowly approached her.

She placed her extended arm between us. "What do you mean if I loved you, Malik? What do you mean?"

She ran her left hand over her hair. "Do you feel love surging between Tre and me?"

I didn't know how to answer. Therefore, I remained silent.

"My wedding and reception were awful. People said they felt love floating in the air. The love my guests felt permeating the atmosphere radiated from your parents' affection. Their love filled the room with a euphoric pheromone. It also confirmed I wanted that type of love in my life."

I wrapped my hands around her waist. "Let me provide, protect and nourish your mind, body, and soul as my father does for my mother."

She pulled away from me and leered angrily. "Now, you want to love me and marry me. I felt shunned at the wedding and reception."

"I was in a state of devastation!"

"All I needed was one look from you saying you loved me. Instead, you gawked at your fiancée the entire wedding. You gave her, your parents, and Tre all your attention at the reception. You left without saying goodbye or dancing with me."

Laughter erupted from her belly, causing her body to shudder. I could feel my skin warming up. "This is not a joke. Don't laugh our love off as if it means nothing!"

"You want to know what is funny? I wobbled my half-naked ass all in your face. You never reacted."

I slammed my hand against the door she flinched.

"You married Tre, not me. I already told you that Raven is my assistant! You're ranting about a kiss on the head and playful banter. Do you understand you married my brother!"

I pulled her into my arms. I was livid, but my love for her did not vanish after she said, 'I do' to Tre. I wish it had. I would do anything to make this woman happy.

"What did you expect me to do? Baby, I was dying as I watched you and Tre dance and kiss. My brother was happy. I could not take that from him. I had to leave before I embarrassed myself and my parents. I wanted to confess my love and beg you to get an annulment. Then I realized that you would have chosen me if you wanted me. So, I bowed out gracefully. I was confused, hurt, and angry."

She inched closer to me. Her sweet aroma filled my senses, and I continued baring my soul. "You were gyrating around in shorts that you should wear in our bedroom. Hurt because you chose Tre. Pissed at love, I wondered if I even knew you."

"I wondered the same!" she countered. "Seven degrees of separation, my ass. What are the odds? All the men in Vegas and I have a one-night stand with my boyfriend's foster brother."

Wiping my hands across my face, I focused on my tone. "You had a once in a lifetime experience. I know I did. Do you think I planned to sleep with you or fall in love? If you loved me, Miya, you would have never accepted Tre's ring."

"I wanted to win the bet," she bellowed in frustration.

"Fuck this bet, Miya. What about love? Our love?"

Shocked by my aggressiveness, she swiped at the tears trickling down her cheeks. Instantly, my demeanor softened.

"This marriage is a lie. You are lying to your heart, body, and soul. I have told my close friends and family about the woman who stole my heart away in Vegas and San Diego. Have you told anybody about me? If you had reached out to me at your wedding, I would have confessed my love for you on the spot. But you didn't. So please stop lying to yourself about loving Tre the way you love me. I hear ignorance is bliss, but come on, Miya!"

She took her index finger and pushed me upside the head. When I did not react, she punched me in the chest.

"Men are always lying. They never want to accept the blame for what they do!" She kicked the door with the back of her foot. "I wish my heart didn't love him." There it was, she finally admitted to loving Tre. I stepped back.

"I was ecstatic you were at training camp. July was a pleasant month. These weeks in August were even better because you were not in them."

I closed my eyes and swallowed hard because my bruised ego was caught in my throat. The temperature in the room shifted along with my mood. The days of women trampling over Malik Walker were over.

If she hits you below the belt, you return the favor.

"You're the one who lied to Tre about him being the first man you ever made love to, not me," I barked. The moment the words slipped from between my lips, I regretted saying them.

Her eyes bucked; she clutched her chest.

I stepped closer to her, and she slapped the shit out of me. I rubbed my cheek and bit down on my bottom lip.

I closed in for a kiss. She threw her head back, knocking it against the doorframe. Her body collided with the floor. She tucked her body into the corner of the door, covering her face with her hands as she rocked and wept.

God did not build my heart for this type of drama. My mind pleaded for me to walk away, yet my heart demanded we stay. I leaned forward to help her up.

"Go ahead. Hit me! I know you want to."

Did I miss the signs of a battered woman, I thought. *God? I'll kill him if he hit her.*

"Miya, has Tre ever hit you?" I was afraid of her response because I loved my brother, but I would beat him to an inch of his life if he struck a woman.

I tried to touch her, but she kept slapping my arm. I bit my bottom lip as her hits intensified. I could taste the salty crimson gliding over my tongue, yet I could not release my mouth from my deadly grasp. The thought of my brother hitting her drove me insane.

"I don't know what to do except stay away from you because my common sense is squandering. I crave you. I dream about you. My heart aches at the mere thought of not being able to touch you," I mumble through clenched teeth.

She rose from the floor and examined me.

"Anger consumed me at the thought of my brother touching you, kissing you, and making love to you. Right now, I want to inflict physical harm upon him because I feel like he has been hitting you."

She jammed her hands into her armpits, soothing herself with a hug.

Miya is rare like Pablo Picasso "Les Femmes d'Alger (Version O)" 1955. Why would a man destroy a priceless masterpiece?

I could feel myself drifting into a blind rage where understanding and wisdom did not exist! Ducking my head into her neck, I ran my right hand across her cheek. "I need you to be honest with me. Does Tre punch you? Did your father beat you? What man has hurt you? They will pray for death after I'm done."

Stepping back, she punched me and then bumped me hard. "Liar." Tears streamed from her eyes. I went to wipe them away, and she hit me again.

"I will never harm you, so please stop. There is nothing you can ever do to make me strike you." She punched, kicked, and slapped me until I stepped back.

"Give me a reason to hate you, Malik. Whack me, then call it a love tap! I know you want to! All men smack women when they don't get their way."

My chest rose to my chin, then plunged to my gut rapidly. I struggled to keep the tears from flowing. My heart could not register her rage.

"You don't love me! You lust after me! You would have never allowed Tre to marry me if you loved me."

"Miya, I could say the same thing to you."

Turning away from her, I went to retrieve my phone. This conversation was going nowhere fast. When I spun around, she was still standing at the door with her hands plastered to her hips.

Who was I kidding? God would never allow this conversation to work out in my favor. I was disobeying His word by touching and lusting after this married woman.

I leaned down and whispered in her ear," I am sorry for violating your space. By the way, this is love, not lust," I insisted, kissing her on the cheek. Another piece of my heart crumbled when she rubbed it off.

"Can I leave now?"

Smacking her lips, she asked, "Where are you going?"

I motioned for her to move.

"Please, Miya?" She sluggishly moved away from the door. "I am going to finish training camp. I need to focus on my career and not this drama. You are with the man you love, right?"

Her face went blank. I battled the tears that generated as I waited for her answer. She looked away, never responding.

"Enjoy your heartache. I will do my best to stay away from you." I stepped out of the door. She yanked me back by my wrist.

"What about the concert?"

I stood mystified. I revealed my heart, fears, and desires, and her last question was about some damn performance.

"We already had our concert. We cried and swayed to the beat. Shit, you even exploded in delight."

"How will I explain your absence to Tre?"

Seething, I snatched my wrist from her grip.

After today, I was leaving all this soft shit behind. I was convinced that shitty mates created terrible boyfriends and girlfriends. I wish I could be a dog because today taught me that women favored them over real men.

We silently gawked at each other until Lauryn Hill's lyrics "Lost Ones" danced down the hotel's corridor, slicing the silence between us. My heart waved a white flag.

I laid my eyes on hers long enough to convey my seriousness. "A good man has no chance in this world. All of you women prefer cheaters, drug dealers, abusers, and deadbeats. Since I am none of those things, it is time for me to admit my defeat."

"Go ahead and leave. Shit, I don't need you. Miya doesn't need anybody."

My body deflated as I implored it to keep walking.

"Fuck you, Malik! Fuck you!"

"Rain On Me"
Ashanti
Miya

ITTER BILE PRODUCED IN MY THROAT as I leered at our fake smiles on our wedding portrait. I picked up the picture slamming it against the nightstand. I watched the glass fragments scatter upon the fluffy beige carpet; temporary relief washed over me. I didn't have proof, but my gut was informing me Tre was cheating.

Last month he crept in at two in the morning using his cellphone light to illuminate his path—the harsh light alerted me to his presence. Anger swept over his face when he noticed me sitting in the chair. "Why are you reading a bible in the fucking dark?"

He punched me in my thighs, demanding an answer. Mentally drained, all I could do was cry. When I glanced at the clock on the wall, I realized I had been sitting there for seven hours.

In San Francisco, I should have begged Malik to assist me with divorcing Tre so we could spend the rest of our lives together. I should have told him that Tre abuses me. However, my pride would not allow me to admit I rushed into a union with a man I barely knew to win a silly bet and pacify Malik's betrayal.

Despite everything Tre has taken me through, I was still trying to make my marriage work, but how can you fix a relationship yourself? Tre and I are like two ships passing in the night. I only received my husband's attention when he was horny. I stopped creating games and outings to bring us closer or spark love.

I had not seen the BAEs in a while and missed Naja's birthday celebration. The small distance between my girls and me has grown into a gap. I could not face them or questions concerning my marriage. I could let them see my crown hanging on by a couple strings of hair because it had surpassed tilting.

I am ashamed to admit I married a man who handles me roughly when he does not get his way. I went from reading books on love, marriage, and sex, to ones about verbal and emotional abuse.

Snuggling in my six hundred thread count sheets and goose comforter, tears of frustration, shame, and pain rolled from my eyes, soaking my bedding.

"Why, Tre?" I screamed, pulling the duvet back over my head. I was just not ready to face the day.

I silently wished it were still yesterday, and he came home. He was making a fool out of me in these damn streets. After today, my life will never be the same. And I felt it in my heart.

I rolled around the bed, searching for my cell phone. I called again. "You have reached Tre; you know what to do at the sound of the beep," his voicemail sang.

Again, his phone went straight to his voicemail.

I yelled at the phone. "Yeah, I realize what I must do! I'm going to leave your cheating butt!"

I called him back every thirty minutes, each time hearing his voicemail. I wanted to stop, but each call broke another piece of my heart, and I needed my soul to eviscerate his existence.

"You have reached the maximum time allowed to leave a message," the pre-recorded voicemail bitch announced.

At this point, I did not understand whom I hated more; Tre or this automated Karen. "Fuck you, and your maximum time allowed bitch!" I cried out, sobbing into the phone.

Anger and rage swept through my body, and my phone flew across the room. I watched in disbelief as my new phone hit the wall, disintegrating on impact, just like my marriage.

I finally dragged myself out of bed to use the restroom. The clock on the bathroom wall said it was ten o'clock in the morning. I stepped into the shower; the reverberation of water pounding on my flesh camouflaged my screams, concealing my tears.

My heart hurt for the love I lost with Malik by marrying Tre. I cared deeply for Tre, but I was in love with his brother. I had genuinely attempted to turn a pile of shit into lemonade by doing everything my mother taught me. I spoiled him rotten. I cooked, cleaned, worked, obeyed, and sexed him on demand.

After my shower, I moped around the house going from room to room, peeping through the doors. By the time I arrived at the kitchen, reality had introduced itself to my mind.

After we were married, I told him never to creep into our house or allow the morning sun to kiss the nape of his neck. I recalled him promising that would never happen.

"Yeah, right? You're a lying motherfucker, Tre." I picked up the house phone to call him.

"Hello," a masculine voice said.

"Who the hell is this?" I rudely hissed.

"Well, um…um…this is Malik. I'm sorry. You shocked me when you answered the phone before it rang."

"I was about to make a call, and you were on my line," I stammered, trying to disguise the hurt and pain in my voice.

"Sorry. I was checking in on Tre." I raised a suspicious brow. I was surprised he called the house phone. Malik always called Tre's phone.

"He left already," I fabricated. Why was I lying to Malik?

"Miya," he shouted, "I am a man of my word. I don't want to invade your space, but I need to know if you are okay?"

I knew he cared deeply for me. I sighed heavily into the phone. The last thing I wanted to do was cry to Malik regarding Tre.

"King, trust me, I'm fine."

I tried to correct my salutation. However, Malik was my baby, my king, and my lover.

"Oh, she called me her king," he taunts. I forced myself to giggle. "Did he hurt you?"

I shook my head from side to side as though he could see me.

"I will never allow my brother to mistreat you. You are a queen and deserve to be treated as one," he insisted.

Tears escaped my eyes, followed by a sniffle. In my heart, I knew Malik should be my husband, not Tre. "We pay for our mistakes."

I scoffed.

Who was I fooling? This entire messy situation was my doing because I ghosted Malik, never allowing him to explain the ring, then I married his brother to win a bet that Naja had already won.

I could hear Deniece Williams's "Silly" playing in my head.

I pushed back the truth, fearing what Malik would do to his foster brother. "No, he did nothing," I fibbed again. "I'm feeling a little under the weather." Partly true because I was burning up with a fever and could barely breathe. "Can we talk later, King?"

"Sure," he responded. "If you need anything, please call Raven. I'm on the road."

The line went silent; my bottom lip eased outward because he didn't say goodbye before disconnecting the call.

As I pulled the phone from my ear, I heard a deep baritone voice say, "I texted Raven. She'll be there shortly with soup, medicine, and tons of Gatorade."

I protested, but I knew he would insist on taking care of me.

"Okay. Thank you. My heart will always belong to you, my king," I blurted, disconnecting the call before he could respond.

I slid down the wall, curled in the fetal position, and cried like a newborn baby straight out of a mother's womb, distraught by the anxiety of childbirth.

I wished Malik were here to hold me tight. I needed to lay my ear on his chest until my heart mimicked his rhythmic beat.

Tre walked through the door around one forty-five as if he had done nothing wrong.

"Hey, baby, I'm just here to change my business attire. Malik and I are going to the gym. I fell asleep at his house last night," he fibbed.

I looked at him, and all I could see was red. I wish I could say it was the blood of Jesus.

"Raven is in the kitchen, preparing me some chicken noodle soup. Malik sent her to take care of me."

His eyes bucked when Raven emerged from the kitchen.

"Cry Together"
O'Jays
Miya

RE AND I SILENTLY STARED AT Raven. "Raven, what state is Malik in today?" A mischievous grin replaced her grimace.

"I'm not sure. Malik left two weeks ago. I can provide you the exact location; let me retrieve my laptop."

"No need, honey. I'm just grateful Malik called you, and you drove from San Diego to take care of me since the man I married was out of town with your boss, his foster brother."

"I told you about that foster shit," he barked.

Raven cleared her throat while typing on her phone.

I could see the gears turning in his head as he conjured another lie. I held my hand in the air as his mouth opened.

Raven helped me off the sofa after insisting I should be relaxing in bed.

I stepped dreadfully close to Tre's face. He leaned back as my hot breath escaped from my mouth and flowed up his nostrils. "How dare you stay out all night long? Then you walk in here, fibbing about where the hell you were and with whom," I barked. "You knew I was sick when you left."

I took a few steps back because the soapy stench from Tre's body made my stomach wrench.

"Are you alright?" he sputtered, trying to hold me up.

I slapped his hand away; as Raven attempted to latch onto my arm, my body crumbled to the floor. He pulled me up, wiping my forehead with a cold towel that Raven handed him. They both helped me navigate the stairs to the bedroom.

"You need to take better care of yourself and stop worrying over me so much. I am a grown-ass man. I will be alright."

Raven huffed at Tre's comment and rolled her eyes.

I inhaled deeply; the same odor smacked me in the face once again. My stomach churned from the disgusting stench that seeped from his pores. A haze of fog invaded my space.

"If you want my queasiness to stop, then go shower!" It was my turn to fan him away like an annoying gnat. "Your bitch's cheap soap and cigarette smoke are making my stomach queasy."

"Shit!" He screamed, removing glass fragments from his left foot, sitting on the bed. "Where did all this glass come from, Miya?" he asked, his lips curled, his brows raised. "Why were you here destroying shit? I told you I fell asleep at Tamia's house. I called. Seeing your smashed phone, I understand why I couldn't get through."

I said nothing for a couple of minutes, giving him an annoyed squint. "Liar! My smashed phone does not affect the service; you know the damn house number. I hate you so much."

"Bitch, watch your tone in my fucking house before I slap your ass well. Now lay down and take a nap. You are talking and acting crazy."

Glancing over at Raven, he spoke, "How long will you be here? Are you going to run and tell my brother I called my wife a bitch?"

"I will clean the glass up and get you another phone ordered," Raven announced, ignoring Tre's existence.

He smacked his lips like a girl.

"Can you go take a shower? You smell like stale cigarettes and rotten ass."

Raven turned up her nose as she stepped in Tre's face. "I'll leave when the Bossman or boss lady tells me to go." She stared Tre down until he blinked.

I rose off the bed, and the room started spinning. "Tre, get the fuck away from me. Your deceitful ass stinks," I whined. "Tell your bitch to upgrade her life and stop buying .99 cent store soap."

"Fine, I'm going to take a shower, and I will tell Malik–I mean, Tamia, to stop buying .99 cent store soap and lotion," he stuttered.

Raven cleaned the glass off the floor and then called my assistant Eva. They agreed to order me a new phone and oversee my work responsibilities. She went downstairs to call Malik, and I could hear her reading Tre like an informative book.

Raven walked back into the room with an apprehensive scowl. "I was going to leave, but Malik has requested I stay until you are well. I'm hoping Tre doesn't make me beat his ass."

"Raven, please don't tell him the truth." She held her hand in the air, and I stopped talking.

"Bossman is my number one priority. He cares for you, so you are my second priority. I would never tell him anything that would mess with his mindset. Bossman worrying about you can distract him from the game. One hesitation or misstep on the field could end his career. My job is to make sure no problems get past me to upset my brother."

Eyeing Raven, I could see she was a ray of sunshine. I admired how she protected Malik and that she viewed him as a big brother, not a lover. Consumed by ignorance and rage, I misinterpreted his sisterly love for her. Damn, I wish I could go back in time to San Francisco. I would tell him to love me better than his father loves his mother.

"I appreciate you. Thank you for taking care of Malik and me," I said wholeheartedly.

An hour later, Tre returned to our room with ginger tea. I was furious at him and wanted to whip his ass, but now my health was more important than he was.

Tre competed with Raven all day long, both spoiling me rotten. I hope Tre understood—I might forgive, but I will never forget.

He pulled me in his arms, and I mustered all my strength to look him in his eyes.

"Tre, we cannot go on like this. I've been slapped and dragged by my hair to our bed because you were horny with rage. All I see in our future is a divorce. I want a divorce."

"Mimi, Mimi, stop talking crazy. I've only slapped you a few times and yanked you by your hair once. Maybe twice. You made me hit you each time

I did. But I never hit you with my fist balled. You wasted time playing around when I told your ass to come to bed because I needed some pussy. I'm sorry, ok, and I promise I will do better."

"One time is too many."

"Hush, baby, go to sleep. I promise tomorrow will be better than today."

Tears streamed from my eyes. "I am sick of empty promises and being disrespected. I need this marriage to be over."

He gripped a handful of my hair, yanking my head towards his mouth, then kissed me viciously. "I will never grant you a divorce."

When I didn't respond or kiss him back, he dragged his sizable body across mine, and we cried.

We may cry together, but we will never make love again.

"(I Just Want It) To Be Over"

Keyshia Cole

Miya

TRUDGING TO THE FRONT DOOR, I wondered how a beautiful sunny day could feel gloomy and gray. The garage door did not work, and I could only envision another repair bill I would have to pay.

I hauled myself into the house, hitting the light switch, and nothing illumined. I called out for Tre, but I heard only the sounds of a grumpy home. I flew into the kitchen and tried those light switches. "Damn these rolling blackouts," I grumbled.

I used Tre's laptop lying on the dining room table. I turned my cellphone into a hotspot and opened his browser. Porn instantly appeared on the screen. He was always watching porn on his laptop. Twice, I caught him pleasuring himself. I questioned why he could please himself without me, but he had to be present if I masturbated. He would always reply, "Because I am a man, and this is what men do. I need you to stay in your pretty box and stop questioning the king of this castle." I started to inform him that the king needed to bring in more money than the queen if he desired to remain the ruler over this castle.

After navigating through every nasty popup worldwide, I finally made it to the Southern California Edison website. The screen instructed me to call the electric company's customer service number.

I hoped the system would acknowledge my phone number, although the account was in Tre's name. I'd usually use his phone during a blackout because the automated system would recognize his phone number and provide details concerning the outage and an estimated timeframe of reconnection. However, the system directed my call to customer service after I keyed in the account number. I scratched my head in confusion and waited for an operator to come onto the line.

"Can I ask whom I have the pleasure of speaking to?" The operator stated the second the music ended.

"Miya Young, the account is under Tre Young. He is my husband."

"How would you like to restore your service? I am showing your balance is $425 in addition to a reconnection fee of fifty dollars and a new security deposit of $500."

Anger swept over my body.

"Mastercard," I retorted, reciting the numbers of our joint debit card.

"I'm sorry, ma'am. Do you have another card? This one did not go through."

My heart dropped into my stilettos. This card should have cleared a charge of one thousand dollars with no problem. We have over eighteen thousand in this account.

I nervously giggled, "Financial planner, my ass."

"Excuse me, ma'am. What did you say?"

I huffed, embarrassment sinking into my soul. To be a suitable helpmate, I deposited five grand a month into our joint house account to cover all the house bills.

After spending the money out of my and Naja's old college account, I spoke to him about spending money without asking me beforehand. He promised it would never happen again, which was a miscommunication on his part. Now this shit! Damn, how forgiving is a woman supposed to be?

Finally, locating my bank card in my wallet, I replaced the Mastercard, pulling out my American Express card. The customer service rep advised me that my power would be back on Monday. Had I known this tidbit of information, I would have never paid her a thousand dollars to restore my electricity. I would have waited on Tre to turn the power back on.

I pleaded with the customer service rep. However, she had no one in my area. They closed at 4:30 pm, and it was four o'clock. I paid an additional $250 for an emergency weekend reconnection. The term hotter than fish grease rang true by the time I ended my call.

Pouring myself a glass of wine, I allowed the warm tears of disappointment to cascade freely down my cheeks.

I called Tre's cellphone. He did not answer. I called him again three more times, and his phone went straight to voicemail.

I swallowed my pride and called Tamia. She always knows my husband's whereabouts. Her phone rang until the automated recorder greeted me. I ended the call, calling her right back; this time, the call went straight to her voicemail.

I had sprung into worry mode. Maybe she and Tre were involved in a car accident or something.

Phoning Lexi, Paxton confirmed he spoke to my husband earlier, and Tre and Tamia were out buying accessories for his Halloween outfit. These days it seemed everyone knew of his whereabouts except me.

Once the worry dissipated, I was pissed again. Fighting the urge to tell Lexi I needed a place to get dressed and stay until tomorrow afternoon. I was not mentally ready to confess that I had married a damn loser. My pride would not allow those words to develop in my mouth.

I bounced my cell phone in my palm, contemplating calling Malik and Tre's mother. She was a charming lady. Every week his parents called the house looking for him, and it pained me to tell them he was not at home each time.

A week ago, Tre kicked me off the bed, and I flew into the dresser, busting my lip. When his mother called, I was ready to tell her they had raised a monster; instead, I requested to speak to Mr. Walker. I planned to ask him to talk to Tre concerning the definition of a good husband. Malik was incredible. Since the same man raised them, Tre had to have some awesomeness trapped in him. The second Mr. Walker greeted me, my throat went dry, and I could not get a word out.

Mr. Walker prayed for me, assuring me I could call or visit them anytime to talk.

Instead of waiting a week to call again, his parents called every day. I think they could tell I wanted to talk to them, and most days, I sat on the phone listening to his parent's views on marriage, wondering if they could tell I was crying. Every call ended in prayer; once I hung up, I read every scripture they quoted. I could see Malik's parent's core values instilled in him. He is such a gentle soul. I wonder what the hell happened to Tre.

My body deflated as I recalled not knowing his mother's number. A dim light lit over my head. Her name and number are on the house phone call log. I picked up the house phone, and the realization of no electricity hit me again.

I honestly did not know how much more of this marriage I could take.

I drive to work crying and back home crying. I became furious the more I thought about the last two months. I inhaled a huge gulp of air and checked our joint bank account. A bolt of sadness struck me.

The bank account was five hundred dollars overdrawn, and my old account with Naja only had $250 in it. I reckoned he left the bare minimum in the bank since he knew Naja would receive an email alert each time the account goes lower than the current amount.

My cheeks blazed hot from the anger brewing in me.

I needed to talk to the man that called himself a husband. I may not have known where he was now, but I knew where he would be tonight. Tre was supposed to meet me at Malik's house at 6:00 pm sharp. We were carpooling to Paxton's friend's Halloween party. I was not in the mood to party now, but I needed answers.

I had not seen Malik since San Francisco, and I was unsure if I was mentally prepared to see him or vice versa. I was afraid I would run into his secure arms and pour out my heart's pain. The other option was to confront Tre at the Halloween party. The BAEs would be there, and for a woman who considered herself to be black and educated, I was making dumb moves and was not ready for them to witness my downfall.

Searching for the paper Tre gave me a couple of weeks ago with Malik's address, I packed a small bag and grabbed my sexy officer outfit for the Halloween party.

I pulled onto the freeway, deciding God and I needed to discuss my marriage. My marriage has been freefalling since August. Once the MLB season ended in September, Tre started staying out until two in the morning. He'll swear he is with Paxton or Tamia.

Last week, Tre pulled into the driveway as I pulled out and headed to work. Lexi once mentioned Paxton had to be home at a specific time. I casually interrogated Lexi on Paxton's curfew. When I suggested implementing a similar rule in my house, Lexi admitted Paxton didn't technically have a curfew. It was an unspoken understanding. He knows to be home before 1:00 am. He can only stay out longer if they are together.

Before I could ask her if he ever violated the agreement, Lexi confessed he had come home late once. She went to my auntie's house and did not come home for days. According to Lexi, Paxton never again walked through their front door past 1:00 am. He even checks in when he is on the road for games. His coach has a curfew set during the season.

If I went to my mother's house for a couple of days to punish Tre, I genuinely do not think he would miss my presence since he is never home.

I have tried everything with Tre, even leading by example. When I went out with the BAEs, I'd call if I would be out later than midnight. To my surprise, I called home one night, and he was there. Then he had the nerve to be angry because I disturbed his game.

By the time I got back to the house, he was in a deep slumber. Tre could not grasp why I was angry. As I explained why I was upset, he looked unmoved. I inquired what he would have done if something happened to me, and I called him, and he was fast asleep. After an hour of arguing, he ended the debate by saying, "I hope you are smart enough to call 911 and not me. What the fuck can I do? I am at home in bed, asleep. I can only pray your dumb ass ain't stupid enough to waste critical time calling me and end up dead."

I cannot describe the hurt his words cast on my soul. In my heart, I knew Malik would swim a million miles to make sure I was safe.

Once the car's GPS directed me to exit the freeway, I snapped out of my trance. I spotted a Starbucks. I grabbed myself a sugary Frappuccino, hoping it would spark my energy. I pulled in front of Malik's house precisely at 6:00 pm. The sun was slowly beginning its descent. I surveyed the street, looking for Tre's car.

An unrestricted view from his front door to the backyard pool lay before me, and I looked through the glass door, attempting to see if Tre was in the house.

Gently knocking, I waited before I banged on the door.

Malik walked towards the glass door, shirtless, wearing a pair of swim shorts; my heart dropped as his dreads glided across his shoulders.

I could swear a beam of light illuminated his path while glorifying his smooth cocoa butter skin. The front of his dreadlocks rested in a man bun as the back draped around his shoulders. I swallowed hard. I wanted to rest my head on his hard pecs and wrap my arms around his powerfully built frame.

I apologized to God in advance because I knew I would seduce Malik tonight.

I needed him! No! I deserved to feel a surge of love emitting from his body and sail through my veins.

"Come Over"
Aaliyah
Malik

THE LIGHT FROM THE MOON GLIMMERED through my house, hugging every curve on her body. A pinch of hope leaped into my heart as she knocked on the front door. I silently prayed she was here to confess her love for me and show me divorce papers. My heart needed her to admit she had been missing me the way I had missed her.

The closer I drew to the door, I noticed her lovely face was etched with fret and disappointment. I swung the front door open and wished she would run into my arms as she did at the Four Seasons.

"Miya, are you okay?"

"Um…. Hmm. I'm good," she hummed. I could hear a hint of sorrow in her tone.

"Get in here, baby. I mean, Miya." The scent of her sweet perfume made my heart race.

Heavy D And The Boyz "Somebody for Me" blazed throughout the house, and she smiled. "I love hip-hop and rap, yet there is nothing that can touch the seventies, eighties, and nineties rhythm and blues," I revealed as my new playlist started playing.

Miya snapped her fingers and swayed to the beat.

"This is one of my favorite playlists. I can turn it off."

She placed her hand in front of me to halt my steps. "Let it play, Mr. DJ. I avidly love what my uncle and auntie call baby-making music. I love Luther, The O'Jays, Isley Brothers, Marvin Gay, and Earth, Wind, and Fire."

We chuckled. "Maybe we can play some of those songs later tonight."

We planted our feet and smiled at each other. Thoughts of our first encounter ran through my mind. I grinned so hard my cheeks ached.

She twirled the ends of her hair. "You know I love a slamming band."

I agreed with my body language.

Waving her Starbucks bag in my face, she asks. "Can I warm my low-fat blueberry pound cake?"

I led her to the kitchen. "Miya, pass me the bag." I waved my hand in her face. "Whatever you are thinking about must be deep. A penny for your thoughts?"

I took deep breaths to slow my pounding heart. Something about this woman turned my world upside down with her mere presence. Was the moon shining upon her or her glory beaming brightly to illuminate her path? She was a testament to God's love for me. Her smile made me feel like I could trounce Goliath. When we shared space, I felt solidarity.

Meeting Miya helped me understand what my parents meant about Sabrina not being my queen.

I sighed to be a better person for Miya. I needed her to see a strong black king deserving of her body, heart, and soul. Since I met her, my relationship with God has grown. I have learned to be a selfless servant and a navigator to lead my household one day. I pray she is the queen in my mansion. I understand that Tre is my brother, yet I cannot help how my heart feels.

Looking at her smile, I knew I could take on the role of provider and protector. I would change any behavior she did not favor, and my heart knew she would do the same. My first job would be to pour into her mentally, physically, emotionally, financially, sexually, and spiritually. My second job would be football.

Miya spun around the white and natural wood kitchen with gold accents. Her sweet floral aroma invaded my nostrils, and my strength reacted. The desires of my heart misled my penis.

I held onto the counter, overcome with emotions.

"I did not imagine your house would look this breathtaking. You would never imagine the back of the house was crafted of all glass from the front door. I bet in the daytime, the sunlight floods this entire space."

"The same way the moon is coasting a spotlight upon your beauty."

She blushed, switching the subject back to the house. "I am in love with this open concept. The bright white sitting room merges perfectly with the kitchen."

I hesitated to tell her Raven helped me design the house. The white furniture was from my old home in Atlanta. Raven refused to get rid of it and buy contemporary furniture. She repurposed most of my old stuff, except the bedroom furniture Sabrina and I had in the master suite.

"You look happy."

I was over the moon. The love of my life was standing in my kitchen, yet I was curious. "I am happy to see you. However, what brings you my way?"

"If you do not want me here, I can leave. Your foster brother asked me to meet him at 6:00 pm. We were supposed to go to Paxton's friend's Halloween Party in Temecula Hills."

I placed my hand on her arm, and electricity surged through my body. Backing away from her, I informed her of my plans. "I told Tre last week, and yesterday I was not going. I was getting ready to go for a swim when you knocked on the door."

She dropped her head and shuffled her feet.

Walking over to her, I lifted her chin with my index finger. "I hate it when you cast your gaze on the floor. How can you see where you are going if you are not looking forward?"

She shrugged, and my heart melted.

The power this woman had over my heart and soul drove me insane. I leaned in to kiss her and then pulled away instead, thinking how ruthless this world could be because the one I loved was married to another.

"Malik, do you think you can call Tre?" she asks, stumbling over her words.

I arched my eyebrow at her. Why would she need me to call my brother? I started to ask if her phone was dead because I had a ton of chargers. I began to speak, and she cut me off.

She swiped a tear from her eye. "Tre has not been answering my calls. When I got home today, our electricity was off, and...."

A lonely tear rolled down her rosy cheeks rendering her speechless.

I pulled her into my arms, and she batted those big nutmeg eyes at me. "Baby, you can tell me anything."

She buried her head in my chest and wept before speaking. "Some nights, my heart is in utter anguish. I lie in my bed and cry, wishing you were next to me. I miss you every day. Lately, it seems like a wish that will never come true."

I sought to make love to her until all her pain diminished and pure happiness remained. However, nothing could transpire between us until she divorced my brother. Looking deep into her eyes, I failed to find the right words.

"Last Friday was one of my heart and soul pillow soaking midnight cries. The more I cried, the more confused I became. Seeing you on the television and genuinely missing your touch crushed my soul. I cried for my failed marriage, and because I miss your heart and tender touch, I need you to love me on a greater level than your father's love for your mother. Am I a fool to imagine a love of this magnitude? Am I crazy for loving you while married to your foster brother?"

Tears streamed her face, and I wanted to bottle all her pain and cast it away. "Baby, I have been living in misery since San Francisco. I should have said yes to you."

I was ready to rebel against the Holy Spirit, which resides within me, until she said, "There is an internal battle raging within me too. My heart yearns for you, but my soul has me heeding to God's word."

Please resist the temptation and fight your desires. My heart yelled at my strength.

"How can you have a marriage if your mate is never present?"

"What does that mean, Miya?" I laced our fingers together. "Do you want me, or am I a consolation prize since you and Tre are having problems?"

Before she could answer, my cell phone rang. The LCD screen revealed it was Tre.

"What it do?" Tre asked the second I answered the call. Releasing her hands, I stepped into the backyard.

I listened to my brother go on and on about not wanting to face Miya because he had fucked up again and felt like a failure. I tried to tell him how he was behaving made him a loser. My brother was slowly slipping back into his old patterns. My heart ached for her.

"Tre, hurry and get here. Me, you, and your wife need to talk."

He tried to feed me some bullshit. I cut him short. Fuck! He had the woman I loved and did not appreciate her.

"Be a fucking man!" I yelled rudely. "Are you cheating on the best damn thing God has blessed you with?"

He disconnected the call and then texted me. Demanding, I let Miya stay at my house and stated he would come by tomorrow to fix things.

Before I could respond, he texted me again.

"What the hell? How do I tell Miya her husband needs to learn to breathe again?"

Closing my eyes, I mumbled to myself. My heart didn't want to lie to Miya.

I scoffed out of frustration and exhaustion.

"Think of a good lie," I muttered into the atmosphere. "You know your job has and always will be defending your baby brother at any cost, even if that means sacrificing your happiness."

"Shh"

Tevin Campbell

Miya

HIS BODY LANGUAGE SPOKE VOLUMES AS I observed him talking to Tre. I eased out of the house, attempting to hear their conversation; He turned around and ran directly into me, squinting his smoky gray eyes.

"Were you ear hustling?"

"Nope," I responded with a smirk. "You were talking loud enough for me to hear. What did your dishonest foster brother say?"

"He is running late. Maybe he is pitching a new business proposal to some people," he fibbed.

I smiled because Lexi had already told me he was out shopping earlier. He got off work way before me.

"You said you would never lie to me. Yet, you are fibbing." The look on his face revealed he was busted. "Don't let Tre compromise your soul or our bond."

His eyes bucked. "Besides, compromising your soul is my job." I giggled, running my hands over my body.

He swiftly looked away.

"Are you going to deny those smoky grays the pleasure of viewing all of this?"

I could see the tension developing in his body.

"I understand that Tre is your foster brother. You say it's your job to safeguard him, but he will have to stand tall for himself one day."

His face went blank.

"You cannot stand in his place on judgment day."

"God will tell you what you need to know when it is time for you to know it," he replied.

I frowned, then pulled one of his dreads. "Remarkably, you just admitted there is something I need to know."

He chuckled. "Stop, baby." I loved the way he always slipped and called me baby.

"Just a Friend" by Biz Markie came on. Malik turned up the volume on his phone. "What do you know about this?" he questioned, pointing towards the speaker under the outside pavilion. He surprised me when he started doing the New Jack Swing and the Burger Bounce.

"Is that all you got?" I teased, then pushed him out of the way and did the same movement, adding the Stanky Leg.

He waved his hands in front of me like a referee. "Flag on the play, Baby, keep it to the late eighties or early nineties with the dance moves. I'm talking about Roger Rabbit, Mary Bop, House Party Kick, Cabbage Patch, Fly Girls, Hammer Time, Running Man, Butterfly, then making that Tootsie Roll. You feelin' me?"

He transitioned into the chicken noodle soup. I hip-bumped him. "Now you are breaking your own rules. Keep it late eighties or early nineties," I taunted.

He chuckled. "I am. Check out the fancy footwork. I'm doing the smurf on my Kool Moe Dee ish."

I smiled. "Deal," I shouted, slapping his hand, breaking into the Roger Rabbit.

Father MC's "I'll Do 4 U" started playing. He started swinging his arms in the air and shuffling his feet back and forth. He was straight up on some Kid 'n Play type shit doing Tom and Jerry. I giggled. I cherished each shared moment, praying this wouldn't be the last.

"You know nothing about this," he declared, singing, and acting out the words the rapper was spitting. He rubbed my back before he kissed me. I blushed, then he kissed my thigh.

The song needed to end soon before I got into trouble. I could feel a tiny spark between my thighs, and I could not allow it to ignite, but then again, I had already repented.

"What's wrong? You're scared of a small peck?"

I squinted my eyes at him, then twisted my lips sideways. "No, I am not, Sir."

I closed my eyes and silently prayed. *"Lord, please help me resist the temptation steering for Malik's sake. Defying you will kill him. All I know is when I am around him my soul feels at home, and nothing or no one in the world matters except him, me, and our happiness."*

"Earth to Miya." I opened my eyes, and he blew me a kiss.

"What are you mumbling, baby? Are you exhausted?"

I giggled, then involuntarily licked my lips.

"The only thing exhausting are your dance moves."

He chuckled. My heart melted.

"God, I promise to repent later. Blame me, not him," I mouthed, gazing upward.

"Don't Let Go"
En Vogue
Miya

MAXI PRIEST'S "CLOSE TO YOU" BOOMED from the speakers. It was time to turn up the heat. I rolled my hips like a Jamaican dancehall queen. Malik nervously chuckled as his eyes locked onto my hips.

"What do you know about this?" I questioned.

Never removing his eyes from my midsection, he quipped, "Dang girl, I didn't know good girls could move their bodies like a snake."

Throwing my head back, I teased, "You don't know? I mean, you honestly don't know."

"No, what?"

"See, I met this fine brother with golden dreadlocks in Vegas, and he composed this swerve in my hips with every rhythmic thrust of his pelvis."

I whined my body to the floor, then brought it back up and let my booty bounce. The erotic sex kitten within me grooved to the beat. I wobbled, dipped, and twerked all in my lover's face.

Malik pretended he was smacking my derriere by playfully slapping the air near my ample bottom.

"What, you don't have any Jamaican moves of your own?"

I could see the lust he had for me smoldering in his eyes. He stuttered and pushed his dreadlocks off his broad shoulders. "I don't know this song."

I teased. "Liar. Liar."

"I will dance on the next song," he replied, gazing at me through lust-filled eyes.

"What about this one?" He stood there quietly, listening to "Black Cat" by Janet Jackson. We danced around the backyard, attempting to reenact Ms. Jackson's video.

I was out of breath and ready to sit when the sounds of Kris Kross's "Jump" filled the backyard. I gazed at him as he jumped to the beat, then started dancing.

"Are you trying to get crunk?"

"Girl, this is a mid-80s and early-90s concert right here," he reminded me while jumping around, waving his arms. "They were not getting crunk back then."

He continued to bounce around me, and I joined in. I refused to let him upstage me.

As the song ended, he walked to a small refrigerator by the BBQ grill to get bottled water. I was headed towards the earth-tone patio furniture to sit when the next song blasted through the speakers. "Oh, shit," I shouted.

He turned around rapidly. I sashayed over to Malik, bent over in front of him, showing him my phat backside as I did the freak.

"Baby Got Back" by Sir Mix-A-Lot provided my hips with the perfect tempo.

"You are my lyrical soulmate," I proclaimed.

He smacked me on my butt, then began freakin' on me. I could feel his penis growing. I knew I was entering dangerous territory, yet I didn't care. Nine times out of ten, I was probably sitting in his kitchen, imagining all of this in my head.

Malik stretched me across his patio sofa with my legs on his shoulders. Janet Jackson and I were moaning in sequence to "Funny How Times Flies (When You're Having Fun)" as he had me for dinner.

"Oh shit! That feels so good," I moaned.

I wanted this fantasy to last an eternity. Usually, I wake up right before I climax. Malik snaked his tongue in and out of my sugary canal.

"Dang, you are doing your thing tonight," I said, complimenting his abilities as I tugged on his hair.

"Oh, lawd," I screamed as his tongue journeyed deeper into my wetness. "You have never made me feel like this," I whimpered.

"Miya, I missed you." This man licked, slurped, and snacked on my love button like I was his last supper. He took off my shirt, planted kisses on my belly, and then devoured my breast in his warm mouth.

I screamed with delight. "Honey, not so loud," he warns.

His tongue slid in my mouth—sweet Belgian chocolate saturated my tastebuds.

"Can I taste you?" I whispered in his ear.

He nodded timidly.

"We should take this in the house," I instructed. "Tre could arrive and hear us."

"Little Secret"

Xscape

Miya

YELIDS CRESCENT IN A SQUINT, THE butterflies fluttering in my stomach ceased. I pulled him closer to my warm flesh.

"No. No. No, Miya."

My eyes bucked when he shoved my hands away.

"This is wrong. We can't do this. My body is on fire, but my heart is full of disgrace," Malik claimed, easing away from me. "There is a battle erupting in my soul. I cannot do this."

Clawing at his shorts, he gently shoved my hands away. "Malik, please play "Lose Control" by Silk." I tugged at his shorts again. "How are you going to deny me in my dream?"

"Miya, this is not a dream, and I cannot lose control. This situation is a nightmare. I am in love with my brother's wife. I am supposed to shield him from pain. My parents expect me to care for my brother and live righteously. It's the way things have always been in my home."

A ton of bricks hit me; my eyes widened, realizing this was not a dream.

"What about your happiness and mine?" I yelled at him as he walked to the refrigerator to get a beer. "You don't want me? Are you creeping with Tamia? Are you in love with your wifey assistant?"

His red eyes pierced my soul. "Honey, Raven is my assistant and play sister. You should know that by now."

I suspiciously nodded. Would Malik lie to me? I wondered.

"Look, If I did love another woman, my life would be simpler right now. You are the only woman I adore. You are the only woman I see, no matter who is present. As Prince said, 'If God one day struck me blind. Your beauty I'll still see.' Your crown is the only one I want to protect, queen."

He walked back to where I was seated but didn't sit next to me on the loveseat. A mahogany coffee table with a mid-century teak leather top separated us. I could tell it killed him to sit across from me instead of next to me.

Tears flowed without restraint as I listened to his words.

"I have replayed all of our conversations in my head. I understand how you and I arrived at this place. In San Diego, I had to take a last-minute physical to ensure I had a future to offer you. I left a note. Thinking back, I should have woken you before I left…."

"I didn't see a note."

"In Los Angeles, you thought your engagement ring was for some imaginary girlfriend. The ring box you saw in the hotel was a refurbished ring for Tre's Mimi."

Holding my hand in the air, I glanced at my ring. "Tre told me he bought this ring," I confessed.

"If I had known it was for you, my love, I would have proposed myself with a brand-new ring. I knew I had won the night we met in Vegas, but you ghosted me before I could tell you how your essence consumed me in the elevator. Never on God's green earth would I have allowed the woman I love to marry my brother or any other man," he confessed, casting his eyes downward.

"Remember, we always hold our heads high."

He slowly lifted his head, forcing a smile.

"I wish I would have opened the box. I almost returned to the hotel to beg you not to marry your girlfriend and marry me. My pride would not allow me to beg for a man. I thought I married someone who loved me more than you. Knowing I felt love oozing from your pores in San Diego. I wanted to love Tre wholeheartedly, but you had already claimed a chunk of it."

He looked away from me, turning his ankles in tiny slow motions. "Baby, we both missed our opportunity. Poor communication, egos, and pride have destroyed our chances."

My shoulders became laden with a heavy and hot burden as I listened.

"In San Francisco, you mentioned a bet. Tell me about it, Miya."

I pulled my core straight and cleared my throat as I struggled to find my voice. "In college, the BAEs and I betted on who would make it to the altar first. They all agreed I would be last. I wanted to prove them wrong and finally beat my cousin Lexi." I honestly admitted. "I wanted to defeat her. The funniest part is that Naja won. She secretly married her childhood boyfriend and trounced Lexi and me."

Malik cleared his throat. "Is Tre the one God has ordained for you or the one you picked based on this silly bet?"

I wanted to lie. I smiled. He knew me so well he'll detect the deceit in my tone.

"The bet," I mumbled. "I settled for one-third of a man."

"Did you want me, or were you looking for a bet filler?"

"Haven't you ever wanted to be first at something or outdo someone because they always seem to come out on top?"

He nodded.

"Tre robbed me of my parent's attention when we were kids and married the woman I love. She and I have a natural connection."

I blushed at his words.

"Yet, I can't have her or stop protecting Tre because it's all I know."

"But…."

"No, buts, Miya. You allowed your competitive spirit and pride to blind you. The enemy played you and blocked you from seeing your blessing. I can say this to you because I was there. I allowed the enemy to trick me into handing him my NFL career. By God's grace, I am back on the field again."

He swept his hand across his face. He pointed at me, then himself. "This cannot happen again. It took every ounce of the Holy Ghost within me to pull away. God would never allow us to be happy. He is not in the business of blessing a man with another man's wife."

"Even if my husband is not a husband?"

He looked away from me.

"What do you want me to do, Malik?"

He shook his head from side to side, never answering.

"How do you end a marriage? What will people say when they find out I divorced Tre to marry his foster brother?"

He finished his beer before speaking again. "Never been married. You were supposed to be my one and only."

"Then prove it. Show me."

"Miya, outside of my beliefs, I think highly of you. That's another reason we cannot cheat. I cannot have you on the road to death. A good girl should not be hiding in the depths of darkness for two hours of delight. I never want you to be a secret. I want to proclaim my love for you to the world."

He paused. I could tell he was attempting to control his emotions.

"I can say you are not ready to divorce Tre. Shit, you're more worried about what people will say than us ultimately being together. Fuck," he screamed, "you do not love me."

I flinched at his words.

"I am sorry for raising my voice and cursing. It's okay, baby. You still love Tre. I must face the fact that Tre has stolen something dear away from me once again."

Tears stung my raw cheeks. "I care for him, but I'm in L.O.V.E with you," I yell.

He stood up and plopped back down. "Please don't cry, baby. I am doing my best to stay on this side of the yard. I thought tough love might help you comprehend our current circumstances. However, it hurts me to talk to you aggressively."

We sat there in silence.

"Miya, what you fail to understand is I don't want you for one evening. I want you for a lifetime. The first time I looked into your eyes, I relinquished my heart to you, instantly enthralled by your essence. I married you in my heart. Our first kiss sealed the deal. Honey, I breathe to love you. Shit, you own my heart. But—"

"But What?"

He ousted a lengthy flow of air. "Our future together is a faded song on an 8-track."

Remember, when your mother hit you as a kid, you would scream and cry, but no sound would escape your body? That's precisely what his words did to me. He leaped off the sofa, raced over, and swaddled me in his arms while gently stroking my hair.

"I will file for a divorce. It should be easy since we don't have kids. God was looking out for me. They say he looks after babies and fools, and I am both. Please give me time."

"I am God's baby boy and a fool in love with you, Miya. But…"

"No, but's – prove how much you love me."

He rocked his head from side to side. I could feel his body inflate under me. "Tonight, I realized I have unresolved issues with my parents and brother. You have unresolved issues with your cousin and husband. After addressing these obstacles, I pray we can move forward."

"Together, I hope." I kissed him on the chest. In return, he kissed me on the forehead.

"Me too. I think we make each other better people, and I see life vividly when we are together."

I rocked my head against his chest.

"This is how I know you are, my queen. I messed up too, baby. I allowed my pride to get in our way."

Tears escaped my eyes and rolled across the mounds on his stomach.

"You and only you control what happens between us next. Concerning your marriage, you must follow your heart. We cannot be alone anymore. I will do my best to stay away from you. A blind man can see how much I love you. I will pray for you and Tre from afar."

I raised my head off his chest and pleaded for him to reconsider, but he refused.

"You can stay here tonight. I will get a room."

I pulled away from him. "No, I will leave, Malik; this is your house," I insisted.

Malik's eyes turned midnight. "What kind of a man do you think I am? I would be less of a man if I allowed you to be alone on the road this late. I'm the type of man that wouldn't be able to sleep until I knew you were safely tucked away in bed."

I relaxed next to him. He gently caressed my cheek. "I worry about you all of the time. I'm always asking my parents to call and check on you."

I smiled brightly. Malik's declaration explained why his mother increased her calls and stopped asking about Tre. "Did you tell your parents you love me?"

"No," he responded. I could hear a hint of regret in his tone.

"It's okay." I took his hand and kissed it.

"I fear being alone with you tonight."

"Look at this enormous house. I can sleep on the east wing, and you take the west wing."

"My bedroom is on the east side," he joked.

"Deal? We both have a ton of praying to do."

We nodded in agreement.

"Can you do me a favor?" I asked him. He nodded. "Can you lock your door, so I don't creep in?"

I poked him in the side, and we struggled to laugh through our torment.

His laughter grooved along my skin, and my heart plummeted into his chest, endeavoring to wrap roots around his heart.

I knew I was going to divorce Tre and marry Malik. What I did not know was how to start the process. Should I wait until after the holidays since his mother invited Tre and me to her house? Malik is protective of his family. The last thing I wanted to do was hurt his mother and cause him pain during the holidays with family drama.

"Turn the music back on, DJ." Malik hit a couple of buttons on his phone, and Janet Jackson's "Let's Wait Awhile" started playing.

Tears flowed freely when I realized Tre might have placed a ring on my finger, but he was not my husband. Malik was. Therefore, his state of mind and heart will be my top priority.

I kissed the tear that rolled down his cheek. I hummed the lyrics from "You Don't Have To Cry" by René and Angela. He tried to catch each tear that fell from my eyes.

I pulled him into an intensified hug, wishing I could absorb him into my soul.

"Malik, love is ruthless!"

"Only when it goes unsaid," he countered.

"Just Be A Man About It"
Toni Braxton
Mya

THE SHEER BRIGHTNESS OF THE MORNING sun smacked me dead in the eyes the moment I pulled my king-sized comforter off my face. It aggressively reminded me that the night had faded, and the dawn of a new day had begun. I shot up from the bed and went into the guest room, ready to give Tre a piece of my mind. The bed was untouched. I searched the house for any signs of Tre's presence.

Since Halloween, he came home late and camped in the guest room. Time after time, I failed to talk to him about our relationship. It's obvious your marriage has ended when your mate lives in a separate house room. Anything I say provokes an argument that ends with me having a new bruise from being rough handled or shoved into a piece of furniture.

I almost had the sheriff deliver the divorce papers to his job but changed my mind. I needed to get through Thanksgiving, and then I could have Raven and Eva deliver the divorce papers to Tre; contrary to what he may believe, I didn't want to embarrass him at his workplace. I was afraid he might become abusive if I pursued that route. Lately, I have been praying this divorce does not get ugly and Tre bows out gracefully.

I wanted my freedom; I wanted Malik Walker, the man I should have married in the first place.

I stepped out of the sliding door onto my bedroom balcony, inhaling the beauty surrounding me. The smog seemed to have vanished as the sun rained over my body. The California skies were a dazzling baby blue and white.

"Father God, please shine your light upon me and tell me when I should serve Tre with these divorce papers." I held my breath, leaning on the rail, awaiting an answer from the Lord. My heart, my ears, or my mind heard nothing. Closing my eyes tighter, hoping God would give me a scripture. Once again, utter silence.

Gazing down at the pool in my backyard, I cringed at my thoughts. I wondered if Tre would die if I pushed him from the balcony.

Strolling into the bathroom to freshen up, I screamed at my reflection. "Fuck you, Tre! I'm tired of your bullshit. I never thought I could conjure up a thousand ways to kill a man until I met you. I'm tired of being tired. I want this marriage to be over already!"

I could have sworn my reflection rolled its eyes at me. Shit, my conscience was tired of me nagging and complaining and not putting any actions behind my words.

Opening the door to the bathroom, I was rejuvenated after my calming shower until Tre dashed past me.

I rested my left side against the bathroom door watching as Tre dashed around our master bedroom.

"Miya, stop standing there and pack your shit. My mother wanted us there for lunch. We are late as hell."

I sat on the bed, baffled by Tre's behavior, clenching the bedspread repeatedly as though it were a stress ball. I looked at the clock. It revealed two in the afternoon.

I huffed. How would we make lunch when he had not been home for breakfast?

Pausing in front of me, he planted a sour kiss on my cheek before snapping his fingers in my face.

I could not believe this man was walking around the house packing, kissing me on the cheek, and lying about his whereabouts last night. He expected me to go to his parents' house, smile, and pretend we were one big happy family.

Retrieving the divorce papers from my computer bag, "Papers" by Usher played in my head as I gripped the documents tightly. I found Tre in the kitchen and slowly approached him; Ignoring my presence, he walked past me, placing his bags by the front door.

"Tre, I'm not going to your parents' house. I need to give you some papers to sign. I wanted to wait until after the holidays, but I cannot. This madness must end. If I wait any longer, I will either go insane, or one of us will lose our life."

"What else is new? You always forget to manage important business," he hissed rudely. "Are these the papers for the house equity?"

I shook my head.

Snatching the papers out of my hand, he scanned them. "I love you, Miya."

"You do not love anyone apart from yourself. You are an emotional and physical abuser."

He sat on the gray sofa in the living room.

"Let me get comfortable while you continue to beat me down," he insists. "I think you are the manipulator."

I could feel tears brewing and my nose stung. Shoving my emotions behind a steel door, I locked them away. Preferring to die a million deaths before I allowed this man to witness another tear fall from my eyes.

"Before we were married, something was off. Nonetheless, I ignored the womanly intuition in my gut to win this damn bet. Oh, how the universe has made me pay for that mistake! According to your parents, a man should pour positivity and life into his wife. You only fed me negativity and death. I feel humiliated. You are controlling and physically abusive whenever you don't get your way. Our bedroom and marriage lack respect, love, and passion. Largely, I'm sick of walking on eggshells in a house where I pay eighty-five percent of the expenses." I folded my arms across my chest and leaned against the wall.

"Don't stop now, Miya. I see you're on a roll today."

"I'm done, Tre! Please sign the divorce papers and end our misery."

"I'm not an emotional abuser. I'm a sex addict! I married you because you were pure and innocent. You were supposed to cure me!"

Stepping closer to Tre, I try to comfort him. "If you would have been open and honest, I would have gone to counseling with you and helped you get through the issues plaguing you. Now it's too late. This marriage has emotionally and physically drained me. I think your issues are deeper than sex. Desiring sex is not a disease. It is a feel-good action to disguise horrendous pain or a copout for unfaithful people to mask their cheating ways. Which one describes you?"

"My therapist says it is an actual disorder. I had my addiction under control until I met you."

Snickering, I couldn't believe he was blaming me for his shortcomings.

"Bitch! I don't see anything funny."

The sympathy I felt for him diminished instantly. I held my hands in the air and retreated.

"What did you think would happen when you sent me into a den full of thirsty women?"

Placing my hands on my chest, I blinked in shock.

"Yes, you! You insisted I hang out with Paxton because you want to be like Lexi so damn bad. You think you're the shit, but you are a jealous, insecure bitch! You will never be Lexi because she is sexy. You are not!"

I wouldn't simultaneously allow Tre to tear me down to the studs mentally, nor was I wasting any tears on this fool.

"So, I'm a bitch. Okay, I see!" Struggling to maintain my stance, I rocked my hands back and forth in front of me, searching for the following words to speak. "Why didn't you tell me Paxton's trips flipped an imaginary sex addiction trigger in you?"

He huffed. "I tried many times, but I knew you would ask a ton of questions I was not ready to answer. I loved you, Miya. I struggled to satisfy my quench with porn. After the yacht trip, I had some random hookups. Then it was not easy to stop. I have spent all of our money on porn, call girls, and strip clubs because of you bitch!" He smacked the lamp off the end table. "Fuck! I hate being a sex addict!"

He sniffled as if he was crying. I chuckled to myself because I had invented that move. I resisted the urge to reveal that my money was safe in my two new bank accounts under my maiden name. So only his ass was bankrupt.

"Does Malik know you are a sex addict and have sex with random strangers even though you are married?"

Tre dramatically gazed off into the distance.

"Have You Ever"
Brandy
Miya

E SHOOK HIS HEAD IN DISGUST. "My entire family knows. Why do you think my mother calls you?" I struggled to hold my emotions in. Has an entire family played me? His mother was as sweet as apple pie. There is no way she and Mr. Walker had been playing me.

"Hello!" Tre yelled as he clapped his hands in the air. "Earth to Miya. Do you know why?" I hunched my shoulders.

Tre smirked. "Why do you think Malik is always looking out for you? Because he is covering up my tracks. He is my big brother, so watching over me is his job."

"Malik would never. I know him better than you do."

He chuckled. "Bitches, kill me! First, you want to pretend you had no clue about my addiction. Maybe you didn't! You were too busy trying to suck my brother's nasty NFL dick. Malik has all of you women dumbfounded." Tapping his finger against his temple, he continues. "He smashes nearly ten different girls a week."

I couldn't believe what I was hearing.

"Sounds like you are the one with nasty community dick, not Malik," I hissed. My heart refused to believe Tre. "Let's talk about you and not Malik. Did you ever care about my life? Did you consider our future while you were screwing all these women?"

He reclined on the sofa, crossing his legs.

"Mimi, Mimi, Mimi. I have never put your life in jeopardy. Malik makes me get checked for diseases regularly." He swung his hands in the air as if directing a choir. "I always used a condom with you. I rarely smash a stranger without one." He chuckled. "Ain't that some shit. I always had to fuck you with a condom—it was Malik's rule, not mine. I guess we can blame him for my addiction igniting again as well. Maybe if I could have felt you raw, things may have been different."

"Do you hear yourself? You protected your wife by using condoms so you could fuck strippers raw. You continue to blame Malik and me. When are you going to take responsibility for your actions?"

"Malik takes care of my actions."

"Damn!" was all I could say. I genuinely married a man I didn't know.

"Baby, do you want to have angry makeup sex? Fuck Malik! I will even hit it raw."

I rolled my eyes so hard that my vision became distorted for a spell.

Tre could have told me he slept with dogs, men, or both simultaneously, and I would have been unmoved. I was indeed over his ass. I had no love, empathy, or remorse for him.

A fire burned in the pit of my gut, igniting my entire body with heat. Fuck everybody's feelings. 'Let's show Tre the bitch he keeps calling us,' my psyche, heart, and spirit declared. I felt complete because we were finally on the same page.

Clearing my throat, I stiffened my spine until I towered with confidence, my hands latched onto my hips. "I thought Malik was protecting me because he loves me. You tend to protect the woman who willingly gave you her virginity on a hot platter," I declared with pride. "According to him, I was the best woman he ever had. He ate me out until I passed out. Shit, he feasted on my yoni so many times I had to rename him Mr. Good Dick."

I placed my hand over my mouth as my mind journeyed back to my second date with Malik. I felt myself blushing, a needlepoint of light pierced my wrath, and joy sprung forward.

Tre's eyes tightened as he walked over to me. My smile earned me a hard slap across my upper cheekbone, accompanied by a couple of crazy bitches.

Tre went into the kitchen to retrieve a beer. Sitting back on the sofa, he glared at me. "Now tell me the fuckin' truth, bitch."

"Nope, I misspoke." My voice cracked like a walnut under pressure. I tapped my index finger against my lips. "I renamed him after my tenth or eighteenth orgasm." I tossed my head back and chuckled.

I fanned myself as I continued to speak. "I loved how Malik's warm raw flesh explored my soaking wet pussy. She gobbled up all his seeds."

I ducked as Tre's beer connected with the wall. "Hmmm." I licked the beer off my lip s, hunched my shoulders then rolled my eyes. "That's why he didn't want your dirty dick in me raw."

Anger flooded his eyes.

I clenched my chin, staring off into the distance this time. "Ya, that's when I gave him that name."

Tre's demeanor changed. He lifted off the sofa and rested his elbows on his knees. "Are you telling me my brother fucked you raw before me and filled your dumb ass full of cum?"

Blinking rapidly, I smacked my lips before I spoke. "Nope! I'm telling you Malik made love to me, and our warm flesh danced to an ancestral drum, and you have never been able to achieve a smidge of that. I tried to love you, but you kept breaking my heart. Malik is the man I dreamed about my entire life. He has my heart, not you. He is the perfect love lyrics over my dramatic beat."

"Bitch, what the fuck are you talking about?"

"Mary J. Blige's album "What's the 411?" is the soundtrack to our pathetic marriage."

"You are always talking about fucking songs and lyrics. Stop being so melodramatic," Tre barked. "Tell me more about your hoeish ass."

Smoothing out my clothes, standing tall, I replied, "I'm not melodramatic. I'm a smooth melody over a dramatic beat."

"Bitch, what? You are not making any sense. Use your own fucking words; I know that's from a damn song."

"Nope, all me. Although, music is the sunlight that streams rays of joy upon this horrendous marriage. Malik understands my musical side because we are soulmates. We work in and out of the bedroom. He is my king." I giggled, looking off into the distance as if this were a dramatic movie scene in a love comedy.

"Bitch you ain't shit. I upgraded you."

I expelled a stream of air and rocked my head from side to side. "You are a wretched man always whining for attention and praise. You can't manage a fucking penny. My other bank accounts are still phat. Without my future husband's money, you don't have shit. So, who upgraded whom? Now fuck your feelings and you."

"Did he fuck you or not, bitch?"

"He has never fucked me," I declared through clenched teeth. I arrogantly tilted my head to the left while lifting my chin. "I guess you didn't hear me. So, let me repeat myself. He has never fucked me. He has only made sweet love to me."

"How many motherfucking times?" Tre demanded, slamming his fist on the coffee table.

A mischievous grin slides across my face. "How many times in one night or how many times did we wake up in each other's arms?"

Seeing the discomfort on his face pleased me.

"When and where?"

Stalling, I glance around the room. "We hooked up in Vegas, San Diego, and at the Four Seasons after you refused me."

Pausing briefly, tapping my index finger against my lips again, I asked, "Does finger fucking and oral sex count?" Before he could answer, I replied. "I'm going to say it counts. So, add San Francisco and Halloween at his house."

I rested my hands on the back of the armchair, waiting for his reply.

"You dirty bitch. Now I know why you couldn't cure me."

"Because I'm not a doctor. Tre, you seriously need help. I hope you understand that self-change starts with self, not Miya."

"Miya, stop talking. Malik runs through women just like me. You were another notch on his belt. I was the one who was foolish enough to marry you."

Giggling at his reaction, I responded, "Once you sign the divorce papers, Malik will be the next fool to marry me."

Tre leaped from the sofa, wrapping his hands tightly around my throat. I kicked. I attempted to scream. I scratched his forearm, but he just kept squeezing tighter and tighter. I could feel myself drifting into the darkness. I fought more arduously, but the dusk was more robust than me.

I felt my knee connect with his balls. My eyes flickered open. He punched me in the face, and the darkness shifted quickly, demolishing more light. The abyss intensified as the light grew to a needle's point.

He was gone after I regained consciousness, and so were his bags.

I wanted to call Malik. I knew he would beat Tre's ass if he saw my bloody nose, but my heart was upset with him, and I didn't know whom to trust anymore. He knew Tre was a sex addict, and he stood by and allowed Tre to marry the woman he supposedly loved.

My consciousness was correct. I needed to leave both Tre and Malik alone.

I picked up my phone and called the one who always cared for me, even though I refused to recognize it.

"Dance With My Father"
Luther Vandross
Malik

A CONTORTED GRIMACE REPLACED MY MOTHER'S BRIGHT smile. I was sick of Tre's antics. Her children were the only people who could alter my mother's mood this quickly. I watched Momma whisper something in Pop's ear. He shook his head before forcing a crooked smile on his face, then kissed her cheek. I would never disrespect my parents, but Tre was slowly ripping our family apart, and we needed to address his issues as a family.

Raven was right; I needed to get all this stuff off my heart before returning to the field. We needed a family meeting, and there was no time like the present.

"Can we sit at the dining room table and have a family meeting?" My mother and father appeared puzzled but agreed.

"Momma, do you believe God outlines all of our lives to help us become the person He has ordained us to be?"

She nodded, still unsure where I was going with this line of questioning.

"I do, Son," my father rapidly replied.

"Do you feel Tre has become the man God created Him to be?"

My mother placed her folded hands on the fourteen-seater table. "Yes."

"I disagree," Pops responded.

"I think God has more for Tre than he has already achieved."

I sneered. "Tre has a decent job, a house, and a wife. I'm referring to his mental health. I believe he could have become a better man if you had stepped out of God's way."

Momma started to speak. Pops placed his hand on her, halting her speech.

"God sent Tre two angels. You and dad were to guide him through his traumatic experience. When we were teenagers, you tried to address Tre's sexual abuse by his aunt. Once he confessed, he could not discuss his past abuse; we all withdrew. You sent him to a therapist and even made me try a couple of times to get Tre to open up. You fired the psychotherapists who pushed him to talk even though you hired them to do just that."

I rested my hands on the table. "Yet Tre can use his abuse to win an argument or get you and dad to give him money. I'm guilty of this, too, because you raised me to safeguard my baby brother."

I paused and gazed at the ceiling, searching for my following words. My father went to the wet bar and returned with a glass of cognac for him and me. He brought my mother a glass of white wine.

"This seems like a sip conversation." Mom and I snickered at my father's joke.

"Mom, you and Pops go out into the world preaching and helping people overcome the same things Tre experienced during childhood. You have taught many classes at church concerning kids who attempt to divide and conquer their parents, yet you're oblivious to Tre's behavior. He is slowly ripping this family apart. I can recall you and dad arguments because they were always about Tre."

"Malik, are you here to trounce me for Thanksgiving?" Mom questioned.

Pops patted her hand. "We raised him better than that, Mary. The boy has something he needs to get off his chest. We will not become the family who sweeps issues under the rug. We are going to be a family that deals with problems head-on. The way we always have."

Inhaling deeply, I nibbled on my bottom lip's dry skin before continuing. "Pop, we have always swept Tre's issues under the rug. Instead of addressing it, we give him whatever he asks because we feel guilty about what happened to him. What about the things that happened to me? We were both children."

Tears flowed from my mother's eyes. Her voice rattled as she spoke. "Were you molested as a kid, Malik? Was it one of your football coaches?"

"No, Mom. Sometimes I wish something traumatic had happened to me. Once Tre and his siblings came along. I received the scraps after a delicious meal. Tre received the main course. His sisters got the soup and salad, and you guys were each other's desserts. There was nothing left for me, Mom. Nothing." I wrung my hands together.

Pops reached across the harvested and sustainable solid hardwood table to hold my hand. I withdrew. "Son."

If I had felt any emotion, I would have cracked and not continued relinquishing my heart issues.

"Tasha was not an excellent mother. I believed I had enough motherly love for all of you."

"My childhood was stolen away from me, Mom. You have an enormous heart, and you share it with the world. I needed more of your heart and time. I have been seeing a therapist. She has helped me deal with my love for Tre's wife. She also helped me realize how I'm always searching for genuine love, yet I'm afraid of it. I imagine someone will steal it from me. My fear allowed the love of my life to slip through my fingers and land in my brother's hands."

"Son, Exodus 20:17 is clear. 'You shall not covet your neighbor's house. You shall not covet your neighbor's wife, or his male or female servant, his ox or donkey, or anything that belongs to your neighbor.' So why are you coveting your brother's wife?" Momma demanded.

Pops dropped his head. "Mary, the boy, is not looking for you to paraphrase a scripture. We taught him the word. He is looking for the same hope and inspiration you give Tre. Do you not see misery engraved on our child's face?"

Momma sprung from the table; my father followed her. Pops gripped Momma's wrist and pulled her into his arms. She laid her head on his chest, and he rested his chin on the top of her head.

"My dear Mary, my queen, I love you, but tonight I need you to remain quiet until I touch you on the shoulder."

My father stroked her back and then kissed her on the forehead. "Open your heart and hear our son. Malik is right. He was an only child, yet he shared his world with four other children. You have an enormous heart. I love how caring you are. However, you continuously blame yourself for Tre being molested by his aunt whenever he visited Tasha."

Momma buried her head into my father's armpit and cried. Witnessing my mom's grief smacked tears from my soul.

"Tasha refused to take any blame for Tre's abuse. She laid it at your feet. You picked it up and refused to allow me to carry that burden for you. Maybe we should have taken Tasha to court. The chances of us winning were slim to none. The lawyer stated we had no legal rights. So, we danced to Tasha's beat, afraid she would rip Tre out of our lives. Queen, that was our only option at the time."

My mother nodded.

"The second Tre informed us we safeguarded him."

"King, he was raped for five years straight and three summers. As a mother, I missed it. Malik was suffering, and I didn't notice. Am I a good mother?"

"Of course, you are. Queen, we can continue to live in shoulda, coulda, woulda, or discuss what we need to do to move forward."

Walking to my mother, I laid my head on her back. "Momma, you are the best mother in the world. I felt secure coming to talk to you and dad. I knew you all loved me enough to hear me out. I admit you would die to defend your kids."

She turned around and pulled me into her arms. Pops wrapped his arms around us both.

"Queen, Tre has to fly on his own. It is time for him to leave your bosom."

Momma stroked the back of my head. "I'm sorry, Malik. We should have asked you how you felt about sharing your childhood, us, and your personal space with four other children. Maybe we should have sent you to a therapist along with Tre."

"I know, Momma."

"Son, this mess with your brother's wife has nothing to do with your upbringing or sharing your childhood with four kids. If this woman is meant for you, I'm sure God brought her to you first. You allowed the enemy to trick you out of your blessing. That's your fault, not mine nor your mother or brother."

I broke my embrace with my parents and leaned against the wall. "He brought her to me three times, but I allowed lust and fear to cloud my mind."

"You fumbled and lost your wife."

"I know. I understand what I did, Pops. Yet the pain hurts the same."

"Malik trials and tribulations come along to teach us how to handle more prominent issues ahead. You allowed Sabrina to be a distraction, and the enemy crept in and attempted to rob you of your career. However, you and the enemy forgot what God gives; no man or evil spirit can steal it away," my father preached.

I nodded in agreement, and my father continued.

"As a reward, God illuminated your future queen's glory. You should have felt solidarity the first time you met her because your missing half reunified your body, mind, and soul. Yet, you and nobody but you allowed lust and fear to distract you from your blessing. The enemy intervened and manifested your fears by giving your brother your wife."

Pops' words were chopping me down quickly. I couldn't do anything but cry because the truth hurts.

"Tre and Miya are not in love. I saw the love you had for Miya at their wedding. You confirmed my suspicions by constantly calling your mother and pleading for her to check on Miya. When your mother and I call Tre's house, he is never there. Since the wedding, I have been praying for you, Tre, and Miya. I knew something was brewing within you at the reception. I noticed your protective spirit and the wrath her outfit conjured in you. Love and regret encased your spirit."

Instantly I felt naked standing there as my father peeled off all my layers like an onion.

"Although you and your siblings are adults, it's still my job to monitor your behavior."

I nodded at my father as a new batch of tears emerged.

"Son, please understand that God will not give you a married woman even if she is your wife. Nor will He hurt another person to bring you joy. God brought your soulmate to you first."

I always thought my mother ran our home. After seeing my father in action tonight, I understood what equal partnership meant. Pops was full of wisdom, knowledge, the holy word, and sound advice. He only spoke when his queen needed defending, reassurance, guidance, or she was too distraught to speak for herself. He knew when to press forward and when to fall back. He is the man and husband I wish to be one day.

Momma ran her hands through her salt and pepper hair. "My feelings about Tre divorcing Miya and marrying you are overwhelming. I have never imagined this type of situation in our family. Your father and I can only pray for you all. Matters of the heart fall beyond collective understanding. Son, only God, possesses the wisdom to alter the heart and mind."

"I'm torn because Miya is an educated queen with a warm heart. I know they are married, but I wouldn't label it a marriage or a partnership. Whenever I call, she sounds as if she has been crying or on the verge of tears," my father added. Momma's facial expression changed.

"Momma, did Tre tell her he was a sex addict?"

"Maybe you should ask your brother. He will be here soon."

Pops gripped my shoulder blade and kneaded it. "Son, can you walk away from this woman?"

Momma glanced at me, waiting for my response. "Dad, I cannot. I don't want another woman. She completes me."

I stepped to the right and eyed my mother. "Momma, she is my queen. Before her, football was an essential thing in my life. Now she is. I pray for her more than I pray for myself. I worry about her all the time. Her happiness is all I desire, even if she picks Tre."

"Oh, Malik," my mother swooned, "you love her unconditionally."

"Son, walk away. If God chose her for you, He will bring her back once you're ready to love her wholeheartedly and vice versa. Until then, cut all communication and focus on repairing your bond with Tre, your mom, and God."

"Pops, I finally understand 1 Corinthians 7: 32-38. It is easy to serve God because he requires us to keep his ten commandments. A wife requires more than the bare minimum from her husband. She requires her husband to place the sun, moon, and stars in the palms of her hands. On top of that, you still must provide God with his bare minimum. I have searched my soul, and I'm ready to please two people. I was afraid to call Sabrina my wife and say God sent her. However, He revealed that Miya is my wife, and the same things I place in her hands, she will place in mine. Dad, I'm ready to love this woman like Christ loves the church. I'm willing to hold on until God brings her back to me."

Pops clenched my chin tightly. "Then use the power and the victory in your tongue. Neither your mother nor I can speak for God."

I nodded, knowing that my heart, body, and soul had to be in alignment before I kneeled before God. "Love is not one-sided. Does she want to be your wife?" my father questioned.

I sat my pride aside and answered with my heart. "She does, Pop."

My mother walked to me with her palms turned to the sky. I gently placed my hands inside her warm palms. She kissed my hands and washed them with her tears. Unashamed of my tears, I felt safe and secure as my hands resided within hers.

"Malik, I had no idea you felt this way. My heart is breaking. I wanted to be there for Tre because it seemed like no one cared for him. I wanted our family to be the family who unconditionally cared for him. I'm not clueless. I understand that Tre uses his childhood abuse to get things from your dad and me."

She wiped the tears from my face. "Malik, I would love for you to think your mother is perfect. And she knows all the answers. Except I'm human and flawed. I am learning and growing daily like you. I'm sorry, Son. Starting today, I will take a more standoffish approach and allow Tre to become the man God has ordained him to be."

Momma and I were hugging when Tre burst through the front door.

"Mommy, did Malik tell you he slept with my wife countless times before we were married?"

"Caravan of Love"
Isley, Jasper, Isley
Malik

RE RAN TO MY MOTHER, YANKING her from my embrace; Tre didn't address my father or me. "Mommy, did Malik tell you he slept with my wife countless times?"

My father kissed Tre on the head and hugged him.

"He did. It is time for your mother and me to allow you and your brother to handle your mess. I have two rules: keep your hands off each other and don't destroy anything in my doggone house. Remember how your mother and I raised you? Mom and I are going down to one of the villas. This way, we will not interfere. If you need a mediator, call on Jesus."

"Mommy," Tre whined, extending his hands to our parents. My mother wrapped her arms around Tre and me and squeezed tightly. My father pried our crying mother away from us before escorting her out of the house.

"What did you do to my mother, Malik?"

I huffed before speaking. "Our mother, Tre. Don't forget she is our mother, not yours.

"She is mine, asshole."

"I allowed you to borrow her. I have her blood running through my veins; you don't."

"You may have grown in her belly, but I grew in her heart."

"Do you hear our sons, my King?"

My mother's wails instantly humbled me. I glanced behind me and watched my father pull my distraught mother into his arms. He consoled her, placed her in the golf cart, and drove away.

I was ashamed of my behavior.

"Baby bro, I will not do this with you. We both grew in her heart. Our mother kept both of us shielded and warm from the harsh elements of the world. It kills me to see her torn to pieces because her boys have fallen apart."

Tre's chest rose as he widened his stance. "You started it by sleeping with that lying bitch Miya. I hope she dies tonight! Shit, I almost died driving up here."

"Where is Miya, Tre?"

He clapped at the air and stomped his feet. "I tell you, I almost died." He scoffs a chuckle. "And all you can do is ask about that lying bitch!"

I stepped closer to my brother and flinched at him. He jumped back.

"You are always bullying me, Malik! I left that conniving bitch laid out on the floor. I choked her until she passed the fuck out!" Tre says, soaring with pride, then chuckles.

Before I could catch myself, I punched my brother in his mouth. The sight of his blood decorating the wall did nothing to halt my advances. As my fist soared to hit him again, something caught my fist in midair and wouldn't let it go. "God, please. Tell your angel to step aside." Instantly Romans 12:17-19 sailed through my heart.   .

Tre massaged his cheek.

Attempting to control my anger, I placed my hands in my pockets, rocking on my heels, eyeing my phone on the table. I needed to call Miya.

I ignored Tre's rants as I dialed Miya's phone. Her cousin Lexi answered her phone, assuring me that Miya was excellent. I could finally breathe again.

"Tell her I love her more," I replied, disconnecting the call.

I turned my attention back to my brother.

"Did she say she loved you back?"

I nodded.

"Did she ask about me?"

"Nope."

"Malik, why couldn't you let me have her?"

"I've allowed you to have everything since we were kids."

"Not true. You get everything. You have Mom and Dad's approval, fancy cars, a mansion, a football career; all I wanted was a virgin to help cure my narcissistic disorder."

Jeremiah 31:3 wailed in my soul, tempering my demeanor. I slowly approached my baby brother. "I do all the challenging work, yet you reap all the benefits. Momma stays praising and encouraging you. She always asks me to push harder and demands that I do better than before. They expect everything from me. Yet, they are happy with anything you give them," I exclaimed.

"Not so!"

"I provide, protect, respect women, and pour into them. Yet, I'm disrespected, and they cheat on me. You treat women like disposable red cups. You tear them down and rip every inch of substance from them, and they love you. Hell, one even married you."

"All the women in my life were temporary. Miya was supposed to be my permanent remedy. She was the cure to my sex addiction, my Virgin Mary. Through therapy, I learned that I use sex to cope with my past and daily living pressures. Since Miya was a virgin, I assumed she would excite me and cure my illness and narcissistic behavior. However, you took that from me by fucking her first."

I placed my hand on my brother's shoulder and kneaded it. "If I would have known Miya was your Mimi, I would never have…."

"You would have never what?"

"No, that's not the truth. I would have married Miya because I fell in love when I laid eyes on her. Her essence called out to me; it was as familiar as breathing. In her presence, my heart felt harmony and wholeness. I'm sorry, but I love Miya more than anything in this world," I confessed.

He sucked on his teeth in annoyance.

I continued to lay my feelings for Miya at Tre's feet, telling him how we met each time we reconnected and my plans to propose, but she ghosted me. I apologized for violating her space and disrespecting their vows.

"Did you fuck Miya out of revenge? I told you Denise meant nothing to me. I had a difficult day at school. She came over, and before you knew it, we were having sex in your bed. Man, you know Sabrina was no good. I was visiting to get some money. You were not at home, and before I could protest,

Sabrina sucked my dick, and I smashed a couple of times. It's your fault for telling her I was a sex addict. I knew then, Malik, I had a problem."

Well damn, I thought. *His confession was news to me. Indeed, my brother has a problem.*

"This is not about those women. Miya erased every awful thing any woman has ever done to me with one kiss. Any anger I had in me diminished in San Diego. I had to let it all go to fill my heart with her, God, and our family."

"Miya was supposed to do all those things to me," he whined. "Instead, you and that bitch have fucked me up even more. You know Tasha's sister constantly raped me. It fucked me up. I'm damaged. Bruh, I'm traumatized. How are you going to fix me, big brother?"

Tre kicked at the air. Baffled by his words, I remained mute.

"What will Tre have after everything is all said and done? You know she will take half of what I got. I will not have anything. Are you going to help me financially?"

"What's Happening Brother"
Marvin Gaye
Malik

RE'S EYES DANCED WILDLY AS HE worked his jaw in a stiff circle. "I have never stopped helping you financially, emotionally, or physically. However, your antics must stop. Me enabling you must cease. Your escapades will not work on mom or me anymore."

"This is all about mom. You're jealous because she loves me more. Fuck, you got, dad."

Wrenching my hands together, I continued. "I cannot want more for you than you want for yourself. I have helped you in abusing other people instead of stopping you. You use what happened to you as a kid to control our family. As of today, I'm cutting you off."

I stepped closer to my brother to hug him. He pushed me away.

"I need a place to live. I have bills. Can you at least give me enough money to cover those expenses?"

"No. Figure it out."

In a rage, he swung on me, landing a punch that clipped my right jaw.

Thoughts of my mother flooded my head. If I harmed him again, she would never forgive me. He approached with his fist in the air. I slapped the sense he lost back into his head. He rubbed his jaw as he mumbled about telling my mom.

"Miya told me how you drained her bank accounts, your back taxes, and the disconnected electricity on Halloween. I give you monthly income to help pay your bills even though you have a decent job. Where did the money go?"

"She told you all this the night you ate her out until she passed out or while you two were fucking in my house?"

"I haven't slept with Miya since you married her. I resisted the urge too. Again, where did the money go?"

"You should know she makes more money than me. The bitch should have been paying all the bills. I'm sick of women thinking men are supposed to take care of them. Shit, why can't a bitch take care of me for once?"

I shook my head. "It is your job to provide for your wife. Miya is the type of blessing that would never weigh down her husband by not contributing to their union. I agree that you may think I have not been a good brother. Throwing money at a situation is different from helping. I sincerely apologize."

"For what? Fucking my wife? Trying to cut me off or trying to turn mom against me?"

I chuckled at the audacity.

"The more you rant, it's obvious the role I've played in your ignorance and downfall. When will you stand up and be a man without my help or our parent's help?"

"You are so soft when it comes to these bitches. Here's a word of advice. Fuck them and leave them before they fuck you over. Women ain't shit." He hunched his shoulders, then erupted in laughter. "Stop falling in love with every woman, you smash!"

Tre needed to open his eyes to his ignorance. "My mother, I'm sorry, our mother is a woman; what about her?"

"Mommy is mommy!"

Tilting my head, I rested my thoughts on my shoulders. "Baby bro, I'm done."

"Mommy will not allow you to hurt her baby boy," he contended. "She will walk through hell to make me smile. Even God stopped you from beating me."

"Because vengeance is His and not mine. Your feet will slip in due time."

"Miya is proof he favors me and not you, Malik."

It was clear my brother was not ready to take responsibility for his actions or willing to change.

"Listening to you, I know you don't love Miya. I understand you may think it is fucked up for me to love her, but I do. If she would have me, I'm going to marry her. I don't care who condemns my behavior or thinks I'm a buffoon."

Defeated, I plopped down on the sofa. I locked my fingers together and tapped them against my lips. My heart was pleading with my brother to step back. I wanted to offer him money to step away, but I knew if Miya ever found out, I would surely lose her forever.

"Tre, I love her. Understand I cannot breathe without her."

"Sounds like a personal problem."

"Okay, baby boy."

"Yea, okay."

Tranquility hovered over me. I smiled.

"I'm going to turn all of this over to God. The only bill I will pay is your therapist if you go back. Mom and Dad have plenty of space. You can live here. Allow Miya to keep the house."

"You want that bitch to keep the house you bought me so she will marry you? Damn, big bro, you are pathetic!"

"I think she has suffered enough."

His shrieking sliced through my thoughts. "Fuck, Miya! I had my house before I met her. You bought it for me, not her."

"Fine, I will buy Miya her own house. Raven will see to it."

"This bitch has your nose wide open. Fuck it! You can have her for a price."

"You cannot sell or give away something that never belonged to you. God will give her to me when we are ready."

"Not if I refuse to sign the divorce papers."

I rubbed my head. He was making it hard for me to keep my hands to myself. "God is greater than you and your manipulation."

"I will never allow you and Miya to be happy together! If I can't be happy, nobody else will be!"

"I love you, Tre."

"Fuck you, Malik," he stuttered. "I hate you!"

He threw a picture frame at me, then headed for the front door.

I closed my eyes, muttering a quick prayer.

"I will never let you be happy with Miya! Never!" he screamed from the hallway.

I picked up the broken frame and spotted how I protectively held Tre's hand while leading him out of a store. Since I was six, my primary job was protecting and caring for my brother.

"Today, I let my brother's hands go and place it in your hands, Heavenly Father. Amen!"

"Nothing Even Matters"

Lauryn Hill

Miya

SNIFFLING, I EXHALED SHAKILY; TRE REFUSED to move out of the house, unbelievable since it had been less than a month since he attempted to kill me. I could not move until I had another place to go. I was embarrassed about the ruptured blood vessel in my eye. My family and the BAEs would want me to relive every abuse episode between Tre and me. Lexi demanded I get a restraining order; I refused. She pleaded for me to leave. I had paid off his back taxes and all the bills in our home. I deserved to be here as much as he did. Shit, possession was nine-tenths of the law.

Two weeks ago, Tre brought a stripper home. I caught them having sex in the game room on the pool table. Distraught, I called Malik, but Raven answered his phone. She probed until I poured my heart out to her.

The next day she forced Tre to leave and instructed him to stay away from the house whenever I was there. After I go to work, he comes home.

Raven repeatedly calls and comes to check up on me. Whenever I questioned her about her Bossman, she supplied me with little to no details. I appreciated him for sending her to aid me. However, talking to him would have been better.

Yesterday was a tough day for me. I missed Malik, and Tre was in the house when I returned from work. He refused to leave and begged me to have sex with him. I called Malik, and again Raven answered his phone. She dodged all my questions concerning him. I snapped and instructed her to stay in San Diego and tell Malik I didn't need his help anymore.

I locked myself in the bedroom the second Tre arrived home. The last thing I wanted was to see Tre or bump into one of his random chicks. I was ready for the weekend to be over as I buried my face in my pillow, screaming into it. I emptied the last contents of the wine bottle into my glass and downed it in one long gulp, wiping my mouth with the back of my hand. Specks of red wine stained my sheets. I studied the spots as the tiny droplets grew.

My body felt soulless. Tears dripped from my eyes and deformed the notebook paper. I tried to balance the pad and pen in my hand. I decided I was going to send Malik a letter.

Dear Malik,

I don't know anything about football, yet I watch it whenever you play. The first time we met, I stood over you. I intuitively knew all I needed in this world was you.

After we made love, you held me in your arms, close to your body, the same way a football player snuggles a football. The players hope they don't fumble the football before reaching the end zone. They hold the ball as tight as possible to secure it.

I'm sorry I leaped from your arms each time you attempted to pull me close to your rib. Congratulations on going to the Superbowl. I understand why you are not accepting my calls. I pray (1 Peter 4:8) resides in your heart, and you can forgive me.

I looked down at the words on the paper and ripped the page from the pad, tossing it across the room with my other failed attempts.

I dialed Malik's number from my cell phone and house phone. A hairline crack etched itself in my heart when the automated service announced, "This number was no longer in service." I needed him to know I missed him, and I was sorry. I could finally envision us together.

I went to the kitchen to get another wine bottle and returned to bed. Tre spotted me in the hallway and gripped my bottom. I shoved him away and dashed into the bedroom.

Tears dropped onto the neck of the bottle as I tried to sip my pain away.

"Lord, I lost the bet. My husband is a sociopath, and my future king has blocked me from his life. God, can you bring Malik back to me? Please! Haven't I suffered enough?"

I sprung from the bed. I needed to have a conversation with myself. I ogled at the reflection in the mirror. A contorted face reflected at me, then spoke, "You settled for a man that was less than our worth. I despise you for not listening to our heart. You allowed your competitive spirit and pride to trick you out of the greatest love we have ever felt and known!"

Broken and defeated, I couldn't debate with my inner soul. She was right. My chest quivered and contracted, but no words escaped my mouth. I held myself tight in a hug and rocked as the Holy Spirit in me cried out to the Lord on my behalf.

Moaning, I hoped God could sense the pain plaguing my soul and wipe the tears from my eyes. Each time I attempted to pray, a deeper moan escaped my body. All I could do was cry out to God. My confused and broken heart forgot how to pray.

I caught a tear on my fingertips and gazed at it. How could something opaque and small contain such an abundance of agony?

"Signed, Sealed, Delivered (I'm Yours)"
Stevie Wonder
Epilogue

Malik

Dear Miya,

My therapist gave me a homework assignment to write you a letter. I repeatedly tried to compose my feelings but only produced love songs. Maybe it's the rhythmic sounds of The Isley Brothers' "Sensuality Pts. 1 & 2" or the cognac and Cuban cigar I'm indulging in, but I feel you need these songs to know how I think, Queen. You need to know I miss you! You need to know my heart will never leave you.

Promise you will listen to these and think of me and only me!
  01) *Forever for Always for Love – Luther Vandross*
  02) *If Only You Knew – Pattie Labelle*
  03) *Knocks Me Off My Feet – Donell Jones*
  04) *You're Always on My Mind – SWV*
  05) *You're My Latest Greatest Inspiration – Teddy Pendergrass*

06) *We Belong, Together – Mariah Carey*

07) *Baby Be Mine – Miki Howard*

08) *No One in the World – Anita Baker*

09) *You Are My Lady – Freddie Jackson*

10) *The Lady in My Life – Michael Jackson*

11) *You Give Good Love – Whitney Houston*

12) *Forever Mine – The O'Jays*

13) *Cause I Love – Lenny Williams*

Love Always,
Malik

ALIK

Dear Miya,　　　　　　　　.

It has been a month with no word from you. I decided not to send another playlist but a letter to express my feelings for you. Raven told me you refused my offer again. Then I heard you're moving soon. I hope you send me your new address.

Besides my mother, your crown is still the only crown I want to support and protect. I hope my tears haven't made me appear weak.

Our courtship, relationship, or whatever you want to call it, is rough on me. I have never experienced this magnitude of emotions nor rebelled against God's word by pursuing a married woman.

I wish you could swim through my heart and feel my sentiments. Baby, you are my soulmate, wife, and queen. Your eyes provided a mirror into my soul. In you, I see endless possibilities and our happily ever after.

Your voice is the perfect soundtrack to my heart and music to my ears. Sometimes I can hear your laughter in my house.

Every moment with you was like a beautiful dream filled with vibrant colors. All my heart's desire is you! I sleep to dream of you and wake to reminisce about us. Some days I sit and imagine how our lives would be if you had married me.

I thought Tre stole all the people I loved. He stole the first people I ever loved from me at age six. My high school sweetheart cheated on me at my house and in bed with him. The next woman I loved betrayed me with a teammate and my brother.

My deepest fear came true when you walked down the aisle to marry Tre. I felt he was robbing me of unconditional love.

I realize now he didn't take my parents. They merely increased the size of our family. Nobody can steal what is yours. My high school sweetheart and second girlfriend belonged to the world.

God intended you for me. He allowed me multiple chances to confess my love for you before your marriage. I feared being blessed with you and losing you to someone else. Fear cheated us out of time.

I pray that God will shed His grace upon us and allow us to become one soon. My heart, soul, and body will remain faithful to your spirit until that day!

Until we meet again, I am holding on to 1 Corinthians 13:13, 'And now these three remain: faith, hope, and love. But the greatest of these is love.'

I place my faith and hope in God. Our love will continuously reside where only God and my family live in my heart.

Love Always,
Your Husband/King/Lover/Protector,
Malik Walker

IYA

I ran my fingertips over the rugged circles on Malik's letter. I imagined him laughing and crying the same way I did as I listened to his playlist.

Dear Malik,

I apologize for waiting months to write back, but you once said, "It is never too late to express your love for someone." I was angry and hurt for a while after discovering that you knew about Tre's past and that you covered for him. You allowed me to marry Tre blindly. I was pissed when you refused to talk to me. How could you change your number and not give it to me?

I stayed at Tre's house longer than I should have. I was waiting for you to rescue me. However, you never came.

I decided to take Raven's advice and talk to a therapist. I needed to get myself together before becoming your wife. A change has come over me.

I was wrong for blaming you and Lexi. I should be the only one held accountable for my reckless behavior. My bad choices were mine and mine alone.

Please accept my most profound apology! Marriage is a serious decision, and I took it lightly to win a bet.

On another note, I bawled as I listened to your playlist and read your last letter. I tried to call you, but you changed your phone number. I drove to San Diego to see you after the playoffs were over, but Raven opened the door and informed me you would be away for a while. I asked her for your new phone number, and she refused. She muttered something about getting permission first. She called and texted you in front of me, but you never replied. Wounded, I walked away.

Since she never called with your number, I can only assume you said, "No."

I started to come to your house again, but my heart could not take any more disappointment and rejection.

I detoured to the hotel where we spent those two glorious days. I was hoping the spirit of our love still filled the room. Someone had reserved our room. Feeling defeated again, I drove back to Los Angeles and snuggled in bed until Monday morning.

These days all I do is work and lay in my bed staring at the ceiling. I can't remember the last time I joined the BAEs out on the town.

I finally understand why you wouldn't tell me what to do. You yearned for someone to finally pick you. Your parents, high school sweetheart, and last girlfriend chose someone else. I am sorry I was no better than they were.

Please understand that my heart and soul desire you. My mind was stuck on winning. Then there was my pride. Pride is the smallest bag we carry, yet it is the heaviest. I allowed pride, fear, and competitive spirit to block my blessings.

It's crazy how wisdom, knowledge, and understanding don't come until the end of a test or trial. While I stood in the storm's eye, I matured as those things rained upon me. I hope it is not too late for us.

You needed to know that my love was sincere, and I am ready to prove it was and still is. You promised to remain faithful to me. I pray you are keeping your promise.

I appreciate your parents. They have been a blessing as I go through this divorce. They refuse to talk about you or Tre, but they have continued ministering to the broken girl within me. Your father said this trial in my life would be over soon. I hope that means Tre will finally set me free.

It's funny. I always thought your mother enlightened me to be the perfect mate for Tre. The veil of doubt lifted, revealing she prepared me to become your wife, queen, and helpmate.

When your father spoke of pouring into your husband and him pouring into me, he knew Tre could not treat me in a manner befitting a queen. Only you can.

I finally confessed my love for you to your parents. Your dad told me to read 1 John 4:18. After reading the scripture, I knew I had to allow love to lead me, and fear had to take a back seat.

Loving you is not a punishment. You once whispered that your love for me was made perfect once it joined the place in your heart where only God resides. I finally understand the magnitude of love.

As my fears and anger dissolved, my love for you beared much fruit. I love you because you first loved me. Your affection has driven doubt out of my heart and life. I promise you will feel loved every single day of your life. I will pour into you daily because I know you will submerge me.

I wish I had offered you my heart the second time God brought us together. Every time I gazed into your eyes at the wineries, I witnessed our love blossom.

I felt safe each time you held my hand and knew you would lead our family down a righteous path. I miss the tranquility I experienced when I curled up in your arms and you rocked me to sleep.

My life feels complete when I am near you. No one on God's green earth can replace you. In my heart, you are my husband. I vow not to take another man into my bed or my heart until we are united.

You once said, "Love is only ruthless when it goes unsaid." I will not allow anything to go unsaid from this day forward.

I miss you, my king!

I created a playlist of all the songs we shared every time we were together. I hope our hearts are unified again soon! Right by your side is where I desire to be.

Your crown is the only crown I vow to protect, my king!

Forever and Always,
Your Vegas Lover/Helpmate/Queen/Wife,
Miya Walker

IYA

It has been two months since I mailed my letter to Malik using my new address. Whenever I heard a knock on the front door, I hoped it was him. I refused to let go and move on. I pulled up to my new condominium and went straight to the mailbox.

I shuffled through the envelopes in my mailbox. My heart dropped, and my hands trembled as I held the letter. My eyes burned with fiery tears, and it felt like a two-hundred-pound boulder lay on my chest.

I blinked rapidly and hysterically shook the letter like an etch and sketch, trying to erase the words.

"RETURN TO SENDER"

Testimony

Life can change in a blink of an eye. A Mustard Seed of Faith can level the playing field.

A regular doctor's visit turned into a life gut punch and a 24 to 48hour-to-live diagnosis. An acute pulmonary embolism had imprisoned my heart and lungs and would chain me to a bed for months. After 72 hours, it was clear that God didn't care about the expiration date stamped on my medical chart.

To pass the time, I listened to music. I believe that music and laughter restore the soul.

Praying one night, I heard a voice say write. I had the time, so why not. Music, prayer, and unexpected tears filled my heart and hospital room as I created these incredible characters. This book poured from my heart and soul.

As I entered the editing phase, my sister passed away from Cancer. The bond we built while in the hospital fighting for our lives was exceptional. This loss crushed me, but I had to be a pillar for my family, so I grieved silently through my pen. I pushed this book back again and wrote two novellas as I worked and prayed through my grief.

I shared this book with some people, and they loved Malik, so I sent the book to an editor. That editor and the one after were another roadblock.

When I tell you the enemy continued to try and claim my life, it was crazy. Ear pain and migraines turned into a tumor on my jugular vein behind my ear canal.

At this point, who wouldn't want to give up, "ME!" I buckled down, strapped on my armor, and started radiation treatments.

My faith made me laugh at the enemy's advances as I held on to the words the spirit of the Lord had whispered to my heart when I was told I had a brain tumor.

I kept reminding the enemy, "If you're attacking me, God has allowed it. If He allowed it, He has already claimed my victory."

The Holy Ghost warned me that trials were coming, but the enemy could not have me. He promised to whip the tears from my eyes. I joked that my old miracles were old and that God needed a new testimony pouring from my heart. I didn't know he would give me three… LOL.

Did I have moments where my faith was weak, and I cried? "Yes." Then I smiled as I recalled God's promise.

The blood clots had placed a cardiac strain on my heart, and I could no longer get upset. Forced to utilize a walker, asking for assistance, and learning essential tasks like washing clothes, bathing, and combing my hair humbled me—a calmness wrapped around my heart and planted roots.

I experienced a rollercoaster of emotions and poured those emotions into this novel as I rewrote each chapter. With each edit, I fell deeper in love with these characters.

I witnessed a change in my thinking and writing. My new perspective could have been my swollen brain messing with me, but I listened.

I found a fantastic editor. I had a couple more edits when shingles joined the party in my mouth and right side of my body. The pain broke me. I started to wonder if God wanted me to write.

Readers reminded me that God doesn't make mistakes.

The road to publishing was rough, but I made it.

Amen!

Lyrics Playlist

Join the party

Listen to *"**Lyrics Between Us**"* playlist.

◊ *Tidal*

◊ *Spotify*

◊ *Soundcloud*

◊ *YouTube*

I hope you enjoyed reading

Lyrics Between Us

Want to chat about this book? Join the conversation with other readers at iamchristat.com

You can also reach Christat
on Facebook (www. facebook.com/iamchristat)
on Twitter (www.twitter.com/iamchristat)
or Instagram (www.instagram.com/iamchristat)

You are just one click away from…
• Being the first to hear about author events
• Exclusive giveaways
• Free bonus content
• Sneak peeks at our newest titles

Happy reading! CLICK HERE TO SIGN UP

Made in the USA
Middletown, DE
14 October 2022

12765393R00161